I0769803

WHERE WHEN IT RAINS

JOHN F. DUFFY

For Dani,
who found me in the desert and led me out.

Part One

I turned about with my heart to know and to search out and to seek wisdom and the reason of things, and to know the wickedness of folly and the foolishness and madness.

— Ecclesiastes 7:25

I was alive. The clock blinked twelve but it wasn't twelve. A square hem of light rimmed the black curtains that made night of day. Behind my right eye the heel of a boot stamped out the seconds while above me a string of pink lights swelled to full brightness before fading to nothing and then back again. Like the room itself was breathing. Like I was in the belly of some greater being. Dom was alive too. The sheet drawn up to her hip. Her bare shoulder, framed by a black bra strap, lifting and falling. She smelled of hairspray and perfume and cigarette smoke, and her exhaled air, still tasting of vodka, found my dry lips even though she was facing away.

I wiped the grit from my eyes. Breathed with the room. Tried to lay hands on my last memory from before I'd passed out. Images like a stack of Polaroids spilled over a table offered a working tale of everything that came before if only they could be set in order. Sleep is like a coma. Time stops. Or your mind stops counting it and the moment of waking is scotch taped to the moment of going under so that it feels like one naturally follows the other. Like that place of nothing never was. But in truth, your body goes on without your mind. The meat and blood keep working without all the knowing that we think is so important. Without the part of us that looks around and names everything and tells a story about where we think we've been and where we think we're going and then doubles down on its madness and adds a why.

Sometime in the night the breaker had been tripped. I had a picture of that. We were naked when it happened. Hip to hip. Me pushing into her. My fingers holding her open because she liked that. Because I liked that. The thud and squeal of the music seeping through her walls was at once quiet, replaced by the wails of drunks and a confused chatter accompanying the opening and closing of closet doors as those with enough wit remaining at that hour went in search of the power box. In that humiliating silence, she'd said something. Words seeking words. But I was beyond speech. Incapable because of alcohol. Incapable because I wasn't in the driver's seat. So I'd fed my thumb into her mouth and she'd sucked on it. Worked it with her tongue. Then the electricity was back and with it came cheers from the backyard. Her pink lights and blinking clock and a heavy bass beat to banish talk and guide my thrusting.

I lifted the sheet and turned my body. Every movement slow. Deliberate, so as not to wake her. My foot stepped down on last night's condom and I had to restrain my gagging. Like I was removing a leech, I peeled it from the ball of my foot. The wriggling thing began to drain onto the carpet so I flung it away and wiped my hand on her sheets. My clothes were there on the floor but my underwear was missing, probably lost in the tangle of blankets. Fuck it. I bundled what I could find against my chest and walked on my toes. Stalked my way to her door. Held my thumb over the lock as I turned the knob to mute the sound of it popping open.

I made my way to the bathroom naked. On the cold tile in the hall my feet left brief impressions of themselves. Passing Jaime's room, I paused to listen to her flat but rhythmic moaning. Someone was doing a bad job fucking her. Or maybe not. What the hell did I know? On the bathroom counter, drops of blood. In the trash, the smallest ziplock bag atop a mountain of wadded tissue. Whoever had barfed in the toilet either hadn't noticed or hadn't cared that some of it had missed the bowl and splattered on the wall. I took a long, loud piss. My dick smelled like latex and salt. I'd have loved a shower, but I never used her shower. It could wait until home. After dressing I felt at the pockets of my jeans. My phone was missing. I swished whoever's mouthwash was there next to the sink, spit, then left without flushing.

In the living room, a guy was passed out on the couch, a

hoodie hiding his face from the daylight that cut through the gaps in the blinds and fell in triangles across the furniture. Another young man slept curled up on the floor, breathing dryly through his parted mouth. A shoe for a pillow, but not his own. The short table near the couch was a mess of red plastic cups. Roxy Music was crooning that there was nothing more than this from an iPod still randomly selecting songs, serenading the unconscious house. In the kitchen, more red cups. Some tipped on their sides. Some upright and holding the last dregs of stale beer. Cigarette butts floating in the golden liquid like dead roaches. Bottles and cans covered the counters and spilled from the overstuffed trash. Most of the after party had been confined to the backyard, but people had drifted in and out through the sliding door to steal beer from the refrigerator or to hide their drug use in the bathroom, not out of shame, but scarcity, and the checkered kitchen floor was now criss crossed with shoe prints. Dance steps in desert dust.

The backyard was a wide patch of dirt and gravel surrounded by a high cinder block wall. Empty plastic chairs left in nonsense patterns were the last evidence of conversations now forgotten. A lone Palo Verde tree grew in the exact center of the yard and a strand of white lights drooped from the corners of the roof over the slab patio to that tree and then back. They were still plugged in but the light they gave was vanquished by the force of the sun. Against the trunk of the leafless tree was a floral print couch, faded and dirty. On it a woman was sleeping with her head turned into the filthy cushion. She still wore her pink heels, and her legs were drawn up in a fetal position, knees to chest. She was using a jacket for a blanket. My jacket.

"That's my jacket," I said, my body casting a shadow over her.

She groaned, settling more deeply into the couch.

"Please, I need my jacket back."

"It's not mine?" she whimpered, still clinging to sleep.

"No."

"Where's my jacket?"

"I don't know."

"Who are you?"

"Riley."

She still hadn't opened her eyes. "Who the fuck is Riley?"

"Look, I need my jacket back. My phone's in the pocket."

"It's cold."

"You can go in the house."

She groaned again. I scanned the yard. One of the plastic chairs that was tipped on its back laid atop a black leather jacket. Fetching it, I patted away the dirt from the leather and brought it to her.

"Here."

She parted her eyes and seeing her jacket she opened them wide. "My jacket!" she said, sitting up and letting my own coat fall to the ground. I picked it up and spun it in my hands to find the pockets. The girl shivered and threaded her tattooed arms into her jacket sleeves then drew her legs up and hugged them. I took a seat on the far end of the couch in the place her feet had abandoned and laid my jacket over the arm.

"Aren't you cold?" she asked.

"No."

She rubbed her legs. "I'm freezing."

"That's because you slept outside." I pulled my tobacco from the inside pocket of my coat and began rolling a cigarette.

With her hand shielding her eyes from the sun she watched me work. "Can I get one of those?" I licked the paper and sealed it shut and handed her the cigarette then set to rolling a second one for myself. "Thanks," she said. She watched me work. "You're good at that."

I grunted and hung the finished cigarette from my lip while I felt at my pockets for my lighter. With fire at the end of my cigarette, I puffed it to life then passed her the lighter and said, "Kinda wish I wasn't."

She lit her cigarette. Handed back my lighter. Blowing out smoke, her voice was deeper. "Who do you know?" She asked.

I wasn't sure what she meant.

"Jaime or Dominique?"

I spit between my feet. "Dom. Well, both of them I guess, but Dom more so."

She began coughing. Phlegm was caught in her throat and she covered her mouth with her fist as she brought it up. Then with her whole body she spit a yellow oyster over her shoulder. She sniffed and spit again. Turning back to me, she smiled. "Sorry."

I shrugged and took a drag.

She wiped her eye with her thumb then flicked away what she'd gathered and in that deeper voice again she asked, "Do I look like shit?"

I squinted at her. "No."

"For real?"

"Yeah, you look fine."

She offered me her hand. "I'm Elise."

"Riley."

"Riley the photo guy?"

"The one and only."

"I've heard of you. You do Ashli's stuff, right?" She took a drag and as she exhaled she pulled at her bleached hair with her free hand, trying to put it some sort of way. "I think I'm still drunk."

I flipped open my phone. My sister had called the day before. Twice. She also sent me two text messages. One wishing me a happy birthday. Then another asking if I was OK. "Shit."

"What?"

"Yesterday was my birthday."

"Oh." She sucked the cigarette hard and her lips popped when she released it to ask, "How old are you?"

I had to think for a second. "Twenty-six." My cigarette smoked to a nub, I dropped it to the ground and twisted the toe of my shoe on the ember. I pulled my jacket on and pocketed my phone. "I gotta dip," I said. "I don't want to be here when Dom wakes up."

"I thought you said she was your friend?"

"I said I knew her."

As I stood up she asked, "Can I get a ride with you?"

"No."

"Wait? For real?"

"For really, real. I don't have a car."

She laughed and her laugh turned into a cough. When she cleared her throat, she said, "I thought you just like, wouldn't give me a ride, and I was like, that's fucking cold." She flicked her cigarette butt and it hit the ground with a flash of red. "How are you getting home?"

"Bus."

"Did you get a DUI?"

"No. Why?"

"Everyone I know who takes a bus, it's because they got a DUI."

"Well, where I'm from it's normal." I walked to the sliding door. My hand was on it when the low register of recently awoken human voices hit the glass. No one was in the kitchen but I wouldn't risk walking back through the house. On the patio there were milk crates full of crushed cans and I picked one up and carried it to the concrete wall running along the side of the house. I tipped the crate, dumping its contents, then set it upside down against the wall and used it as a step. With both hands I was able to push myself up high enough to throw my leg over the wall. Sitting there as if mounted in a saddle, I waved to Elise. She stopped pulling at her hair and waved back and coughed and said, "Happy birthday." My head started to swim. I kicked my second leg over the wall and scooted forward, falling to my feet and hands in the front yard. Dust rose from beneath my shoes and I clapped away the dirt from my palms and made for the sidewalk without looking back. A clean escape and the new day blue and warm like all other days.

Finding the exact right moment to begin a telling is impossible because every moment before is of equal if not greater importance, so I started there. Right in the middle of everything. On top of the iceberg as it were. I don't often think about that morning. About any of the mornings. Because when I do I wonder if given the chance, would I do it differently? If doing it differently would have brought us all to different ends. What small kindness would have saved their lives? What words spoken? Or maybe left unsaid. But there is no doing it differently. No trick of gravity that sends sand upward through the pinch in the hourglass. Where in time that part of the story is told, I am what I was, no different than the mountains or the valley, all an exact sum of the eons of weathering they'd been subject to. Down to the minute. To the second. To whatever the pieces of a second are called when they get chopped up and looked at through a microscope. The truth is that back then, I was still in love with it all. With who I had become. The part that I was playing. Riley, the photo guy. Ashli's photo guy. My name loosely strung to hers a passport to every party, a seat at every table, a bottle or a can or a rolled up twenty passed my way. Head nods and hugs and so many smiles when I entered a room whether I was pointing my lens or not. And all of it by accident. See me there. Shipwrecked by fortune. A merry fool tripping towards tragedy who either could not calculate the consequences of his actions, or who simply refused to try. Hungover. Self satisfied. Waiting for a bus.

None of it would have happened if I'd stuck the landing. I always stuck the landing. Or limped away. But not that one. Not that time. When I woke up in the hospital, a machine beeped along with my beating heart and the bright light hitting my blurry eyes fed a rising pain in my head, a hammer striking solid steel behind my right eye, the ring of it spiraling down into my gut where it stirred a nausea that came in waves. I didn't know where I was. A moment before I'd been running back up the steps. A light drizzle had glazed the concrete. The generator was grinding and choking to power the lights and its exhaust mingled with some unknown smell.

When the nurse came in she explained everything. My friends had called the ambulance. The doctors had put me in an artificial coma while they worked to reduce the swelling in my brain. She asked me if I knew where I was. "Arizona. Somewhere in Phoenix." Then what year it was. "Two-thousand-six. I hope." She smiled and said that it was and later the neurologists came as a group to assess me. They said maybe a lot. Danced away from certainty no matter my question, always finding the safety of cautious statements about how I would fare. About what would remain and what would be lost. They were hopeful when they heard my speech. When they watched my gait. When my pupils tracked their moving fingers and pinholed down to hide from their flashlights. My body seemed to have lost nothing, but they warned that wouldn't necessarily be so for my mind. Non-battered brains are hard enough to understand. Twice a day they came as a team to ask me how I felt and twice a day I told them that I was fine. Eager to get back to my life. A few days later they agreed and discharged me into a foreign land.

On the sidewalk in front of the hospital, with everything I

owned strapped to my back and absolutely no idea where I was or where I should go, I called the team manager.

"Holy shit, he lives!"

"What's up, Jake?"

"What's up with me, what's up with you, man? How's the dome?"

"All good. They let me go, so, you know, I'm ready to get back in the van."

He was quiet for a second, then said, "Ry, I'm sorry bro, we had to move on. We stuck around for a day, but you know how it is. We had stops to make. We couldn't wait."

"I get it. No doubt. But can't I like, fly to where you are?"

"Dude, I'm sorry, but we filled your spot. When you went lights out we brought in this kid from Tallahassee who fucking rips. Nico Ortega. You heard of him?" I was thinking about the question when he went on, "Doesn't matter. Look, we still got mad love for you. You're still on flow, and maybe in a few months we can fit you in again."

My shoulders ached under the weight of my bag. I sat on a bench. "So what am I supposed to do?"

"About what?"

"About being stuck here."

"Right, I hear you. Let me get back to you in a bit. I'll make some calls and figure out what we can do."

A bus stopped for me but I waved it away. The driver scowled and closed the door and pulled off down the road. Palm trees lined the streets. Almost all of the buildings were painted a stark white. A blue sign pointed the way to Old Town, so I followed it. I tried to skate, my wheels *clacking* on the brick sidewalk, but I quickly felt unstable, and listed to the side. After hiking the weight of my bag higher onto my shoulders, I reset my feet and pushed along again, but the faster I moved, the more my head would spin. It was the oddest sensation, the image of the world before me turning over like a framed picture affixed to a spinning fan. It wasn't enough to know that the lateral tilting of the ground was an illusion produced by my own head, because within that head, the unconscious motors of balance were fully convinced and responded in kind. After veering into a light pole, I stopped. Stood still. Blinked and breathed and waited for the dizziness to pass, but every time I tried to skate, it returned, dragging me left or right against my intentions. So I gave up. Strapped my board to my bag again and walked. Laughed at what I believed was only a temporary circumstance.

My shadow was two steps ahead of me as I passed boutiques and cafes. The sky was cloudless and blue and the air was warm and the sum of it felt like vacation. Like whatever home was not. A woman in white pants and a wide hat with lips too big for her face walked toward me carrying a tiny dog against her chest. As we passed each other, the dog growled and the woman hurried her step. At a restaurant called Saladas, on a wide patio within a railing of welded iron, tall white tables were hidden from the sun beneath yellow and red umbrellas emblazoned with Mexican beer logos. A sandwich board advertised one dollar tacos. I counted the money in my pocket. Twelve bucks. Figuring I could eat and still afford a bus to the airport, I climbed the short steps up to the patio deck and walked to the bar, taking a seat on a black stool. The bar top was a mosaic of glassy blue tiles that together made the image of ocean waves and waiting for service I ran the pads of my fingers over them. A smiling Mexican set a basket of chips and a molcajete of red salsa in front of me. He stood staring and when I thanked him he hurried away. I was crunching a chip when Collin slapped a menu in front of me. I asked for water.

He flipped a glass in his hand and filled it with a soda gun. "What else?"

"I'll get some food."

"No. What else are you drinking?" He set the water in front of me.

"Just the water."

"You're sitting at a bar."

I looked to an empty table, then back to him. "Should I move?"

He shook his head. "I'm fucking with you. Know what you want to eat?" I ordered three beef tacos, and he tapped my order on his monitor. The back of his right hand was tattooed with a shamrock.

"Are you Irish?" I asked.

Turning, he crossed his arms and looked at me puzzled. "No. Why?"

Pointing to his hand, I said, "The clover. I just thought..."

Before I could finish he examined the back of his fist. "What, this? It's a lily pad."

"Really?"

"No, of course I'm Irish. Can't you tell by how handsome I am?" He smiled proudly, his teeth slightly out of alignment, his nose one that had been broken at least twice, his right eyebrow fractured by a thin line of scar tissue. He crossed his arms again. The back of his other hand was tattooed with a cricket.

"What's the cricket all about?"

He used the index finger of that hand to tap his head, and said, "Got a cricket for a conscience." When it was clear that I was confused, he asked, "Pinocchio?" He hung motionless for a second, waiting for me to get it, and when I didn't, he brushed me off and vanished into the restaurant. I ate chips and sipped my water slowly, wary to ask for a refill. When Collin returned he had my food, and as he set it before me he asked, "How much did they take out?" I stared at him as he leaned back and pointed to my head. "You're brain. How much did they remove?"

I touched the stitches on the shaved side of my scalp. I hadn't considered what I must look like. "I was in a coma," I said, almost apologetic.

"No shit?"

"No shit." I bit my first taco in half and chewed.

"Have anything to do with that skateboard?" he asked.

After chewing a bit more I got out a "yep," then stuffed the rest of the taco into my mouth.

"What were you doing? I mean, besides something stupid."

I gulped water and with my tongue wiped my back teeth free of tortilla pulp so I could speak. "Switch backside-flip to front board down an eight stair rail."

"I have no idea what that means, but it sounds hard."

"It is." I bit into my second taco.

"Not wearing a helmet, I take it?"

I grimaced.

"I'm kidding. Helmets are for pussies."

I laughed as I swallowed. "Totally."

"So you must be good."

"At skateboarding?"

"No, oil painting. Yes at skateboarding."

"I am."

"So what happened?"

I took up my glass and shrugged. "Even good people fuck up."

"Not as bad as you."

"Not if they're lucky."

The ticket printer started grinding. A white slip of paper slowly curled from its opening. Collin tore the paper off, read it, then set it on the end of the bar. He reached into a beer cooler, pulled out three green bottles which he held against his chest with one arm, then with the other, quickly *snicked* their caps off with a shiny bar key. The bottle caps hit the ground like shell casings and he spun the bar key on his finger before sliding it into his back pocket. He set the beer bottles atop the white ticket and forced a lime wedge into each of them then returned to where he'd previously been leaning. "Where were we?"

"I fucked up."

"Right. Did it hurt?"

"I don't remember."

He smirked, "If you don't remember your mistakes, you're bound to repeat them."

I sat back. "Yeah, but forgetting means we won't be afraid to try again."

"Will you try again?"

"That trick at that spot?" My head rocked side to side as I considered it. "Maybe. I don't know. Hard to say. It's doable. I think what fucked me up was the rain."

Collin's eyebrows went up. "You tried it in the rain? Man, you are dumb."

"Drizzle really. But the ground was getting slick because of the dust. Maybe I should have hung it up, but the whole crew was there. I had only landed that day and I was being filmed for a big company video, and I felt I had to prove myself."

He uncrossed his arms. "Wait, are you a pro?"

"Not yet. Trying."

Collin looked to his left. Two young women were walking up the patio steps and making for the bar. Both of them were skinny. Each wore tight white pants and opened toed shoes and wide sunglasses that hid half of their faces. They were bleached the same blonde and had the same tan. Only their colored halter tops could differentiate them. "Collin!" they exclaimed in near unison. He stepped out from the bar and passed behind me on his way to greet them. He hugged each woman in turn and asked them what they were up to and when they said they were so bored he told them he would make them shots and as he passed behind me again on his way back to his station, he leaned to my ear and whispered, "Yo, do me a solid. I forgot these bitches names. Introduce yourself to them."

They raised themselves onto the stools to my right. I turned to them. Cracked a big dumb smile. Prepared myself for the nervous kick in my gut that was always there whenever I introduced myself to a girl. But it never came. I waited for it, but in its usual place, I felt nothing at all. Less than nothing. If these women told me to go fuck myself, I would simply have returned to my basket of chips no differently than if they'd told me the time, and that lack of attachment felt new. And fascinating. My dumb smile grew wider, and I said, "I'm Riley," and I extended my hand to the woman nearest me. She turned, and though I couldn't see her eyes, her chin went up and I knew she was examining the Frankensteinian mess of stitching and scar tissue on the side of my head. I kept grinning and let my hand remain floating in that space between us.

Collin began shaking a silver tumbler full of ice and liquor and said loudly over the noise, "Ladies, this is my boy Riley. He just woke up from a coma."

Both of their mouths fell agape. One said "No way!" The other said "Shut up!" The woman closest to me took my hand and as she gave it the limpest of shakes, she asked, "Were you in a coma for real?"

"For really, real. Six whole days. I just left the hospital about an hour ago."

"That's fucking crazy!" The second woman said, leaning around the first and dipping her head to examine my surgical wounds over the frame of her sunglasses.

"I'm Lacey," the first woman said.

"Chantal," said the second.

Collin set four glasses in a line on the bar and passed the tumbler over all of them, a strainer holding back the ice and allowing only a brilliant red liquid to pass through. Each of the women took a glass and Collin took one as well. The fourth glass remained and Collin nodded to me, "That's you."

"Oh, I can't pay for that."

Collin's eyes peeled back and I knew immediately that I was ruining something.

He said to the women, "His brain is still a little fucked up." They laughed and he glared at me until I picked up the glass. It was already fogging. "Sluts for my sluts," Collin said, and everyone held their glasses high, so I imitated them. They touched their glasses so I sent mine into the mix to be clinked and when every glass had touched every other, we drank. I expected the fire of alcohol but the drink was entirely sweet. The cold of it almost painful against the back of my throat. With their glasses drained the women thanked Collin and said they were going to take a table and asked him to send out margaritas. Special ones. They each gave me a short wave and fell away to a corner of the patio where they took refuge beneath the shade of an umbrella.

"I was serious," I said, when the women were out of earshot. "About not being able to pay for that drink."

"I know," he said. "Don't worry about it. You did me a solid. I couldn't remember their names for the life of me."

"Do they come in a lot?"

"Enough. I fucked that Chantal girl a few weeks ago, and if she found out I didn't know her name..." He let the sentence die.

"She'd be mad?"

"I don't know about mad. It probably wouldn't help my chances of fucking her again though. Want a beer?"

"I'm broke."

He sighed and planted his hands on the blue tile so he could chastise me. "Clearly, I don't give a shit. Do you want one?"

"Sure."

He pulled a bottle of Sol from the beer fridge and *snicked* off the cap and tucked away his bar key as quickly as he'd drawn it. He pressed a lime wedge into the mouth of the bottle and set it in front of me. Condensation ran from the glass to the grout between the rough-edged tiles of the bar top. Collin set to the work of building two margaritas, still talking to me.

"You said you'd only landed the day you got hurt?"

"That's right."

"From where?"

"Chicago."

He began shaking his tumbler. "So what's the plan now?"

"Waiting on a plane ticket home."

"What's at home?"

I sat up to answer but no words followed. Collin crouched as he poured the contents of his shaker into two glasses with salted rims, closing one eye and watching the liquid with the other to make sure his pour was even.

"Nothing, actually," I said, learning the truth of the sentiment as I spoke it.

He stood straight again. "Got a girl there?"

I shook my head.

"A job?"

I kept it shaking.

He tossed the ice from his tumbler into a sink and asked, "Then why go back?" Before giving me a chance to respond, he lifted the margaritas, and said "Hold that thought." Carrying both glasses in one hand, he went to Lacey and Chantal and I could hear the chitter of their high pitched voices as he delivered their drinks. Collin said something. Then there was a low murmuring. Words too faint to confirm.

When Collin came back, I asked, "Were those the special ones?"

He stared at me.

"The margaritas."

He waved his hand like he was erasing something from the air between us. "Special means they want me to sell them bars." Looking very dumb for the second or third time that afternoon, I sat blankly until Collin said, "Xanax." He walked away again, disappearing into the dark of the restaurant, so I studied the customers scattered about the patio. Their beauty, or their obvious efforts at it. Women trim. Tan. Men muscled. Tan. Above them the sky was cloudless, a perfect aquatic blue defying reality with its even tone. It looked airbrushed. A Hollywood backdrop that could be rolled away if only anyone cared to see what lesser world it concealed. With my thumb, I pressed the lime wedge into the neck of my bottle and sent it into the golden beer like a diver. Millions of bubbles spontaneously came into being, all of them rushing upward in a dense cloister that formed a scaffold of foam, lifting the fruit like a champion carried on the shoulders of a mob of frenzied admirers. Taking a sip, the effervescence of the bubbling beer found my lips and nose, citrus tickling at me before I even drank.

As the afternoon grew long and the patio grew busy, Collin continued to stop and talk with me in spurts, always setting a cold bottle in front of me if the previous one was near empty. The sky slowly turned orange as the sun fell away in the west, and the air had the smell of orange blossoms floating on it, and the smell of the air and the color of the sky joined in creating the spectacular illusion that it was the setting sun itself leaving behind the fragrance as it receded from the world. Something to remember it by. I was stuffing another lime into another beer when my phone rang. It was Jake calling to tell me that the company could fly me home. There was a red eye to O'Hare that left at ten. The fizz from my beer was jumping. Escaping the mouth of the bottle. Bursting just above the rim. "Who do you know here?" I asked.

"In Phoenix? A few people. Why?"

"I'm thinking about staying, but I need a place to crash."

Jake told me that was a wise move. Being closer to L.A. He said he would make some calls and get back to me. When I clapped the phone shut and set it on the bar, Collin was popping the caps off a collection of bottles. *Snick, snick, snick.*

Then the rattle of caps on the concrete floor. "You need a place to stay?" he asked.

"Maybe."

He set the bottles on their tickets in the well then returned to me. "I got a room."

"Seriously?"

"What, you'd rather live with a stranger?"

"You are a stranger."

He held his arms open wide and feigned insult. "Riley. Baby. How could you say that after all we've been through?" When I smiled he shifted his tone. "Seriously, I got a room. And if you take it, then I can make sure you pay me back for all the beers I've been floating you."

"I'll need to find a job first."

He scoffed. "Work here. I can get you a job. You ever worked in a restaurant before?"

"No."

He made a dismissive gesture. "You'll figure it out."

"I don't know how to make drinks."

"You won't be. Bartending isn't something you just waltz into. Half the waitresses here want bar shifts. I can get you barbacking though."

"What's that?"

"Monkey work. Fill the ice. Fill the beer fridge. Wash glass. A guy with half a brain could do it."

"Sounds perfect."

"When Rich interviews you, just make sure you tell him about your five years of experience at that one bar in Chicago."

"I don't have five years of experience."

"I know, dummy. But you say you do. He's not going to check."

"So I have to lie?"

"If you want the job."

The nosebleeds stopped after maybe a week. The chapped lips took longer. Desert air is always hunting moisture and the body needs to adjust. To learn to defend itself by clinging jealously to what it has. It probably didn't help that I was drinking so much.

In those first days and weeks, I had tried to skate, but when after only a moment my balance invariably failed me, I'd stop. Sit. Wait for the world to right itself. Retreating to the apartment I would tell myself that I just needed more time. That my injury was severe and that of course it wouldn't be so quick to heal. So I'd skip a day. Maybe two. Go to work with Collin at Saladas and distract myself with the ins and outs of bar life.

It was easy enough. Stock beer. Cut fruit. Collapse the cardboard. Most importantly though, we had to make the customers feel good. Feel cool. Like by spending money at our particular establishment they were involved in something that mattered, and so alongside alcohol we dispensed hugs and handshakes. Memorized names and favorite drinks. In the beginning, I made sure to never let Rich see me standing idle, even if that meant washing glasses that were already clean. Then one night I caught him asleep in his office and I cut that shit right out.

As we worked, Collin and I sipped beers and snuck shots, and then at midnight we clocked out and wandered up the road to finish getting drunk with our coworkers. I had no mattress then, only blankets I'd bought second hand and laid out on the carpet in the center of my room. But when we would burst through our apartment door in the deep hours of night, loud and slurring, I'd crawl into that simple bed and lie motionless under the humming fan and become further intoxicated by the breeze drawn in through the open window. I couldn't name the plants that made the air not my air, but I was excited by it. By all of it. By my lack of tethers. My freedom to be anything. Waking at some hour past noon I'd take coffee and cigarettes on the balcony, and so long as I kept my back to the wall, rigid and true, that combination of nicotine and sun were always enough to chase away my hangover. To rekindle my faith that I would get better.

But I didn't. And losing heart was a process. Hopscotching across the stages of grief. In those first days, when the idea that I might never skate again came to mind, I banished it immediately. Not possible. I just needed more time. But as the spring grew warmer and I still wasn't able to ride straight down a sidewalk or ollie up a curb without my vision losing its hold on the X Y axis of the world, the notion dug in. Made itself comfortable.

At the hospital the neurologist spoke to me with a dry expression and an explicit warning against hope. He referred me to a physical therapist, a skeleton of a woman who laid me out on a table and gripped my skull and twisted it quickly to the side before sitting me up again. She repeated the process several times over the course of an hour, saying something about microcrystals that might be caught in the wrong part of my ear canal. She said she could make me right as rain. After her treatment, I pushed across the parking lot. Tried a slow moving kickflip and caught it by the sheer grace of muscle memory but had to step off because I was back in the tumble of a clothes dryer. I was forced to sit while the world righted itself. Forced to contemplate what I was before. What I was now. Seated on a red curb, my fingers walked the spinning wheel on my upturned board like a man running in place and slowly falling behind. Then it was on to a night of drinking. Ignoring. Pretending. Forgetting.

Denial carried me until it didn't, and when it finally failed I tried bargaining. I made a promise to myself that I wouldn't lose touch. Skaters were my people. Since junior high they'd been the ones I could connect with because they understood what I understood. They'd felt the freedom of movement and speed and the total decoupling of a human stride from the bonds of gravity, and they'd seen the banal architecture of modern civilization as the carnival attraction it was when bent to our secret purpose. Just because I couldn't be a part of the show didn't mean I was ready to live without its shine. That I even could if I wanted to. So that first summer, I bought a camera. The best available on the consumer market. And I went out in search of subjects.

Summer in Phoenix is hot. They call it a dry heat and they aren't wrong. It's dry the way the inside of an oven is dry, and when you step out into it from the safety of air conditioning you feel very much like you are baking. Like hidden away under your skin your muscle is browning and tightening into bands of desiccated sinew. Anyone who would still skate in such misery was someone I wanted to know. I went to the parks at night when five degrees could be shaved off the day's temperature. There might be three guys there. There might be nobody. The night I met Caleb he was the only one under the bright lights floating across the gray concrete expanse of Pecos Park, his white T-Shirt too weighed down by sweat to billow behind him. I watched him back disaster the high transition then launch a huge indy grab over the hip. He was exactly who I wanted to know.

"Hey," I said, waving.

Caleb was sitting on a ledge chugging water as I approached. Replacing the cap on his jug, water ran down his chin and he wiped it with the back of his hand. "What's up?" He said.

"This is going to sound weird, but I'm trying to be a photographer, and I was wondering if you would be cool with me getting some shots of you."

He looked at the camera hanging from my neck. "Is that a DSLR?"

"It is."

"You got good lenses?"

"Two, so far."

He stood up and wiped his forehead with his shirt which was already halfway dry. "OK."

I shot a few pictures that night and promised I would email them to him after I did color correction. We exchanged numbers and soon I found myself introduced to his friends. Some of them local guys. Most of them transplants from cold places. They were all at least good, but a handful were great, and they all skated for the love of it. Because it had taken over their hearts the way it had mine. Because as young men they had looked around at the world that was being offered to them and decided there was little in it that they could feel any kind of way about. Out of all of them, Caleb had real talent. He could be the next thing. And getting to ride along in the car, to soak up the energy he and his friends manifested on the way to a spot, the buzz generated by their laughter and preposterous slang set to the soundtrack of whatever music they played to amp them up, I hoped it would work. That it would catch me like the net between tightrope and circus floor.

And for a while it was enough. To be there for the *clack clack clack* of their wheels moving over the cracks in the concrete. For the *smack* of fresh wood as an ollie launched them into the air. For the *skreeee* of trucks on a steel handrail and the shouts of genuine elation as four wheels came back to Earth with a body perfectly balanced above them. Knees bent. Hair flowing. The casual ride away from something that should never have been. Something impossible. And after the hugs and the hand slaps, there was me in the center as everyone came to see the shot, to study it in detail as our gathered hands defended the image from interceding light.

That first summer, I split time between working and getting wasted with Collin, then on my days off, shooting photos and getting wasted with Caleb. As the quality of my pictures improved, I sent them to the magazines. Thrasher. Transworld. Skateboarder. None were ever purchased, but a few were selected to be run in the open submissions sections in the back pages. Most of my photos ended up on people's personal Myspace profiles, and there was a certain glory to that. To being the guy everyone relied on to capture their ability. To provide evidence of their worthiness in the thinnest of subcultures. It was all I had. I held it tightly.

In late summer, maybe early fall, Caleb invited me on a night mission. Ernie Moreno was in town and looking to hit a spot. A nine stair handrail outside an apartment complex in Scottsdale. They needed a photog. "Dude, of course," I told him. Ernie rode for Real. He was a full on pro. Any decent photo of him could easily sell, if not to a magazine, then to one of his sponsors who might use it in an ad. It could change my life.

Caleb picked me up in his truck. Driving to the spot, Ernie and Caleb passed a joint back and forth. Ernie offered it to me as he blew out a plume of thick smoke, but I held up my hand and he gave it back to Caleb. Spinning his thumb on the wheel of his iPod, Ernie controlled the music, never letting a song finish. With each track, he'd say, "Have you heard this? This is sick," or, "Bro, this song gets me so hyped," then a hard stop in whatever was already playing as a new song intervened. Songs started. Rose to crescendo. Then cut away before resolving. Never allowed to fade.

When we arrived at the spot, Caleb and Ernie stayed in the truck for a few minutes as I examined the rail, crouching here and there to look through my viewfinder. I returned for my flash kit and the guys followed along, gliding on their skateboards. As I erected stands and placed flashes, they paced out the distance of the run-up, mentally accounting for where they would throw down their board. How many times they could push. Where they would have to snap their ollie. With my gear in place, I squatted in the gravel next to the sidewalk, a lantana bush clawing at my back. Caleb and Ernie took turns practicing the run-up, getting a simple ollie down the set. Then a frontside one-eighty. Backside one-eighty. I took pictures the whole time, using their warm ups as my own, tuning the settings on my camera and the exact pivot of my body needed to capture whatever happened.

They were making confident attempts at the rail when a squad car slowed along the curb.

"Time's up, boys," the officer called through his open window.

We all waved in a sign of surrender. As the car drove away, Ernie said, "Fucking pigs."

"It's whatever," I said. "I'm surprised we lasted this long on a weeknight."

"True," Ernie said. He wasn't too upset. In the short time we'd been there, he'd stuck an incredibly smooth switch flip crook down the rail. Wiping his forehead with his shirt, he asked, "Yo, can I get a look at the sequence?"

I scrolled back through the photos on my camera and let him hold it so he could watch the ten picture sequence of his best trick of the night.

"Bro, that's so sick." He passed the camera to Caleb, who looked and confirmed that it was, in fact, sick.

The squad car rolled by a second time as I was stowing the flash kit in the truck bed. Caleb fired the engine and asked what the plan was. In the middle seat, Ernie flipped open his phone and clicked through messages. As we turned onto the road, I cranked down my window and lit a cigarette. Caleb was suggesting a different handrail when, with a gentle blue light glowing on his face, Ernie asked, "You guys want to go to a party?"

Following the directions Ernie read from his phone screen, we wound through Scottsdale until we came to a three story condominium that was protected by a white stucco wall. Ernie had to call his friend on the inside for the gate code, and as we hopped out of the truck, he asked if I would bring my camera. "I want to show my homie the sequence," he said. I didn't want to have to guard my bag all night, but I wanted him to like me, so I agreed. Ernie sniffed his armpits. Not liking what he found, he asked Caleb if he had any deodorant. He didn't, so Ernie unlooped the pine tree air freshener from the rearview mirror and wiped it under his arms. Caleb laughed, then did the same. Withdrawing it from under his shirt, he held it up to me and asked, "Want some?"

The complex looked like a resort. A central courtyard surrounded a pool which glowed like an emerald for the series of lights fixed just beneath the surface of the water. Terra cotta tiles traced the irregular shape of the pool and beyond the tiles were white deck chairs, two at a time, with circle tables of glass to separate every pair. Islands of flowering plants were ringed by the same terra cotta as the pool, and at the center of each island a palm tree grew to the height of the third floor balconies above. The palm trunks were kinked and bent like worms hardened by a sun that came too quickly after a storm, and their fronds were heavily pruned, leaving only those that stood straight up, giving the heads of the trees the look of an embarrassed show dog. A din of music fell from the third floor and drew our eyes skyward to where a number of people stood leaning against a white railing. We took the nearest set of stairs and walked single file, Ernie at the head and me trailing as we passed through that group of people who looked us up and down and immediately knew what we were by our matted hair and torn shoes.

After a photo session, I always ended my night drinking somewhere. Usually at one of the skate houses where too many young men lived in too few rooms. Where the cigarette burned carpet was never vacuumed and the piss stained shower was never scrubbed clean. Following Ernie into that condo, with its intentional selection of matching furniture and framed art hanging on the walls, I felt like I'd stolen something. Like of course I'd be caught. Every bit of available space was occupied by a body, and as we pressed through them, heads turned to view us and then turned away again because we were nobody. The kitchen and living room were part of the same great room, and moving towards the fridge where we hoped we could find beer, a girl in a tight cheetah print top with her hair teased out and sprayed in place saw us and yelled, "Oh, my God! Ernie!" She opened her arms and stepped close to him. Bright lipstick. Thick eyeliner. A bottle of champagne held by the neck like a dead goose. They hugged.

"Hey, Kaitlin," he said as her chest touched his.

"It's been forever," she said, the word forever coming out as if it were three words and not one. "Want some?" she asked, offering the champagne. Ernie lifted the bottle high and took a swallow. White foam burst from his mouth and he held his hand against his lips to restrain it.

"Who's this?" she asked, a painted fingernail alternatively pointing at Caleb and me.

Ernie wiped his mouth with his wrist and told our names and Kaitlin welcomed us. She explained that the beer in the fridge was fair game but to leave any liquor bottles the fuck alone. Also not to smoke inside.

"Do you know who's here?" She ignored us to focus on Ernie again.

"Who?" he asked.

"Jordan!"

"Jordan?"

She rolled her eyes and pushed Ernie's shoulder. "Jordan Bell! Remember?"

"Oh!" Ernie said. "Yeah, I remember her. Sorry, it's just been a long time."

"You absolutely have to come say hi." She took Ernie by the hand and he didn't resist her at all as she tugged him away, yelling as their bodies were swallowed by the crowd that Jordan was going to be so blown away to see him, the words so blown away spaced and emphasized as if they were all of equal importance. Caleb said "Beer?" and I said "Beer," and together we inched toward the refrigerator. We each took two cans of PBR, snapped the first one open, and drank. Not saying anything. Just sipping. Watching.

The party was undeniably fashionable. Effort everywhere, even in the tossed and tousled hair that was massaged into apparent ad hoc position and then crystalized by creams and gels. Overwhelmingly, the look about each person was that of a penthouse punk. Tattoos on the visible skin. Tight jeans. Faded Tees. The occasional blazer on a guy or pair of brightly colored heels on a girl. Everyone rough at a glance but tailor fit upon inspection. There was a clear intention to look poor without having to suffer being poor. To appear battered while being wholly intact. High end heroin chic, like grad students who wanted jobs at rock labels or art galleries.

My third and fourth beers in hand, I squeezed through the crowd as it leaned and shifted to the music and headed for the balcony. My cigarette makings were in my camera bag, and removing them I stood against the stucco wall as I sprinkled a pinch of shredded tobacco into a rolling paper. A woman was leaning over the railing looking out on the night until she noticed me behind her and she turned to face me. "I could never figure out how to do that," she said.

Smoothing the wet glue strip onto the paper beneath it, I held the finished cigarette up and said, "I've had a lot of practice. Want one?"

She stood in shadow, but I could see by her outline that she smiled. "Sure."

I held out the cigarette and she came forward to take it. When she had it in hand, I said, "One dollar."

She dipped her head. "Take debit cards?"

"Cash only," I said.

As I set to rolling another cigarette, she examined the one I had given her and said, "No filter?"

"Nope."

"Isn't that hard on your lungs?"

I was pinching and rolling as I answered. "Yeah, but that's probably a good thing."

"Why?"

"So I don't smoke too much." I put my cigarette to my lips and patted at my pockets for my lighter. Finding it, the woman raised her cigarette to her mouth and I beckoned her toward me. I clicked the lighter and lit her cigarette and then my own, seeing her face for the first time in the brief orange glow. Breathing smoke, we retreated to our starting positions, her against the steel railing and me against the wall. We were quiet for a moment and then she tapped the railing at her hip and said, "You can stand next to me."

I shook my head and blew out a cloud. "No I can't."

She laughed. "You can't?"

"It's too high," I said. "I have vertigo."

"For real?"

"For really, real."

She turned and looked behind her, examining the drop, then crossed the gangway and leaned against the wall next to me.

"I'm Michelle," she said, transferring her cigarette to her left hand so she could offer me her right.

"Riley," I said, shaking her hand.

"Where are you from?"

"How do you know I'm not from here?"

"No one's from here."

I blew a stream of smoke. "Chicago. You?"

"Milwaukee."

I held out my fist, "Midwest love."

She touched her knuckles to mine.

I liked Michelle right away. She was dressed differently than all the other girls at the party. Fashionable, but not pretentious. A well fit denim coat over a long dress that fell to her heavy boots. Long necklaces. Bracelets on her arms that jangled when she lifted her cigarette for a drag. She was tall and trim and pretty. Best of all, she could spar with words without being aggressive. She was funny in a way that felt like home. We talked for a while about where we were from. Where we worked. Who we knew. When my last beer was empty I said I was going in for another and asked if she needed a drink. She said no, but waited for me to return and when I did she asked me how long I'd been in the valley. I said it had probably been about six months. I was feeling the buzz of the alcohol and the music and the night air so full of perfume and hairspray and chlorine and whatever floated up from those bushes with small red flowers, so I said something that made her laugh, not because it was funny but because it was naive. Something about the energy of the valley. Something about how it was probably impossible to be depressed there.

Her hands were in her jacket pockets and she didn't look at me as she said, "Oh, it's possible."

"Coming from the dreariness of Chicago, I don't see how." My gaze was fixed on the shifting palm fronds out beyond the railing and the black starless sky behind them.

"Give it time," she said, looking to that same black place. "This is just a city, Riley. The same as any other. It's just people going to jobs, and paying bills, and falling into routines."

Waving my beer can like a conductor's wand, I said, "But there's something else to it. It's hard to explain. It's a vibe."

"A vibe?"

"Yeah. Something I can't put into words, but that I can feel."

She gave me a look like I was an idiot but that she forgave me all the same. "Stick around," she said. "You'll change your mind."

"Betcha I won't."

"Betcha you will."

"Fifty bucks!"

"Fifty thousand!" She shoved my chest.

"Deal!" We shook hands with an exaggeration of motion.

"You better be good for it," she said, releasing her grip.

"I've got it on me."

She laughed, then we stood quietly looking away at the night, neither of us in a rush to fill the void. A camera flashed to our left. A group of girls were huddled together while another aimed a small camera at them. Reviewing the picture on the glowing LCD screen, they bemoaned it in turn, complaining about their red eyes and how the flash made them look ghastly. They lined up for another attempt, and by the time they were expressing their dissatisfaction with the second photo, I had my own camera in hand.

"Do you want me to take it for you?"

They assessed me silently, unsure of why I was speaking to them. But in the end my professional rig won over their curiosity and a black haired girl said sure and the group of them all squeezed together for a third time, shoulder to shoulder. With a fast lens and an open aperture, I released the shutter several times. Showing the girls the pictures, they lit up, overly satisfied with how they appeared.

"Katie, you look so good," one girl said of another.

"No way. I look like a goblin. Gina, you look totally hot," another girl said of the first.

"Shut up. You're fucking gorgeous. I'm the one who looks like a bloated corpse," the last girl said.

After they took turns degrading themselves and highlighting the beauty of their friends, one of the girls finally said, "This picture is seriously good. It looks like it should be in a magazine."

"How can we get this?" Another asked. "Do you have Myspace?"

I was typing my email address in a text message when one of the girl's took my arm and dragged me into the condo. She was loudly explaining to someone I couldn't see that I had an epic camera, and she spun me to face an awaiting couple, demanding that I take their picture. The girl sucked in her cheeks. The guy pretended not to notice I was there. I pulled focus on them and released the shutter. Before I could even get their contact information, I was yanked across the floor to where a group of girls sat piled on the sofa, one in fishnets and combat boots lying across the laps of four others who sat tightly together, all of them with wild, large hair, dyed by the layers or spotted in the manner of a leopard's fur, two with piercings in their lips, one with piercings in her cheeks, all of them with tattoos running at least halfway down their arms. I took several shots of the group and was then further pushed and pulled through the room, my shoulders gripped from behind so I could be pointed at the right set of subjects, a human tripod. Dragged about by drunks, filling my memory card with pictures of everyone in attendance.

Not by her own request, but because of the interest so many others had in being photographed with her, one young woman ended up before me more than any other. She was strikingly beautiful. Tall, with hair dyed a perfect primary red, she had razor hips that peeked out over the top of her skirt and high cheekbones that were just as sharp. She wore a yellow tee shirt with the sleeves and neckline cut away. Her arms were tattooed from shoulder to wrist and her breastbone was inked with the image of a raven in flight, wings spread wide beneath her collar bones, in its clutches an hourglass, within which a vortex of sand slipped through the bottleneck of the time piece and fell grain by grain into the lower bulb where was depicted a desert scape. Backdrop of mountains. A saguaro. A sunset. I couldn't see this tattoo in its entirety that night. Her shirt covered most of it. Later though, I would come to know it to the line.

The demand for my camera ended with the same spontaneous indignance as it had begun. A murmur of voices on the balcony rose to a commotion. Something was happening. Some spectacle that triggered a bubbling excitement in the inebriated mass. Bodies shuffled toward and through the door as if some gravity had caught hold of them and drew them out into the night. I followed, but only after replacing my camera in my backpack which put me at the rear of the line. On the balcony, I gathered from the rising clash of drunken exclamations that he was nuts, that no way was he going to make it, that sure he could, that it actually wasn't that far. The mob turned where the balcony wrapped around the side of the building. Ahead of me, everyone was taking turns climbing an iron ladder and stepping onto the roof where they disappeared from view. When my turn came, I gripped the rungs and breathed out. Looking directly forward, I hoped I could make the climb, but after ascending only three steps, the whip and toss took hold in my skull. I closed my eyes against the mania of the ladder before me spinning hard to the left, which I knew it wasn't, yet I'd seen all the same. With paced breathing I retreated downward, and when my feet were back on hard ground, I let my grip remain on the ladder until my brain again agreed with the simple up and down of reality.

From the roof there were only a few voices. The crowd had hushed. Desperate to glimpse what was happening, I hurried along the balcony to the far end where the *L* shaped building hooked to the right. A chant came loud.

Caleb! Caleb! Caleb! Caleb!

I was able to see him there. Small against the black sky. Peeking over the edge of the roof, his eyes measuring the gap before him the way he had measured so many sets of stairs, so many drops from a higher parking lot to a lower. I kept my back to the wall as my heart began to thud. Caleb walked backward slowly and I knew he was counting the steps, calculating the necessary stride in reverse, having decided on the placement of his final foot. I considered texting him. Telling him not to do it. But I knew he wouldn't pull his phone from his pocket. He'd probably already handed it off to someone else. Even if he read my warning, it would have little power against that thunder of voices hailing his name. And then it was too late. The chant went quiet. Caleb took a running leap. My every muscle went rigid as his arms windmilled against the air, his legs pedaling an invisible bicycle until at once his limbs fell tightly in line with his body and he was like a man in a coffin. His shoes hit the surface of the water and he was gone, plunging fast to the bottom of the pool. The splash he made sent a wave in all directions that lapped over the terracotta lip and onto the pool deck. He stayed under for some seconds and when his head surfaced a cry came up from the roof. Arms were thrown into the air with the involuntary hysteria of a revival. Applause followed. And cheers. Caleb swam slowly to the edge of the pool. Raised himself to a knee. Then his feet. Sopping, he wrung his shirt. Pushed back his hair. Looking up to the crowd that had encouraged him to throw his life away, he pumped his fist, and finding me where I stood alone, he smiled. I shook my head but couldn't help but smile back, swallowing my envy.

The revelry on the roof died before Caleb crossed the courtyard for the stairs. I waited for him on the third floor landing. His shoes squeaked as he trotted to me, leaving wet waffle prints in his wake that vanished as soon as they were deposited. "You're insane," I told him. We clapped our hands together and pulled each other in, shoulder to shoulder.

"I knew I'd make it," he said.

"I'd hope so."

Someone gathered an iPod and speakers from the condo and transported them to the roof. The party was up there now. Out of reach. Caleb had gone back up to see if Ernie needed a ride home. Taken with his brief celebrity, he stayed there for a while. I couldn't blame him. I wished I was him. It was something I could have done and would have done in another time. From the roof there were voices and laughter and music, and above it all, a black sky robbed of the cosmos by the haze of orange city light. Legs dangled over the edge and the amber glow of cigarettes danced and swirled like pixies, giving evidence of people who were but silhouettes from where I stood, and when they flicked their butts outward, their fire gained in brightness for the space of a second as it found velocity against the air, tumbling then vanishing before touching ground. Beneath them all, I stood alone, smoking and counting the only lights that dared cross the wide night. Blinking from the wings and tails of commercial airliners, pinpricks of white grew into false stars one by one as they cleared the sharp pinnacles that palisaded the valley, a steady stream of them drawn in from the east, stretching back to the places everyone wants to escape. Back to the great plains and the great lakes where the west is still a thing imagined.

Michelle found me there and stood beside me, rolling her eyes at Caleb and his stunt. At the encouragement it had assembled. At my blithe shrug when she spoke of it. At herself and everyone else there gathered, drunk and so joyously adolescent under that great twinkling funnel of hope. Yesterday's refugees. Young and alive and beautiful. Proof of concept. Or so convinced.

Time was a wheel of seven days. Black and white squares on a sheet of paper pinned to the bulletin board outside the manager's office. Drag my finger down the column on the left. Find my name. Drag right. Find my shifts. They never changed. Hungover again, hair of the dog, try not to puke. Punch in. Suck it up. Count down. Punch out. Tuck the cash in your pocket and if you're smart you hide half of it from yourself.

I was riding a bus when I first saw a copy of The Valley. My clothes smelling of spilled tequila. My socks wet with the dishwater that gathered on the floor behind the bar. I stepped on it. The magazine. And I wasn't the first person to have done so. As the bus bounced and rocked and made its way south, boredom took me and I picked up the battered thing. Read an interview with a man who'd bought a one million dollar Bentley at the Barrett Jackson auction. An article about the projected future of Tempe's economy when light rail construction was finally complete. The bulk of the magazine's pages were host to advertisements for local restaurants and real estate agents. It was entirely disinteresting and wouldn't warrant a read outside the context of an after work bus ride except for those last four pages. A miscellanea of low resolution party photos taken at clubs and bars around town. All featuring beautiful people. Mostly women. A few men. Shot after shot of people angling their faces into the flash, champagne flutes and martini glasses held high. Cleavage. Eyelashes. Ass. At the bottom of the page there was an email address for submissions. Compensation negotiable.

At home, I slapped the filthy magazine on the counter. Brought my laptop to the couch. I had been taking photos at parties for what must have been a month by then, because people liked it, and by extension, me. Scrolling through a memory card, images flicked between shots of skaters in tattered clothes hucking their bodies over gaps and girls sucking in their cheeks and holding up their fingers like mock scissors poised to cut away their own lips.

After that first party where I'd been commandeered as a photographer, I received dozens of messages and friend requests on my Myspace. Everyone wanted to know when I could get them copies of the pictures I had taken. I'd spent at least a day adjusting for color and contrast before sending them out, and within hours, the photos began showing up as profile pics. More friend requests poured in. There was one from Michelle. There was one from Dom. Faye. Thea. Kevin Black. Sophie White. Kelly Sex. Billy Fucking Reed. At least two Heathers and three Taylors, all with made up last names. People I remembered photographing and not. The only person who didn't send me a friend request was the young woman who I had photographed the most. It was easy enough to find her, though. She was in everybody's top eight. Big red hair. Big red lips. Perfect skin. Perfect tits. Fuck me eyes in every single shot. Her name was Ashli Rose.

Messages in my inbox asked when I would be coming out again. Where would I be shooting photos next. Would I be at Yucca Tap on Monday? Palo Verde Lounge on Wednesday? People I'd never met wanted me around and that wanting was a palliative I didn't know I needed, but I must have, because I went to the bars and to the after parties after the bars. Where back home I'd have felt awkward walking into a stranger's house, here, with my camera bag hanging off my shoulder, I entered with confidence because my presence came with purpose. Night after night, I made my way to different corners of the east valley. Wherever the text messages said everyone would be, I went. Sometimes Collin would come, happy to secure new customers for the pharmacopeia of pills he hid in his pockets. Sometimes Michelle would pick me up, and that always felt best. She knew everyone and everyone knew her. Also, she never drank, but didn't care that I did. If I was wasted by the end of a night, she would steer me into her passenger seat and deliver me home, smoking the cigarettes I rolled for her and laughing along at whatever blathering nonsense fell from my mouth.

As these nights came and went and came again, I became a known entity. Riley. The photo guy. Where at first I was reserved in asking someone to take their picture, I quickly learned that modesty was not a celebrated virtue. People were eager to be in front of my lens. In time, I began playing coy myself, leaving my camera packed away, casually smoking and drinking in the company of new friends until at last someone would ask, "So, Riley, are you going to do the photo thing tonight? Just wondering. No pressure. It's cool if you don't." I would exhale smoke and nod. Stub out my cigarette. "Sure, if you want."

When I submitted the first set of pictures to The Valley, it was just to see if I could make a little extra money. Of the thirty or so I sent, they bought five. One of them was of Ashli, and they sent me back a note that said, "more like this." I was nervous when the photos ran. I wondered if people would feel betrayed in some way. As though we had some unspoken agreement that our nights of drinking and staggering and talking so loudly about absolutely nothing at all were a secret we kept between us. That our desire to be seen was born in the saddest place inside of us and was never to be shared. That in fact, there was some humiliation in posing for the flash. In knowing which was our good side. In being so goddamn in love with ourselves.

But I was wrong. There was no shame or embarrassment. No scowls when I raised my lens or hands pushing me away. Only glee. After that first run of pictures in The Valley, people made poorly veiled efforts to look disinterested as I entered a room, shaping their bodies, tilting their chins just so. If I walked by a table at a bar without stopping to frame up those huddled around it, they would be all the more posed on my next pass, elegant mannequins laughing loudly so I couldn't help but turn to see.

I was finishing a cigarette in the parking lot behind the PV Lounge when the door swung open and Ashli stepped out. A group of people followed her but hung back near the white block building as she crossed to where I leaned against the chain link fence.

"You're Riley, right?"

"Yeah." I lowered my cigarette and held it away from her and offered my other hand, saying, "Ashli, hi. We've met, but we haven't, like, *met* met."

She more touched than took my hand and said, "I know. I've seen you. Listen, you sell pictures to The Valley, right?"

I looked to the crowd behind her for some clue to her mood. "Yeah, well, sometimes, but I don't..."

She raised a hand to stop me. "Have you heard of AZ PM?"

I shook my head. "What's that?"

"Just another shitty, local nightlife magazine. But it's a weekly."

"OK."

"You should sell to them, too."

"I should?"

"Yes."

"OK."

Her eyes went to my camera bag on the ground next to my feet, then came back to me. "Are you going to be at Casey's tomorrow night?"

My cigarette ember burned my fingers so I dropped it to the asphalt and stepped on it. "I have to work tomorrow night, actually."

"Where do you work?"

"Saladas. In Old Town."

"Interesting. OK. I'll come by to see you some time."

"See me?"

She cut me off. "Can you be at the after party tonight?"

"I was probably, yeah, I mean, I could go, yeah.."

"Cool." She raised an eyebrow and stabbed my shoulder with a fingernail. "Don't miss me."

"Yeah. No. Of course not."

"Now give me a hug." She brought her body to mine and gave me the slightest hug I'd ever received. Her thin hands rested on my shoulders as though my body was a sculpture of ash she'd rather not destroy, and as soon as her breasts met my chest, she withdrew, but not before a curl of her cherry red hair fell and grazed my face, the least of it glancing off my lips for one wonderful half of a half of a second, long enough only for me to believe that she smelled of pomegranate and rain, but not long enough for me to be certain that I'd smelled her at all. That she wasn't a dream.

She turned and her entourage was already holding the door. Ashli walked into the square of golden light emanating from the bar, and when the last of her friends had followed her inside, the door slammed shut, leaving me alone in the dark.

I submitted the photos I took that night to The Valley and AZ PM, as Ashli had instructed. Each magazine bought one of her and a selection of others. In the weeks that followed, I spent fewer and fewer nights squatting at the bottom of a handrail or kneeling against the embankment in a drainage ditch as some misfit threw his body into the pavement over and over again, torturing himself, ripping the skin from his palms and elbows in order to switch flip this or nollie heel that, but instead, walking tall among perfect bodies in crowded bars, extending my camera high above my head to capture a group of stylish twenty somethings who all knew how to accentuate their figure by rolling their shoulder back as they crooked their arm and laid their hand on their hip, and to the person, they loved it when the flicker and flash was centered on them.

Time was a wheel of seven nights. Black and white square

tile floors sticky with beer and scuffed by heels. Hugs hello. Hugs goodbye. Inaudible words under the weight of music. Cigarettes and beer. Shots passed around. Hold them high. Drink them down. Try not to puke. Out with the camera. Pictures to remember what the poison in our blood erased from our minds. Know something happened but have no idea what. Log in. Upload everything. Power down. Pass out.

John Parson was from Prescott. His family had lived in Arizona since before statehood. A former marine with a thick beard and a voice winnowed by dry air and Marlboro Reds, Parson had bartended at Saladas for years, but despite the better money, he refused to work nights. His willingness to work the Sunday morning open meant I could sleep off most of my hangover before clocking in as his mid at noon. A man of habit, he always had the beer stocked, the fruit cut and the newspaper crossword finished and tossed into the trash by the time I stepped off the bus and climbed the patio steps to the bar.

The Prospector was another man of habit. Every Sunday he sat in the shade of the veranda and drank two Bloody Mary's. He called it his church. His long, gray beard and wide brimmed hat earned him the nickname, though none of us dared say it to his face. His real name was David, and he was a retired tax assessor by trade, though an amateur historian to speak with him. It was a rare Sunday that I arrived and he and Parson weren't into it on some facet of local lore. The Sunday they ran down the tale of the Baron of Arizona, there were jack-o-lantern lights strung behind the bar and our table tents offered a candy apple margarita.

"He went to Spain to prove it wasn't true!" The Prospector said, his fists balled on the bar in front of him.

"What wasn't true?" I asked, hanging a towel off my belt.

Parson caught me up on their conversation. "Back in the eighteen hundreds, when the US bought what is now Arizona from Mexico, they agreed to honor all the existing land titles, and there was this guy..."

"James Reavis," The Prospector said over Parson's words.

"Right, James Reavis," Parson went on, "who claimed that he had title to about a quarter of the state. He said he'd gotten it in a trade with a guy named George Willing, and the whole thing became a decades long scam. Reavis was getting mine owners and railroads to basically buy their land back from him. He went to these crazy lengths, forging paperwork, placing survey stones out in the desert, and he even went to Spain to plant fake documents in their archives."

"Which Johnson eventually proved were forgeries," The Prospector added, tomato juice clinging to his mustache. I signaled to him by wiping my own face where a mustache would be if I had one, and taking my cue, he dabbed himself with his napkin.

Parson propped himself on the bar next to me. "So I was just telling David that my great, great, grandfather was offered half of the claim by Willing before Reavis even came into the picture. Willing was in Prescott trying to officially record the claim, but he didn't have enough money, so he offered my great, great, grandfather half of it if he'd pay the recording fees, promising him they could make a killing selling people back their silver mines."

"That's funny."

The printer started grinding. Parson reached over and ripped off the white ticket. He read it, then bent deep into the beer fridge. Coming back up he said, "Reavis was a master forger, and when he took the claim he generated hundreds of documents to back it up." Parson opened four bottles of beer he'd been hugging to his chest and set them on the ticket in the well.

I said, "If you project enough confidence, you can fool almost anyone."

"Even yourself," The prospector suggested. He held up his empty glass. "Another one of these, when you have a second." Parson took his glass and set it in the sink. He went to work on making a Bloody Mary and The Prospector fixed on me, linking his hands as if in prayer. "He made mistakes, Reavis. He convinced a lot of people that he owned a significant portion of Arizona, but this actually caught the attention of Washington, as of course it would. They asked the Surveyor General to look into Reavis's claims, and in his final report he noted that the pen used on a lot of the documents wasn't a quill. You know, a feather pen. But that it had a steel tip."

"Takes a keen eye, I suppose."

"In all things," The Prospector said. Parson set his fresh drink before him and The Prospector removed the plastic spear with two olives impaled upon it and pulled away the first of them with his front teeth.

"So that's how he got caught?" I asked.

Parson was reclining again, arms folded over his chest. "Yeah but the guy didn't give up. He actually doubled down and married a Mexican woman he met in California, and together they claimed she was the heiress to the original land grant." He chuckled, and went on in his hoarse rasp, opening his arms so he could hold his hands wide and with gesture, suggest the grandeur of the story. "The guy had gone from first claiming that he'd gotten title to all this land through a partnership with another guy who happened to be dead, and when that started to fall apart, he was like, 'Hey, turns out, when I was on vacation I happened to meet the long lost heiress to that exact same hundred year old land grant, and guess what, we fell in love and got married.'"

"Sounds like a bullshitter's, bullshitter," I said.

"It worked though!" Parson laughed.

"For a while," The Prospector corrected. "For a while." He took a sip from his drink then set it to the side. He spun his stool at an angle as if to address not only Parson and me, but the rest of the patio and perhaps the patios beyond. "Reavis became very wealthy. He'd been paid out millions of dollars selling land that was never his to begin with. He bought properties across the US and an estate in Mexico. Had a mansion right over in Arizola. He even found himself a lovely woman. The so-called baroness of Arizona. He dressed her up in the latest fashions and she joined him in the high society life and I'm sure after a while they both began to believe their own lies. I don't see how they couldn't." The Prospector was no longer looking at us and he stroked his beard as he stared away up the road. The printer set to grinding and Parson ripped the ticket and moved to the beer fridge. The Prospector was talking again, but more quietly now, as if he wasn't sure of the words he was about to speak until he heard them leave his own mouth. "I don't believe a person can live a lie effectively without first convincing themselves that there is a greater truth to it," he said. "Their whole scheme involved convincing other people, regarded people, of the validity of their position. But when you go about curating the perceptions of others, you need to make them want to believe you. It's not enough to show them some old paper. It's not even enough to come with a good story. You need to bring them in, and the best way to make someone else believe a thing is to believe it yourself." Without looking, his hand found his glass and carried it until the straw was at his lips.

"A healthy dose of fear goes a long way too," Parson said, returning from the well. "When everything you've ever worked for is on the line and someone comes waving official looking paper in your face, it's hard not to be a believer."

"What happened to him in the end?" I asked.

The Prospector snapped from his trance. "Oh, he went to jail. In a fit of hubris, Reavis sued the US government, which of course meant they sent out the dogs of war. They went over everything with a fine tooth comb. Every document. Every scrap. And the whole edifice collapsed. When he got out of prison he was broke. His wife left him. He died poor. They made a movie about him."

"The American dream," I said.

The Prospector grinned and gave me a wink. Sitting back, he let the sun fall on his face until it hurt his eyes. "Fascinating thing about the guy is that, in a sense, he really cared about

Arizona. He had big ideas about building dams and canals to irrigate the desert."

"Do you think that was part of him believing his own bullshit?"

The Prospector spun his glass in small circles as he weighed his thoughts. "Could be. Could be that in his mind, as the Baron of Arizona, he felt some responsibility towards actually cultivating his charge. That in all his time here he couldn't help but witness real need. Just because he'd attained his high station maliciously, doesn't mean he didn't look out from that elevated position and see all there was to be seen. You have to imagine him a cursed man in that regard. He knew his fraud, but it gave him a true calling, one he could never pursue in good faith after his lie was exposed."

"Heavy is the head," I said.

"Heavier yet when the crown is make believe."

"All that glitters."

The Prospector tipped the rim of his glass at me. He moved the straw aside and gulped his drink until it was empty. He set a twenty dollar bill on the bar and placed his empty glass atop of it and stood. "Make sure Parson cuts you in on that."

Shake was everything. A rock and roll dance party held every Saturday night at a shit bar in a white brick building with no windows, only a black door beneath a glowing red sign that said, ROGUE. On any night of the week, The Rogue was just another dive bar. Quiet. Dark. A place to get drunk for less than twenty bucks. But on Saturdays it offered an experience bordering on religious. A service for those whose only God was the immediacy of the moment. Whose choir of angels were music, fashion, and sex. At Shake, one sought not the animation of the holy spirit but the electricity of their fellow damned. No hymns. No psalms. No falling on one's knees under the weight of divine touch. Only movement and sound. Strobing red light and music so loud as to forbid the possibility of conversation. Perfume and hairspray and sweat infecting the air. And so many happily heathen twenty somethings eager to erase whoever it was they had been back wherever it was they had come from. Congregating in a tight mass, bodies pressed on bodies, all moving as one wretched organism over a checkerboard floor sticky with spilled beer and tracked with grime.

The walls of The Rogue were black, or a color close enough in the low light to convince the eye that they were. A pool table in the center of the space was useless except as a repository for spent bottles and cans. The long bar was lit only well enough for the two people staffing it to dispense the simplest of mixed beverages into disposable plastic cups, and over their heads a mounted TV always silently played some ironic film. *Conan the Barbarian. Barbarella. Legend.*

Lining the wall opposite the bar was a row of booths of torn and taped black vinyl, each shaped around a circle table of painted black wood that was inscribed endlessly with names and symbols meaningless to all but those who'd drunkenly etched them with their keys. The last booth in the darkest corner was by some unspoken yet universally understood covenant reserved for Ashli Rose and whoever she tapped to surround herself with. Never actually sitting on the seats, but rather up on the top rim the of the booth, using the cushion as a footrest, Ashli and her chosen few sat with their backs against the wall high above the flow of undulating hair-dos and drinks held aloft to avoid spillage, as the gathered crowd drifted in a slow and endless circle. Beside the bar, just to the left of the door, the dance floor. An elevated stage one had to climb upon and jump down from, the dance floor on Saturday night was never not full. On it we gave command of our tender flesh to David Bowie, to Billy Idol, to Joy Division and New Order. Gave willingly and received in kind. Painted by the swirl and slash of red and white light, girls and boys all dressed in whatever they thought would make them look their most fuckable, because to find someone to fuck, was of course, the point. Some made unafraid by alcohol. Some made certain by cocaine. Everyone seeking to affirm that most fragile of beliefs. That they did in fact exist. That they were in fact young. That it was in fact now.

The first time I went to Shake, I was still burdened. To ignore what I thought of myself and what I wanted others to think of me in the way dancing requires was something foreign to my body. But at the ripe peak of my drunkenness, Michelle dragged me up, and to Dramarama's *Anything, Anything,* she shook her hips and head and tossed her brown hair wildly. Her eyes closed, she smiled wide. I stepped to the hammer of the drums and she took my hands in hers, pulling me in as she sang along with the blistering chorus, and though her voice was entirely drowned out I followed her lips as she yelled *marry me marry me marry me*. On successive Saturdays, it grew easier. Entranced by the volume of the music and the heat of the bodies all shifting and moving as one, I learned to love giving in. On the dance floor, no one was judging your movement, only your refusal to commit to it. It wasn't a sin to be bad at dancing, only to restrain yourself from enjoying it. It was how we shed our skin. And as long as I wasn't near the edge, as long as I stayed safely cocooned within the throng of dancers, my vertigo never came to call.

By the time I brought Caleb to Shake, I'd become a regular fixture. The bouncer, Clint, waved away my ID and instead shook my hand and thumbed me towards the door. Inside, Caleb followed me to the bar where I skipped the line and stood in the well. The blonde bartender with feathery hair came to me smiling. She stepped around the bar and gave me a hug.

"Who's this?" she asked, screaming to be heard.

"Caleb." I shouted back. Then to Caleb, "Faye."

Faye pulled my hand, leading me down a hall lined with empty kegs to a storage room. I waved for Caleb to follow. With the door shut behind us, we could hear each other but it didn't matter because we didn't say anything, only watched as Faye pulled a hidden whiskey bottle from behind a box on a shelf, unscrewed it, took a swig herself, then passed the bottle to me. I took a deep swallow, then handed the bottle to Caleb who did the same. After he drank, Faye took the bottle, replaced the cap, and hid it away again. "You doing pictures tonight?" She asked.

"Yeah."

"Come get me now before all my makeup runs and I look like a wet dog." She went up on her toes to kiss my cheek. Back at the bar, she snapped two cans of beer and I adjusted my F Stop before taking a series of pictures as she poured liquor into cups, her back slightly arched, her tits pushed out, her chin held up and to the side in a way that made her jawline look thin and angular.

We took the beers and Caleb tried to set down cash when I pushed his hand back towards his pocket. I jerked my head toward the crowd and he followed me through the tight mass of bodies to the back booth. Ashli was sitting up against the wall in the center of a group of people. Some I knew. Some I didn't. Seeing my camera, they all readied themselves by looking as disinterested as possible, posing in a way that hid the fact that they were posing. My flash blazed like lightning as I stepped and reached to find different angles.

"I'm going to go get a few of the dancers," I yelled to Caleb who was waiting at my elbow. With my camera held over my head I squeezed sideways through the crowd, occasionally stopping to get a shot of a good looking guy or girl. If they leaned into my ear to ask who I was, or who I worked for, I handed them one of the cheap business cards I kept in my back pocket. Reading it, they would smile and nod. At the dance floor, I climbed up to the DJ booth where there were a few inches of space I could plant myself. I photographed the DJ first. Pinching headphones between his shoulder and ear, he pointed at me and squinted, like there was something we both understood. Artists in the trenches working towards a common and necessary goal.

Everything I shot of the dancers was a smear of color. Faces detached from their owners' bodies. Lipsticked smiles implied but without edge. Waving arms only arcing trails in space. Whole humans reduced to simple trajectories. An honest portrait of matter on the go.

Jumping down from the dance floor, I returned to the back booth. Caleb was where I'd left him. I was packing away my camera when someone tapped me on the shoulder. I turned and they were pointing at Ashli. She curled her finger, beckoning me, then spoke into the ear of the guy sitting next to her and he climbed down from the booth leaving an open space that Ashli patted with her hand. I awkwardly climbed through everyone's legs until I was sitting next to her. She leaned in to hug me.

"How are you?" She yelled into my ear.

I nodded.

"After party at Kevin Black's house tonight. You must be there!"

I nodded again.

"I have a favor to ask you."

I mouthed the word *what*.

"We'll talk later," she screamed into my ear.

I nodded.

The guy I had displaced next to Ashli returned to the booth. He carried ten shots of yellow liquid, five per hand, his fingers like pincers threaded into the mouths of the clear plastic cups. He set them on the table and began passing them up. After everyone had been given a shot, there was one left and I pointed to Caleb. The guy handed Caleb the remaining cup and everyone raised their drinks high and touched their cup to all others then poured the liquor down their throats, only finding that it was a small amount of Red Bull and a large amount of vodka as it passed their tongues. The empty cups were all stacked upside down in a short tower. Caleb added his to the stack, and seeing him, Ashli leaned into my ear.

"Who's that?"

Her hair fell across my face. So close to her neck, I breathed in whatever that smell was. A perfume, or maybe just her. I was loud but tried not to hurt her ear. "Caleb. My skate friend."

She looked at him and he must have felt her gaze because he looked at her and smiled.

"He looks familiar," she said.

"He jumped off the roof at that party a while back."

She looked at me wide eyed, as if what I'd said was too incredible to be believed. She briefly studied Caleb again, then shook her head. "I don't remember that." Out of some devotion to Caleb or maybe to time itself, I leaned into her ear, ready to give further detail, as surely she couldn't have forgotten something so irregular. So recent. But the first notes of Depeche Mode's *Precious* blared loudly and the crowd screamed their approval and Ashli's arms flew above her head and she rocked at her waist. Flirtatious. Giddy. A girl seated across from her did the same and Ashli reached for her hand. Together they climbed down from the booth, and followed by several others, Ashli led the girl through a crowd that was all too happy to part for her as she made her way across the bar. She climbed onto the stage then reached back for the girl's hands and pulled her onto that full dance floor where more than enough space was made to accommodate them. Right up front. Right in the center.

The girl was alluring, but not seductive in the effortless way that Ashli was. Ashli moved like the song had been written for her and every next note could only sound should she allow it into existence. She knew she was being watched and wanted and despised and her body was daring the world to do any damn thing about it. Her friend though, she danced like she had to. Like it was necessary. A last alternative to blood letting. Eyes closed tight. Hips spiraling and arms winding in coils as she reached for the lights above. Her mouthing along with the music that things get broken a promise or a prayer. That was the first time I really noticed her. Dominique.

Michelle drove. Thea was in the passenger seat riding on Walker's lap. Caleb was in the back seat with me, very drunk and asking questions too loudly.

"Where are we even going?"

"To the after party," I told him.

"But where is *that*?"

Thea leaned forward so she could see Caleb between the seats. "Kevin Black's house."

He looked at me, his face scrunched. "Who the fuck is Kevin Black?"

"Just a guy," I said, my voice low, hoping he'd match my volume.

Thea yelled, "He's Michelle's ex-boyfriend!"

Michelle's eyes went to the rearview mirror. "And he's a fucking asshole!"

"Yeah he is," Thea said, nestling back into Walker's body.

"I gotta piss," Caleb said, and then he laughed for no reason.

The road was empty of cars as we drove through Mesa. Bodegas still had their lights on but their parking lots were empty. Above the road, orange lamps shone from poles that bent midway up their masts, looking as though they were bowing to our car, a long line of them like humble servants guiding us across the night. Passing under them, the flicker of golden light washed our faces again and again. Caleb pulled himself between the two front seats and yelled, "Where are we even going?"

Kevin Black's flat ranch house had a squat palm tree in the front yard that looked like an outsized pineapple. In an older neighborhood, every house on the street had a box air conditioner mounted on the roof. A crisscross of power lines ran the alley behind the homes and the black wires between them rose and fell like yawning waves against the night sky. Arriving cars parked on both sides of the street facing whichever direction was convenient for the driver. We crunched over the gravel yard as a group, breaking around the great pineapple and reconvening on the doorstep. No one knocked. We went right in.

"Oh God, he is playing his own album," Michelle said the moment she stepped into the foyer and heard the electronic beat layered beneath a distorted vocal track. In the living room we were eyeballed by the quiet pockets of people who stood with bottles and cans in their hands, their bodies slowly shifting to the music as if it were an automatic response. Caleb slipped away to find a bathroom and the rest of us filed into the kitchen where a whispered conversation stopped as soon as we entered. Heads turned our way only enough so that we could be viewed through the corners of eyes. We retaliated by pretending not to notice. A guy with hair swooping over half his face asked if we wanted drinks.

"What do you got?" Thea asked.

He showed her a bottle of peppermint liqueur.

Thea winced. "Oh God. Gross."

"There's High Life in the fridge," the guy said.

Thea asked if there was ice. There was, and except for Michelle, we all let the guy pour us a half cup of the liqueur. He said it was better with Sprite but that there wasn't any Sprite. Caleb rejoined us in the backyard. He must have been bouncing his head to the beat of the song playing loudly on the speakers because Kevin Black walked up to him and said, "You like that, huh?"

"Yeah, it's pretty tight," Caleb said. Kevin beamed and the rest of us hurried to the far corner of the yard where a set of wicker chairs were arranged in a circle.

"Poor Caleb," Thea said.

"Poor Kevin," I corrected. "They're about to talk in circles until the sun comes up."

I rolled a cigarette for Michelle and then another for myself. With Thea and Walker we sat watching the door that led to the kitchen as more and more people who had been at Shake filtered into the yard. Some collapsed on the old couches under the awning. Some stood teetering in clusters of three and four. A girl threw up in a dark corner while a guy rubbed her back and spoke encouraging words. From our camp we commented on everyone's clothes. On how drunk they seemed. On who they were fucking or who they used to fuck. We said nothing that wasn't sarcastic or mean and we knew that really, we were still waiting. For what, we couldn't possibly say. Not with words. All we knew is that every night begins with potential for something to happen, something worth witnessing, something you might just experience from the center and that that moment will be great. So you pick your clothes carefully, you set your hair just right, you look in the mirror and hope that you're good enough and then you travel out into the world to coalesce with everyone else who has set themselves on that same course, seeking that something the pulse and velocity of youth have convinced you is out there to be found. And for a time, it feels like you're closing in on it. One drink. Two drinks. Three. Five. Ten. The hours slide by and then the inevitable happens. The night is no longer in its becoming but a thing on the wane. Somewhere behind you the great fire of possibility has been extinguished and only smoldering dread remains. Disappointed and a little embarrassed, you smoke a cigarette you don't even want and know that everyone's hearts are falling into sync. It's time to admit defeat. Time to sneak away before you're the last sad person to realize they should have snuck away.

But then the kitchen came alive with voices. Loud and enthusiastic. A group of people who'd only just arrived brought with them a welcome electricity. The music that was playing stopped and the Wolf Parade song *I'll Believe in Anything* replaced it and Kevin Black hurried into the house to protest but it was too late. A chorus of laughter inside reenergized those of us languishing in the yard. Ashli came out onto the patio followed by a crowd and they formed a circle around a stone bar top. Under strands of red lights shaped like chilis, they talked all at once. They laughed all at once. And in doing so, turned back the clock.

Rising from my chair, I said, "I need to talk to Ashli real quick."

"About what?" Michelle asked.

I was already walking away. "I don't know." Drunk, but able to pretend that I wasn't, I went to where Ashli stood, her pale skin made red by the lights dangling above. At her elbow, I looked down to the marble bar top and the two lines of cocaine awaiting her.

She turned to me, realized who I was, and said, "Riley. Perfect," then bent her nose to the rolled up twenty in her hand and in two short strokes snorted away the white powder. "Fuck. Fuck. Fuck." she said, her head thrown back, eyes blinking furiously. Then she pulled me into one of her fragile hugs. "You made it. Good." Releasing me, she pushed away the guy who had been next to her and guided me into his place. My body moved as directed and once standing where she wanted me, she offered me the rolled up bill. On the marble slab were two lines of cocaine. "Here," she said, and as though it had been my intention all along, I took the twenty. Gestured it as if to say "Cheers." I'd never done cocaine before. I'd never been offered it before. Until that moment, the prospect of using it had always terrified me, especially since my fall and the subsequent dysfunction of my brain. But Ashli stood me in front of it like it was mine, like of course I would do it, like obviously I did this kind of thing, like as soon as this simple formality was out of the way we could get down to whatever business between us so desperately needed attention. So I bowed to the twin rails of powder, and pinching my left nostril I snorted deeply with my right, taking in both lines in quick succession. There was ice behind my eyes. Cords and veins hidden in my dark sockets flash frozen then shattered as my cortex was slapped with an open palm. I jerked myself upright, dropped the rolled bill and blinked uncontrollably. "Shit!" I yelled.

"It's good, right?"

The next person in line was snuffing away while I was still pinching the bridge of my nose against the lightning racing from my face outward to my fingers and toes. Opening my eyes wide, I was somehow taller. Broader. Ready to crush coal into diamonds. Ashli was circling her hands, talking about a favor she needed. Photographs. She liked the pictures I took. They had helped her at work. How'd they help her at work? She was a dancer. A stripper? Yeah. You didn't know that? How would I know that? But that's cool. She was a featured performer now. She had big crowds. Huge. She was making more money. So much more. That's great! Was working fewer hours too. Cool! That's so cool. Seriously. But listen. She needed more pictures. A lot more. Not for The Valley. No? No. Fuck The Valley. She was going to be a Suicide Girl. A Suicide Girl? Yeah, a Suicide Girl. What's a? It's a website. For models. But not, like, regular models. Hot girls, yeah. But like, alt girls. Girls with tattoos and piercings and shit. No way. Yeah. It's like Playboy. For hot girls. Underwear. Bathing suits. Got it. Some naked. OK, wow. Could I do it? Do what? Take the pictures. Sure. Of course. Anything. Anything? Awesome! How many? When? I mean, a lot. How soon can you? Whenever you want. OK! Awesome. Fuck yeah! This'll be great. Yeah? I mean, you're so beautiful! Yeah? Totally, it'll be easy. Yeah? Here's the thing. I can't really pay. That's fine. Yeah? Yeah. Are you sure? Totally. Fuck yeah. Just let me know when. Fuck yeah! Awesome!

I don't know how long it went on like that. It could have been five minutes, it could have been an hour. I was locked on Ashli's face and with her locked on mine I was unwilling to do anything that might encourage her to walk away. I ignored everyone around us as they chattered on, as they chopped up more lines of coke, as the laughter in the yard grew louder, as that laughter moved to the roof and turned to howls and then bottles shattered in the street. It was when the music disappeared that I finally stopped talking long enough to hear the angry voices in the house. The authority with which they gave instructions. The weight of their boots on the floor. And then as though we were all attuned to the same psychic frequency, everyone in the backyard began running for the high cinder block wall that enclosed us. I was dragging Ashli by the hand when the first officer came hunting into the yard.

Feet lost high heels. Denim wrapped legs scrambled on the flat, gripless surface of the gray wall. A flashlight beam wheeled side to side until it fixed on me as I made a basket of my fingers to hoist Ashli by the foot so she could toss her body onto and over the wall. Shadows were jerking and dodging in every direction. As she finished her climb, Ashli's shoe mashed my cheek, turning my head to where I caught Caleb at full sprint. Despite his drunken state, his feet found the corner where two walls met and he ran vertically up their faces like he was climbing a ladder. Behind me, the distinct *whoomp* of a body hitting the ground, losing all of its breath beneath the weight of a jangling officer. A voice demanded that I stay put and someone screamed that they were hurting their arm. I backed from the wall, and with two bounding steps, I leapt, caught the rough surface of the top layer of block and pressed myself upwards. A hand was reaching for my leg as I rolled over the wall. On the far side I crashed into a dry bush that shattered beneath me, shards of it sticking into my shirt and arms. People fled in both directions down the alley. Ashli was nowhere in sight. I ran to the left first, but dug my shoes into the grit, sliding to a stop to switch directions when blue and red lights flashed in the gap where the alley opened to the sidewalk and the silhouette of someone ahead of me threw its hands into the air. Charged with the terror of being caught using illicit chemicals and simultaneously by the power of those selfsame chemicals, I ran so fast I almost fell forward over my feet. Before breaching the sidewalk, I slowed to a trot and looked up and down the road. A squad car with its lights off was turning onto Kevin Black's street. When it was out of sight, I walked in the opposite direction, toward the glowing Filiberto's sign on the corner. At the window I ordered french fries and a coke. Sitting at a picnic table beneath a buzzing light, I dipped fries in ketchup while my heart tried to punch a hole through my chest. I texted Michelle. Some minutes later, she pulled into the parking lot and saved me.

It took two days. Maybe three. Photographing and delivering several different sequences of Ashli. Hundreds and hundreds of shots in which she starts clothed and slowly strips away layers until she's naked, posing in every inviting way. Leaning against a wall. On her knees, pressing her tits together. On all fours in underwear that only just covers her pussy, her painted fingers teasing at pulling it away, eyes half open, mouth begging sex. We stayed in a hotel suite to do the work. Eating take out. Smoking on the patio. Hours on hours of creeping madness and animal desire that moved alternately like minutes or days, depending on which chemicals were most recently stuffed inside my veins. Before I'd taken a single picture, Ashli called some guy named Troy and asked him to deliver cocaine. Standing in the room's kitchenette, he flicked open a knife to cut a line on the counter for Ashli to sample. At sundown, she sent me out to buy several bottles of liquor. For her it wasn't enough to shoot the photographs. She insisted on reviewing everything. Retouching what could be improved with Photoshop. Reshooting what couldn't. She wasn't going to fall into the shuffle of endless Suicide Girl profiles. She was going to have the most popular, most viewed, most downloaded portfolio on the site. And that was just the beginning.

Midnights bled into dawns with me staring at my laptop screen, and if I couldn't airbrush away another minuscule mark or imperfection, Ashli would chop a line of coke and put it in front of me. If I hesitated she had me snort it off her body, so I learned to hesitate. Her blue eyes fixed in mine. Her lips parted, but only just. "Riley..." she'd say, dragging my name out. She knew I was weak. Simple. Easy to bring to heel. When the blow had me erratic and unable to focus, talking too much and losing track, forgetting instructions she'd given only minutes before, she'd pour some vodka over ice and stir in red Gatorade. "Drink this," she commanded. And I drank. Then back to trying on outfits. Mixing and matching. "Fishnets or no? What do you think?" She would stand in the mirror judging the cut of bikini tops or spin in slow circles on her tiptoes and ask me what I thought about different colored panties. "Do you like the G String?" The cocaine had me rabid. Tooth and claw. Ready to pin her down. So I locked myself in the bathroom and jerked off. More than once. I had to. I think she knew I was doing it. I think she liked that I was doing it. That I couldn't help myself. That with so little effort she could slip into my mind and walk around kicking at the machinery of neurons and glands and then laugh at how I yipped and spasmed in response. Naked and sitting close to me as I scrolled through my camera evaluating what we'd shot, she would let her hair fall on my cheek knowing damn well that it was on my cheek. She teased me. It was how she passed the time.

During the few hours when she allowed us to sleep, we laid next to each other in the room's only bed. I woke with her arm over my chest. Her breath on my neck. I didn't move because when she opened her eyes she would understand her mistake and withdraw that arm. Turn away. She dreamed of someone who wasn't me. Someone better than me. She didn't love me and I knew that, but I didn't care. I was in bed with Ashli Rose. And for the first time since I rose from the dead earlier that year, I felt present. The future and the past had been obliterated by her steady breathing. Those were my seconds. My minutes. She didn't know it but I was collecting them. Banking them. Because I knew that when she awoke the clock would start again and she would regain control of the room, of me, and whatever triumph I'd succeeded in gathering would be scattered like blowing sand. But truly, that is the story of everything, isn't it? We grasp what we can and then grain by grain it's taken from us. The accident of our happiness is set right by the persistence of time. But knowing this we grasp all the same because our knowing cannot help us.

Sunlight warmed the room and as her mind passed through the liminal band between sleep and wake she groaned, and in a low voice asked, maybe me, maybe herself, "Are you anything?" Too afraid to speak, I only breathed and followed the paint lines on the ceiling where light met shadow until I felt her body tighten and stir. When her eyes opened, mine were waiting. She sat up, her face confused as she assessed her surroundings. Assessed me. She shook her head and said more to the room than to either of us, "I don't think so," and she walked to a shirt that was draped over a chair. Pulled it over her body. Went to the toilet and peed with the door open while I put on the coffee. She brushed her teeth and I brushed mine and we were side by side in the mirror. Real people in that way the morning makes you real. She looked great. I looked worn. Weathered. Not by wrinkle or gray hair, but by my pallor or some light missing in my eyes, aged. She spit and I spit. I found my makings and took a seat outside. She sat in the chair next to me where she rubbed grit from between her toes and told me she'd like a cigarette. We smoked and said nothing and while I showered a car came to pick her up. Wrapped in a towel, I read the note she left in place of my flash drive. *Thanks Ry.* She was gone and I was alone and there in the vacancy of the room, I had deja vu.

———

The coffee maker gurgled and spit. When I removed the pot to pour myself a cup, the drips that continued to fall hit the hot plate, sizzled, and vanished. I was on my way back to the couch, bringing the mug to my lips when Collin's door opened and a blonde woman slipped out. I moved out of her path. I would have said hi, but before I could swallow my coffee she opened the front door and vanished into the harsh light. Collin exited his room a moment later. Walked to the bathroom and pissed then crossed the living room for the kitchen. As I sunk into the couch with my laptop balanced on my legs, he poured himself a cup of coffee, reached into a cabinet for a green bottle of whiskey, unscrewed the cap, and let a heavy slug of the liquor top off his mug. Without breaking focus on my laptop screen, I asked him who the girl was.

"Kate," he said, his voice still sandy.

"She looked nice."

"She was nice." He snorted up something thick, spit it into the kitchen sink, and ran the faucet to rinse it away.

"Where'd you two meet?"

"Saddle Ranch."

"What were you doing at Saddle Ranch?"

"You know me." He paused his sentiment to spit once more into the sink and rinse it down, then rounded the countertop and came into the living room saying, "I'm always mixing business with pleasure." He sat on the cushion next to me and looked at the photo I was working on. "Damn, who's that?"

"Dominique"

"She's a babe."

"Yeah, she's alright."

"She cool?"

"We've never really spoken." Collin lifted his mug for a sip. His knuckles were torn. He had a cut on his upper lip. I asked him what happened.

"Guy was wearing fucking rings," he said, dabbing at the cut. I clicked over to the next photo that needed retouching. Faye from The Rogue. Collin asked, "Those tits real?" I told him I wouldn't know. He swallowed coffee and nudged me with his elbow. "For a guy who hangs around so many babes, you sure don't get much action, do you?" I told him that I do OK and he looked at me like what I'd said was not only an obvious but pathetic lie. He snorted, "What, the dumpster blow job?"

At one of those early Shakes, when I was reeling drunk, I'd gotten a blowjob as I steadied myself against the dumpster behind the bar. I didn't remember much about it. A slurping sound and the stink of trash. I have no idea who the girl was, only that she had brown hair and when she spit my come out it landed on my jeans. I wondered if we ever saw each other again. If she remembered it better than I did. I'd been too proud when I told Collin about it the following day and he'd made fun of me, so I never told him about any of the others. Like Cara. She took me to her place after a night at Furio. We fucked and then when she slept she pissed the bed. The next morning she tried to blame it on me. Said I was disgusting and told me never to call her. Jackie was beautiful. Truly. On two different nights she let me fuck her, but each time I was so wasted I could barely get hard. I couldn't bring myself to try a third time. Or to tell Collin. I changed the subject, "Speaking of action, did you have to fight for Kate's honor, or what?"

He set his mug on the coffee table and turned towards me so he could gesture his way through his telling. "Get this, right? I'm sitting at the bar, waiting to meet a guy..."

"Business or pleasure?"

He scowled.

"Go on," I said.

"Anyway, this drunk asshole comes and stands in the well, trying to holler at the bartender. And Kate has to get around this guy to pick up her drinks. So, very politely, I say 'Hey, she's trying to get through,' and the guy turns and sees Kate behind him, and you know what he does?"

"What does he do?"

"Nothing! Just goes back to hollering for the bartender, who is ignoring him on purpose so he'll get a fucking clue and walk around to the line." I clicked to the next photo on my screen. To the next girl. Seeing her, Collin pointed. "Goddamn! Who's the dime?"

"Ashli Rose."

"Is that her real name?"

"I never thought to ask."

"Now, I know you haven't fucked her."

"Obviously."

"Where was I?"

"Drunk guy needs to get a clue."

"Right, but of course he doesn't, because he's fucking faded, and when Kate tries to reach past him to pick up her drinks, he bumps into her, knocks her tray over, she drops everything, and so I walk over to him and say right to his face, 'Hey, dip shit, you need to move.'"

"Let me guess, he appreciated your even tempered approach?"

"Yeah, and now we're best friends. No. He called me a jerk off and pushed me away by putting his hand on my face."

"On your face?"

"On my fucking, face." He sipped from his mug. After he swallowed he said, "So, obviously, I couldn't have that. I had to drop him."

"And now you and Kate are in love."

He faked a laugh. "Yeah, no. But it was a good ice breaker. She and I got to talking, I stuck around after her shift, you know how it goes." Selecting the next file from a menu, Michelle's face took over my screen. "She's cute," Collin said. "Why don't you hook up with her?"

"I'm actually waiting for her to pick me up. We're getting lunch."

"Daytime date. How grown up."

"Not a date. It's not like that with her. We're actually friends."

He scooted closer to me. "Go back to the first picture again."

"Which one?"

"The little Mexican girl. With the juicy ass." I dragged my finger on the trackpad, clicking on the frame of a different image. When the picture of Dom came up, Collin said, "Yeah, her!" He sipped his coffee. Leaned in. "She's fine. I gotta come out with you more."

My phone vibrated on the counter. As I started for the kitchen, I told him, "There's a party tonight if you want to come." I read my text, and when I folded my phone shut again, Collin had my laptop resting on his legs. He had a broad, leering grin on his face.

"Hey!" I said, rushing back to the couch.

"I had no idea!" He teased. He had clicked through my open tabs and found pictures of Ashli topless. I grabbed the laptop and he laughed, "Riley! How could you not tell me?"

"There's nothing to tell," I said, powering the computer down.

"Nothing to tell? You're Larry Flynt!"

"Hardly."

As I hid my laptop away in my closet, Collin called from the living room, "Yo, where's this party at tonight?"

"I gotta go," I said, passing him as I headed for the door.

"Is Ashli Rose going to be there?" He followed me. "Or that Dominique, girl?"

"I'll see you at work," I said over my shoulder, as I stepped onto the balcony. The sun was bright overhead and I took the stairs at a trot.

In the parking lot Michelle was propped against her car. Seeing me, she opened her arms. "Hey fuck face!" She was wearing lipstick. I couldn't help but smile when she smiled. We hugged then slid into the car. Michelle spun the wheel on her iPod and asked, "Is Casey's O.K?"

"Casey's is fine," I told her.

We were both in sunglasses as she merged into traffic and headed south towards Tempe. I set my makings on my lap and began rolling a cigarette. Knowing Michelle would want one too, I made hers first, taking care to get the shape exactly right, to keep the thickness even from end to end. She didn't even finish saying, "Can I get one?" before I was handing it to her. With a smile and a laugh she thanked me and held it patiently between her fingers. When my own, slightly less perfect cigarette was between my lips, I reached over the center console with my lighter cupped in my hand and flicked it. Michelle leaned to the waiting flame and sucked her cigarette to life. I lit my own, and we both smoked and didn't feel the need to say any damn thing at all. It was one of my favorite things about her. She had the ability to be with a person without feeling the need to fill every empty second with talk. We rolled our windows down and enjoyed the sublime act of smoking in a car on a beautiful sunny day while music added a soundtrack to the moving pictures flashing by. Strip malls and strip clubs. Under the 202 then over the lake. The peak of *A* Mountain jutting above Sun Devil Stadium and the evenly spaced palm trees between us and the tennis courts. We turned west and were slowed by traffic on University Drive as so many tanned and blonde bodies filled the crosswalks.

"Must be between classes," I said, stuffing my cigarette butt out the window.

"It's always like this," Michelle said, bracing her arm on the door frame and resting her head on her fist.

The car crawled as we passed the campus. *Turn Into* by The Yeah Yeah Yeah's began playing on her stereo and Michelle turned up the volume and sang along. Her voice wasn't great, but it was honest, and her hair floated and bounced as she swung her head. She looked at me with that smile that was permanently engraved in her face and said, "Sing!"

"I don't know it," I told her.

She drummed her hands on the wheel. Her bracelets jangled. The unmistakable sound of skateboard wheels came rushing up from the bike lane and I turned to see a guy with a mop of tangled hair and a backpack kick-push past us. He weaved left and right through the swarm of people crossing the road, ollied up the curb and disappeared somewhere ahead. I cracked my door and spit on the blacktop.

Casey Moore's is an Irish pub set back in one of Tempe's older neighborhoods. A converted house, the restaurant has a wide brick patio ringed by a high wall of wooden pylons standing on end, shoulder to shoulder, all strung with white lights. In a square booth built around a square picnic table large enough to host a family, we sat across from each other. Me with a Guinness, Michelle with a Coca-Cola. The few palm trees standing about provided no shade.

"I don't know how you tolerate us," I told her, as she sipped her drink through a straw.

"Who?"

"All of us. You're always stone sober and putting up with drunks."

She shrugged. "I don't know. It's funny, I guess."

We each had a cheeseburger. I finished mine in minutes but Michelle ate hers slowly. Chewed thoughtfully. I was on my second beer and smoking a cigarette before she was onto her second half.

"How's the fake grass business?" I asked.

She held her hand in front of her mouth, swallowed, then said laconically, "Booming."

"But never blooming."

She dropped her head. "You're a dork. And grass doesn't bloom."

"Yes it does. It just doesn't make a big flower because it's wind pollinated. It doesn't need to attract bees." She dunked a fry in ketchup and looked at me skeptically. "I mowed lawns in college," I explained

"I guess I've been in the desert too long." She bit her fry and when she'd washed it down, she went on. "Work is fine. Bookkeeping is boring, but there is always something that needs to be done and my boss is good to me. How about you? How's Saladas?"

"I finally got a bar shift."

"When?"

"Tuesday morning."

"Well that'll be jumping."

"Gotta start somewhere."

"Save your money."

"Why would I do that?"

She took another small bite of food and covered her mouth as she chewed. "So you can quit selling pictures to those stupid magazines."

"People like it."

She cocked her head to the side and even through her sunglasses I could feel her judging me. "Ry, it's so gross."

"Taking party pictures?"

"Not taking them. Well, maybe a little. But mainly the fact that there are magazines buying them."

"And one website now, too."

"Exactly! *Ugh*, it's so..." She didn't know how to end her sentence so she sipped her drink instead. I knew what she was trying to say and I knew that if I thought about it at all I would agree with her, but at that moment I wasn't ready to say so out loud, so instead I took a double gulp of my beer that was warming in the sun. She wiped her mouth and crumpled her napkin onto her plate. "I've just been thinking about everything lately."

"Well, don't do that."

She was looking everywhere except at me, but her gaze couldn't leave the sunlit patio, walled in as it was. "It all just feels so fake. Like, what are we doing? Every night is the same. Every week is the same. And those magazines glorify it, making it seem like we're all a part of something enviable, like we're living lives that other people should aspire to. They trick people into thinking they're a celebrity because, because what? They're popular in some hipster bar scene? It's such bullshit."

"You like it when they run pictures of you."

Her shoulders fell. "You're right. I do. Or I did. And now I'm asking myself why and I'm embarrassed for myself."

"Embarrassed might be a bit much."

She sat forward. Spoke with force. "It's not though. Getting satisfaction out of...of all this." She lifted her hands and spun them like a magician preparing to release doves from her sleeves. "It's all so meaningless. Finding value in being known by a bunch of people who are desperate to be known. The whole scene is a pathetic circle jerk, but nobody is willing to admit it."

I considered telling her about the work I had been doing with Ashli, how she'd been accepted as a Suicide Girl and how her pictures were getting millions of views. Instead I snuffed my cigarette in the ashtray, took the last swallow of beer from my glass and asked, "Why did you move here?"

She groaned. "I was following a boy. We'd been dating for a few months and he wanted to live here."

"Why?"

She laughed loudly, "I don't know! He just did! He was obsessed with the idea of it."

"Where is he now?"

She slapped her hands on the table, "Back in Wisconsin!"

"Figures."

"We broke up, like, two months after we got here and at some point later he was over it and moved home."

"Why did you stay?"

"I don't know," she said, the sun glinting off her dark lenses. "I think because I was afraid that if I went home it would be admitting that I'd made a mistake. People would say I told you so, and I didn't want to hear it."

"Are you happy here at all?"

"Sometimes. When it's good. There are days when I think about leaving."

"Where would you go?"

"I don't know. Somewhere where life isn't just one big party."

"That reminds me, there's a party tonight."

She grit her teeth. Her arms and hands tensed like the news frustrated her down to the nerve and bone. Then, with a sigh, she relaxed and asked, "Where?"

"Pit Home."

"*Ew*! Ry, those boys are gross! I know they're your skate friends, but they're filthy. And they don't respect women."

She wasn't wrong. The last time I was at the Pit Home there was a paper on the fridge that had a list of points one could score by engaging in particular sex acts. Coming on a girl's face was worth fifty points and it wasn't even a top scoring item. "I know," I said. "But the Baker team is in town and Caleb is hoping to link up with them."

Michelle groaned again. "I don't know."

"At least it's not for party photos."

"Fine. But if one of those boys says something nasty to me I'm going to punch them in the mouth."

"Can I sell a picture of that to a magazine?"

She laughed. "Yes!"

We split the check and she drove me home. In the parking

lot of my apartment we hugged and she jumped back behind the wheel and said "see you tonight." She threw her car in gear and waved at me with her fingers, a punk song blaring from her open windows. *The Approaching Curve,* by Rise Against. She was singing and beating on the wheel as she pulled onto the road. Michelle was cool. I always thought so.

Pit Home was the name given to a three bedroom house in Tempe. At any given time, upwards of ten guys were living there. The permanent residents called themselves the Pit Crew, and the transients who slept on couches and floors were their friends and friends of friends who traveled in from different corners of the US to hide. From winter. From failure. From an expectation that they'd get a job and give up their silly dreams already. A drained pool in the backyard was the reason the leaseholders had selected the house, and its condition on their taking possession of the home - a foot of brackish water, decomposing palm fronds, a naked Barbie stained by leaching tannins - was what earned the house its namesake.

Cars lined the street. Collin and I had to park a block away and as we neared the house the low rumble of bass moved over the ground like gasoline fumes. The front door was unlocked and immediately upon entering the music doubled in volume. Collin followed me down the hall through a thick cloud of weed smoke, a gray helix phantom twisting at eye level, as flanneled young men with tangled hair and torn shoes slapped my hand and pulled me into one armed hugs. I introduced Collin to each of them, and because he was with me, his gold chain and clean white sneakers were overlooked and his fist was bumped when he held it out. Save a uniformed cop, I could bring anyone to that party and they would get a pass. My story was known. I was a worst case scenario. A cautionary tale that no one wanted to believe and that no one would heed because, truly, how could it even be heeded? A walking, talking, purple heart that appeared like a ghost of Christmas to remind them of just how lucky they were. I was pitied.

In the kitchen, one had to ease their way along the counters if they wanted to move through the space at all. A crowd surrounded the table in the center of the room watching the final act of a game. The players, a guy and a girl, each held an index finger on the rim of a sauce pot. Between the heads of the people in front of us, the guy said "Slosh bucket...one!" He kept his finger on the rim of the pot while the girl yanked hers away. The room erupted and the winner was grabbed by the shoulders and shaken vigorously while the loser hung her head and clutched at her hair. A chant began. *Drink! Drink! Drink!* Even Collin and I joined in, pumping our fists as we yelled. The girl lifted the pot by its handle and began slurping down whatever ill concoction of beer and liquor it contained. Grimacing and wiping the spilled liquid from the corners of her mouth, she lowered the pot to cheers and applause. A hand fell on my back.

"What's up, Ry!" It was Bradley. One of the Pit Crew. I introduced him to Collin and asked if any of the riders from Baker were there.

"Spanky and Slash are still here. A bunch of the other guys already split for the hotel. Beagle's here. I think he's still filming the pool sesh if you want to check that. The keg's out back, too. If they try to charge you for a cup, tell them I said you and your homie are covered. If they give you any shit, come find me."

On the cracked and spit stained slab, we waited in line for a red plastic cup full of foamy beer. Behind the kid operating the tap there was a wide acacia tree strung with colored lights and further adorned with an assortment of doll parts. Limbs. Torsos. A lot of heads, many with their eyes burned away by cigarettes, their long yellow hair, tangled and frayed, affixing them to the branches. Unluckier dolls with softer bodies had been skewered in place on the tree's three inch thorns. Raggedy Anne, crucified upside down, what of her red yarn hair hadn't been burned and melted into a plastic scab was cropped close to her head, and her only remaining eye made her look as if she was giving all onlookers a happy wink. A naked Cabbage Patch doll, tattooed with curse words written in black magic marker, its lower half missing, had been impaled like a macabre Christmas star at the apex of the tree, clouds of cotton entrails spilling from her gut, yet smiling and offering the world a hug all the same.

In the pool, a skateboarder with long hair flowing behind him was carving the shallow end before pumping into the deep where he rode frontside up the steep wall and locked into a smith grind that he only held for a second before kicking his board away and sliding down the gray concrete on his hip. The skaters watching from the deck tapped the tails of their boards on the ground, the *smack smack* of it their approval of his attempt. Encouragement to try again.

Haggard furniture was scattered about the gravel yard. Collin blended into the mix to find buyers for his bottle full of Klonopin and I spotted an empty plastic chair where I could watch the show. Caleb, standing on the pool deck with the tail of his board under his toe, bent and wiped the sweat from his forehead with the lower half of his shirt, then pushed off with one step and rode toward the lip of the pool. He snapped an ollie into the shallow end, pumping his way through the deep and carving a figure eight to gain speed. In the shallow again, he locked onto the coping and sat on a long, curving five-oh grind, his steel trucks *schralping* against the bullnose rim before he rolled back in. Boards *smacked* on the concrete and Caleb was moving fast again as he rode straight up the deep end wall where he sat on a blunt stall for only a second before flicking a kick-flip. His vertical board spun a full three hundred and sixty degrees tip to tail, and hanging against gravity, when the grip tape was facing his feet once again, his shoes found their home over the bolts and man and board fell back into the pool together, backwards, his wheels meeting the concrete and carrying him swiftly into the bottom of the basin where he rode fakie up the hump into the shallow end.

"Fuck yeah's!" and "Hell no's!" accompanied the chorus of smacking skateboards on the deck. Caleb climbed out of the pool and he was picked up around the waist and jostled by the long haired skater who was crazed with joyous disbelief. A man with a video camera rushed over to Caleb and put the lens in his face, collecting his smile, the tremble in his voice and hands that were high with the adrenaline of having done something on the edge of impossible.

The next skater was in the pool carving a line, and Caleb slipped away, returning a moment later with a red plastic cup in hand. He took the open chair next to me and I congratulated him on his run, telling him that it was sick, that the back wall of the pool was no joke.

"Thanks man. It took me a minute to bring that blunt flip back in."

"It was perfect."

"I got my feet over it a few times, but I was too scared to put it down."

"Having the filmer from Baker here was probably good motivation."

"It definitely helped."

Someone passed him a blunt that smelled like grape Kool Aid and we talked a while about the spots he'd been going to and the tricks he'd been getting on tape. I apologized for not having been around as much and he shrugged and said it was no big. After the bars closed a second wave of people filled the house with noise and began streaming into the back yard. Among them were Michelle and Thea, who looked lost until they saw me waving at them. "Have to punch anyone?" I asked.

Michelle smiled, "Not yet."

"Who you gonna punch?" Thea asked. She was drunk.

"Gross boys," Michelle told her.

We stood in a circle and smoked and told stupid jokes. Collin joined us and was far too amused by how drunk Thea was. She repeatedly told a story about a guy she'd seen at the bar earlier that night who wore an eye patch that she'd been convinced was a fashion accessory. Apparently, she asked to see his eye hole, and the guy had angrily told her to fuck off. Collin laughed at each of her sloppy tellings, probably because with each one she embellished further, adding questions she never asked about whether or not the man's brain was visible at the back of the socket and whether or not the hole ever leaked any kind of goo. As Thea laughed and stumbled into Collin, I felt the pressure of a set of eyes fixing on me. Dom was on a couch at the far side of the pool sitting next to a guy in a leather jacket who I recognized but couldn't remember where from. She was looking at me. Michelle caught me glancing back.

"Troy's a piece of shit," she said.

"How do you know him?"

"He was friends with my ex. He's a junkie."

Dom smiled at me and I guess I probably smiled back.

As the night grew cool, our group moved into the house. Still wall to wall with bodies, we passed through the kitchen where dice rattled on the table and someone screamed "Four five six!" and that was followed by heavy groans as a pile of dollar bills was drawn in by two sweeping arms. In the living room, Caleb was on one end of the couch. Next to him the curly haired videographer, Beagle, was sucking on a nearly exhausted joint. At the other end, a man in cowboy boots who was entirely too old to be at the party was losing his grip on consciousness. His eyes only slits in his face, he was grinning and nodding, but not to anything anyone said. He wore a suit that probably fit him nicely when he'd first put it on, but as he melted into the couch, it was clear by the wrinkles in the fabric and the misaligned buttons on his shirt that he'd had a day, or perhaps a few.

"I've got a good couple of minutes of footy," Caleb was telling Beagle. "It's not like, a full part or anything, but definitely, I have some clips I'd love to show you."

Beagle dropped the ember of his joint into a beer bottle he

held between his feet. His eyes were glassy and red but he spoke as if he was entirely sober. "You need to come out to L.A. sometime, man. You just need to hang out. You know? Get to know everyone. Let them see you ride. I obviously can't promise you anything. I'm not the guy, you know?"

"For sure," Caleb said.

"But who knows, it could happen."

The cowboy nodded and said, "It could," as if he was not only part of the conversation, but even remotely aware of what was being discussed.

Everyone got quiet and stared at him and Caleb sat forward and asked, "Who even are you, bro?"

The cowboy started laughing, his head lolling in circles as though his neck no longer had the bones necessary to hold it aloft. His body convulsed with silent laughter.

Beagle said, "He's fucking toasted, is what he is," then added, "Listen, I have to find the guys. We gotta be on the road early for Tucson." He said goodbye to Caleb and waved to the room as he left his place on the couch. Michelle left too. Thea was struggling to stay upright and needed to be taken home. We hugged and she asked if I needed a ride. I told her Collin would get me home. She twice asked if I was sure and I twice told her that I was and as they walked out the door, Thea was telling Michelle about the man with the eyepatch, insisting that he was faking it.

Caleb and I returned to the patio and tried to coax the keg into giving us each a last half cup of beer. In the basin of the pool, a pile of wood and cardboard and brittle palm fronds had been set on fire. The concrete walls shimmered orange and red as the fuel crackled and snapped, sending a stream of sparks upward where on hitting the colder air they folded like a cresting wave, like an unseen hand there in the night would not permit their escape. Caleb pumped the keg tap and I held the hose, splitting its trickle evenly between our cups. Dom came over and spoke to me. That was the first time. The hole in the ground behind her aglow with the growing fire, she said hey. I said what's up. She said keg's killed. I said we'll see about that. Caleb said something I can't remember. Dom had black hair and brown skin and she was pretty and I thought she had such lovely eyes. I told her I liked her tattoo. She pushed her sleeve higher so I could see all of her shoulder and said La Catrina. I said nice. She asked if I skated. I said not anymore. Someone inside screamed, "Fuck! He pissed himself!" and we all went to see.

The cowboy was fully out. His crotch stained with moisture, a puddle had formed on the tile around his boots. Girls whooped and backed away pointing as guys from the Pit Crew ran into the room and began cursing, asking the ether who the man was, how he'd come to be blacked out on their couch, what should be done with him. In a revelry of drunkenness, when the man couldn't be awoken with screams or slaps, it was suggested that he be laid out in the yard. Not wanting to touch his piss covered body, an unspoken decision to lift the entire couch was made and a rush of hands joined in levitating the piece of furniture off the floor, down the hall, and then out the front door. Rapt with the hilariousness of the effort, guffawing partiers huzzahed at a drunken rejoinder yelled from the crowd suggesting that the man be deposited far down the road. Taken by the spirit of the moment, Caleb and I joined the others in raising the couch high above our heads, and as a team we howled as we marched the sleeping man down the street like a living deity on his litter, a troupe of girls in tow following on only to witness the spectacle through to its end. Reaching the stop light, it was decided to cross the street and abandon the man, spontaneously dubbed Cowboy Pissy Pants, in the drive-through of a Dutch Brothers coffee franchise. Despite the raucous bobbing and shifting of his unlikely conveyance, the man never stirred. One of his boots had fallen off as we crossed the road and it was run over by passing cars. A girl with flowers tattooed on her hands kissed him on the cheek and relieved his billfold of all the cash it contained, and then begrudgingly split it amongst her female companions who demanded a share. We laughed as we made the return walk. Collin swerved in the lane as he drove us home some time later. The next day, from the safety of my bed, I wondered at the state of the cowboy's mind when with the rising of the sun he'd have found himself cold and wet with his own piss, lying beneath the frozen blades of a prop wind-mill, the aroma of fresh coffee on the air, unable to purchase a cup. Would he remember the night with shame? With glory? Would it be a story he would tell?

Jesse was there at open. I still had a cutting board on the bar covered in limes that I'd halved and then halved again, their juice running everywhere. He sat and I placed a bowl of chips and salsa in front of him. Then a menu. He had a book with him and when I took his order he laid his hand on the cover.

"Can I get a Crown and Coke, please?"

"We don't sell whiskey. How about a tequila sunrise? They're on special."

"Fine. No grenadine though."

I made his drink and served it to him and joked, "Tequila high noon." He didn't get it. Every few minutes he looked towards the entrance. Drummed his fingers on his book.

"Waiting for someone?" I asked.

"Yeah." He looked to the road.

"Friend?"

"Business associate."

"What kind of business?"

"The private kind."

I threw my hands up. He ordered lunch and checked his watch. When I set his food down I saw the title of his book, *Curse of the Lost Dutchman*. While he chewed I asked, "Fiction?" He looked at me quizzically and I pointed to the book. He shook his head and wiped his mouth.

"I don't like fiction," he said.

"What's it about?"

He set down the taco he was about to bite. "You sure ask a lot of questions."

I spun my bar key on my finger. "Slow shift." He bit into his food and chewed, looked at the road, then his watch. "How late are they?" I asked.

He wiped his mouth and hands and dropped his napkin on his plate. "You find being nosy helps the tips?"

"Sometimes it's worth the pay cut."

"Your dime. Thirty minutes. Tell you what," he shook his glass so the ice rattled. "I'll trade you one of these for the inside scoop."

"Deal."

"Give me some good stuff," he said.

I reached for a high shelf and grabbed a bottle of reposado and showed him the label, then poured two ounces of it into the glass and topped it with orange juice and set it before him on a clean napkin. "High noon."

He sipped the drink and said, "Gold." My face remained blank so he went on, "The book is about gold. In the Superstition Mountains. I'm a treasure hunter and I am going to find the Lost Dutchman's gold mine."

I looked at the book cover then back to him. "What's with the curse?"

He sucked air between his teeth then said, "People die up there. Often in horrible ways."

"Define horrible."

"In the old days it was usually murder. People were found decapitated or shot in the head. Peralta family was all cut to pieces. The Apache say the gateway to hell is up there."

I looked to the sky in the east where I knew the Superstitions stood even though I couldn't see them for the buildings across the street. "Who's the Dutchman?"

"The old German bastard who originally discovered the gold."

"Why didn't he take it all?"

"Got sick and died."

"Why didn't anybody else take it?"

"Cause they die trying."

"Not to rain on your parade here, but what makes you different?"

He raised an eyebrow and also his drink. "I know where to look."

"How's that?"

He tapped his temple and refused to say more. A group of people were coming up the patio steps. Jesse turned. Hoping but failing to find his associate, his eyes followed a red head as she and her friends took a table in the shade. "Damn," he said, then looked at me, "No shortage of gorgeous women here."

"And not a drop to drink."

"What's that?

"Forget it."

Ashli came to the bar and stood next to Jesse. I walked around and she gave me an air thin hug. "It's been a night," she said.

"How can I help?"

"Shots for the table and something to sip on?"

I recognized her female companions, but the two men in the group, looking sleepless with their stubble and sunglasses, I'd never seen before. I asked, "Who's the crew?"

Without looking in their direction, she said, "The one that matters is an agent. The other one is nobody." She stole a cherry from my fruit tray and pulled it from its stem with her teeth, gripping it with her pursed lips before biting it in half.

"I got you," I told her.

"You always do." She blew me a kiss and walked away. Jesse watched her go. Behind the bar I started pulling bottles from shelves and filling a tumbler with ice. As I shook it, Jesse drained his glass and pushed it forward. "One more," he said, "With the grenadine this time."

After bringing a tray of shots and two pitchers of margaritas to Ashli's table, I made Jesse his drink and asked him, "If you know where the gold is, why do you need a business associate? Why don't you just go get it?"

He couldn't help but steal looks at Ashli as he answered my question. "Because the Superstitions are protected parkland." He tasted his drink and perked up. "The grenadine is pretty nice, actually." After another, larger sip, he said,

"Anyone who actually finds the gold has to sneak it out without the feds noticing. My associate, let's just say, he can help me with that."

"Well, I'm sorry he didn't show up."

"Me too. He's a busy man though." Jesse snapped his credit card down.

I ran it and handed him his receipt and a pen. "Tell you what, Jesse," I said, reading his name as I passed his card back to him. "You ever find that gold, you come back in here and let me know. I'll trade you another drink if you tell me the tale."

He was still fixed on Ashli as he said, "When I find that gold, I'm going to be a federal criminal. I won't be anywhere near the state of Arizona, that's for sure."

"Then just send me a postcard with an X on it."

"Why an X?"

"Because it marks the spot."

My delight was boundless that first year because everything was new again. The details of the set. Stucco houses. Block walls. Serrated plants. The gravel along sidewalks or sometimes laid as front lawns, brown on brown on brown until I looked closer and my eye caught the bands of lavender, the shades of pink. Sprouting from the spread of grit, a palette of frosty greens. Something that looked like rosemary. Something that looked like sage. Cactuses of all kinds defying everything I'd ever known of vegetation, hedging parking lots and planted dangerously close to walkways. Barrels with their white needles and yellow fruit. Saguaro standing high as houses. Ocotillo like some primeval cephalopod trapped head first in the ground, tentacles baked crisp and impotent by the sun. Passing cactuses I always examined their spines, some thin as hairs, others thick as three penny nails, all of them begging me to press my palm gently to their tips. To test them. To test myself.

The valley is an uninspired patchwork of sprawl. A grid of asphalt stretching mile upon mile across the plain with wide lanes laid to accommodate the personal automobile in a way the cities of the east were both too old and too dignified to deliver. Sand colored strip malls trace the roads boasting a repetition of chain stores with their familiar logos stamped again and again from east to west, their ugliness certain but restrained or somehow tempered by the foreground of flora and its aroma. Lantana. Oleander. Yucca. Flowers offering an impressionist's buffet of color at eye level while the coarsely barked mesquite trees shade them with drooping leaves, soft and broad like ostrich feathers that wimple in the breeze. Citrus fruits grown in yards or as a simple hedge to beautify the median splitting traffic, as if their splendor was a thing unknown. Palms, some low and fat, some tall and perplexingly slim, draw attention up and away from the mess that man has made in service of his wants, lifting one's gaze to the sky that during the height of day is a Caribbean blue, and that on any given evening might grab you by the throat when the sun begins to fall behind the mountains in the west, choking you with awe at that nuclear drop of honey that in its setting irradiates the strands of cloud visible to the eye and the sea of ozone and exhaust otherwise hidden, a cavalcade of particles jockeying up and down by order of mass that renders a tangerine blast to blot that whole side of the world, blacking the faraway peaks and the nearby fronds while an oil slick of violet and rose bleeds away from the blinding gold belly of it all.

Back home the setting sun felt like a call. Like an invitation to somewhere better. Every day it rose to take me by the arm and scream in my face that I live, for God's sake, while there was still time. And then it would run west, and in its last gleaming turn to see if I had followed, and because I hadn't, twilight was always a thing of sorrow. It was different in the valley, having finally found where it was all those years that the sun snuck off to every evening. Certainly, there was blue water somewhere lapping at a damp shore, a place beyond the mountains where the world truly said goodbye to the light, and maybe its song would one day draw me there to witness that holy thing, but there in the valley, at the end of that first year, everything was in its exact right place. I was in my exact right place. Far from every set of eyes that had watched me in my becoming, far from anyone who could upend any attempt I made at evolution by calling me a liar. A fake. In a place where everything was new to me, I could be new to it. My island somewhere in the unmapped sea. I was suddenly and fervently in love with it, and with all the permissions it granted me. I decided that what I did there didn't count. The record of my life, the story other people would know of me, my actions cumulative, the good and bad all counter stacked and judged, it didn't include the desert because the desert wasn't real.

I had lived in a real place. An overcast brickyard of steel and diesel where the clock of life couldn't be ignored. Always ticking. Chiming the hours. Tallying them and multiplying them by a wage before deductions. In that real place, our lives ended slow and fast all at once, and what we made of ourselves in the shrinking space before the final hour was all we would be, all we would say. And in that real place, the sky was so often gray. A dreary cap on dreaming that spit rain at us, weathering, wearing, turning iron to rust.

But not here. Not far away, stockaded by mountains in a city where seasons had little say. Where the turning of the year was mapped on the table tops of restaurants and denoted only by the upcoming drink special or prix fixe menu. Not in a place where Christmas lights wound up the trunks of palm trees but stopped at the fronds so that after nightfall, all there was to see against the dark was a glowing column. Rows of them along the roads. An absurdity that went unquestioned because native eyes had never seen it any other way. Light for light's sake. To illuminate our path to the next booth or barstool. Meaningless here where years didn't end, but simply reset. Where time folded in on itself, and as the calendar turned, we celebrated with debaucherous parties. With girls in red skirts trimmed white drinking martinis they stirred with candy canes. With fireworks and shot glasses and flames in gas heaters that popped in the wind as everyone counted backwards from ten before kissing someone new. With missed phone calls from my sister that I never saw until the morning after and short text messages telling her that I was fine. That no, I didn't need anything. That no, mom didn't call.

We felt like we mattered. Those of us chosen. Only one hundred invitations had been sent. A message on Myspace giving us date and time, but no address. That would come an hour before the party. We were told to keep quiet. Told we had been hand picked by Ashli herself. I got a text message, too.

Bring your camera.

I called Michelle to see if she'd been invited.

"Yeah, but I'm not going."

"Why not?"

"Because Thea wasn't invited."

"They say it's a small space."

"Oh bullshit, Ry. Ashli is just a bitch and she wants her birthday to be exclusive to make herself feel important. I'll get more satisfaction out of not going."

"Lunch tomorrow?"

Her mood changed. "Let's do it."

When I learned the location I understood why it had been kept secret. Why we were told to park several blocks away and to arrive in small groups. Thirty stories high, Centerpoint Tower was still under construction. With work on the half built condominium stalled for ambiguous financial reasons, nothing had been done in months to complete the steel and concrete skyscraper that reached higher into the Tempe sky than any other building. The security man was a part time bouncer at Cabaret, and he'd been paid to ignore the one hundred young partiers, who in twos and threes slipped through the gap in the chain link fence that surrounded the footprint of the site. He even gave an elevator key to those who came early with the generator, the DJ equipment, the coolers full of ice and champagne. Guests had to take the stairs. Six hundred steps in a concrete well. The night was cold and no one was dressed for it. People took short breaks on the landings to catch their fogging breath as they hunched and babbled and took sips from hidden flasks and cursed their habits and choice of shoes before setting off to climb again.

In the dead middle of the thirtieth floor, a folding table held the DJ's laptop and two large speakers. Strands of lights ran from pylon to pylon, small *X*'s of black duct tape fixing them in place. Stepping out of the stairwell and onto the bare concrete, not a person was without trepidation. With no glass in the would be floor to ceiling windows, there was nothing to keep the cold night from our bodies and nothing to keep our bodies from falling to the street below. Standing alone, Billy Fucking Reed had his headphones covering one ear, his face lit by the laptop screen before him. Wary voices were hushed the instant he dropped the needle on Blur's *Girls & Boys,* and the beat grabbed hold of everyone who in their tight dresses and tight jeans couldn't help but dance to the open coolers where the green necks of champagne bottles poked through blankets of ice. It was the only way to stay warm. To be a body moving among bodies. To numb the skin and the mind with drink. Corks ricocheted off the raw concrete ceiling and soon were shot through the wide open windows to loud cheers. If anyone feared that the world below would hear the noise we were making and look up to see the glow emanating from the highest floor of what should have been an unoccupied building, they didn't act on it. They couldn't. This night was a story in the making, and one had to shape how their place in it would be told. Knowing that all acts would be amplified, caution and exuberance alike, people got to the work of aggrandizing themselves in real time. Eschewing reason. Embracing risk.

I went first to the DJ table. Stashed my camera bag. Billy passed me a whiskey bottle and as I drank from it he shouted into my ear, "Nothing goes online! Pictures are for Ashli only!" I gave a thumbs up. Screwed on my flash. Took a few shots and tweaked my settings. Despite the fact that we were all committing a crime, there wasn't a person who didn't want to be photographed. To have it known that they were one of the select few who had attended the party of the year. I was moving into the crowd when the grind and squeal of the construction elevator came clear through the music. Worried heads turned to watch it settle into place. I readied my lens, knowing that when it stopped with a jerk and clang and its yellow cage door accordioned open, it would be Ashli making her entrance. What I didn't expect was her to be on the arm of a man. Watching through my viewfinder, they appeared in the dim light. Her date was tall and broad with dark features. He wore a white suit that matched Ashli's form fitting white dress. Her hand was in his as she danced her way to the cheering crowd. An aisle was made for their passing and the pair moved to the center of the unconstructed floor where the throbbing mass of dancers closed behind them, insulating Ashli from the great and present danger she'd invited everyone to experience. To subject themselves to in her honor.

I didn't know who the man was, but I knew he was more than me. Bigger. More fit. With the look of money. And something else. People tried to be close to him without being too obvious about the fact that they wanted to be close to him. With the opening drum hits of *Tear You Apart,* a blue strobe light flicked on and Ashli climbed onto the DJ table with a champagne bottle in her hand. The crowd threw up their arms. Her flipbook body shifted like something inhuman in the flickering light, there and then gone, there and then gone, as the fingers and hands of those beneath her reached from the alternating blue and black like so many drowning souls desperate to be pulled upward. I tried to photograph the scene. There was nothing to pull focus on. No consistency of form or light. I turned off my flash and shot from the hip. Pointing the camera and releasing the shutter with no sense of who was before me or what I might capture. After each click, my LCD screen showed liquid flesh. Humans untethered from space. Disembodied features and faces that could equally have been expressing the throes of blissful agony or tortured delight, ethereal as they exhaled fog and their bodies steamed in the on again off again blink of the strobe.

With the next song, Ashli pulled her date through the crowd and found me. She yelled into my ear, "I need a picture." I raised my camera to frame her with the man, but she said, "No, over here." Leading her date by the hand, she went to the edge of the building where a pane should have been and struck a pose, behind her the lights of downtown Phoenix standing aglow against the night. I tried walking to where she stood, but I made the mistake of looking past her to the city below, to the dotted lines of intersecting streets that led all the way to the dark spread of mountains, and I felt as though I'd stepped on a carousel already in motion. I paused to focus only on her, on the truth of the unmoving world before me.

"Come on!" she yelled.

I took another two steps forward and my stomach lifted while my brain did a somersault. I lowered myself to one knee and put my hand on the floor, begging it to convince my mind that down was down.

"What's wrong with him?" her date asked.

"Riley, get up!" Ashli yelled.

I held up my finger and took a breath. "Give me a second."

She yelled at me again and so I got to my feet and walked forward, but after another step the floor decided to switch places with the ceiling and I was forced to sit. "Riley!" Ashli yelled, "Get up!" I looked at her like a dog who knew better than to piss the carpet but was too old to hold it in. "I have vertigo," I said, and her face soured, like I'd made the word up. I took deep breaths. Fell forward and fixed my eyes on the concrete between my two hands. Ashli's date complained that

I was taking too long. He waved someone over. Told him to take my camera so they could get this fucking picture already. I struggled to my feet and pushed the interloper away. "Stand together," I barked, restraining the roil climbing in my gut and lurching forward against the chop and tilt my wounded mind invented. Lifting my camera, the couple lifted their faces. I choked back bile. My right leg shook like a nerve had been cut and the muscle could no longer receive command. I released the shutter. Watched the shot materialize on the screen. Held up my thumb and screamed, "Got it," over the music and voices and wind. And then with a bright smile, Ashli dragged her date passed me, back into the warm heave and swell of the party. I sat. Scooted away from the open wall. Braced myself against a pylon and drew slow, full breaths until the horizon sat level and my limbs quit their trembling.

When I was ready to walk again, I packed my camera and went to the coolers in search of a drink. Meltwater leaked on the floor. Every bottle was empty.

"Wanna share?" a woman said from behind me. It was Dom. She held out a bottle by the neck. I took it.

"Thanks." I tipped the bottle back slowly so it wouldn't agitate and start to foam. I passed it back to her and she took a swig.

"I'm Riley," I said.

"I know." She offered me the bottle again. "Everyone knows everyone."

"You got the big invite," I said, after a heavy swallow.

"Ash and I work together. Well, we did."

I handed her the bottle. "You a dancer?"

"Cocktail waitress." She drank and then touched the back of her hand to her wet lips. "Ash quit, thanks to you."

"What do you mean?"

"The modeling thing took off."

"Suicide Girls?" I asked, taking the bottle.

"That and now other things." I offered her the last of the

champagne but she said, "You finish it." I took a swallow then held the bottle high over my open mouth to gather the final drips. "Do you want to dance?" she asked. She smiled with the question and I liked that she wasn't coy. That she didn't need pretense and that she wasn't ashamed to ask for what she wanted. I liked her body too.

"Sure."

Safely kept in the thick crowd, we danced to Joy Division warning that when routine bites hard and ambitions are low that love would tear us apart. We heard without listening and let the alcohol take us, the strobing light and snare hits dicing time into thousands of pieces, disconnecting them so that each moment was its own, owing nothing to those that came before or after. She pushed into me and our hips declared their intentions. She kissed me and the dry champagne was still on her tongue. Kissing her back I felt like I'd fallen onto a conveyor belt. Like some simple animal hanging by its leg in a silver clamp that would carry it to its death. The end was written and I knew what it would be but because I had started there was nothing for me but to be carried along and witness all that would happen in between. We danced in the pocket of heat those one hundred humans created in that vacant loft, pressing our thighs together only to split and spin as the music demanded before coming back together to satisfy the call of our aching flesh. When the music suddenly stopped and the flickering strobe was halted, casting the whole room in a deep blue, it was Ashli who screamed out, "Security got a call! Party's over, bitches!"

On the street below, Dom took my hand and we slipped through the gap in the fence. People were splitting up, scattering like rats. I suggested a bar but Dom suggested her house. She asked if I could drive her car because she was pretty drunk, and I asked if she minded if I smoked and she said not at all. On the road I realized that I was drunk too and I labored at my focus, checking constantly that I was going exactly the speed limit, steeling my arms so the car wouldn't swerve. At Dom's house, her roommate was watching TV in the living room. Dom introduced me and I waved and said hi and Jamie said hi and Dom said come on and I followed her to her room.

She closed the door behind us and swatted a switch on the wall. Only the pulsing pink string lights came on. She went first to an iPod and played music, clicking the volume up several times before coming to where I stood and shoving me backwards onto her bed. We kissed as she undressed first herself and then me. We had sex. Loud and sweaty. Skin smacking skin. Her nails digging into my ass as she pulled me into her. She came once and I slowed but she said don't stop and she rolled onto her hands and knees. I was nothing but body. No thoughts. No voice. Only my senses and their approval of all of her. How she looked. How she smelled. And my God, how she sounded. Moaning. Her back arched and eyes closed and mouth open as she fell into her pillow. If I roared as I came I wouldn't be surprised. I'd like to think that I did. After ripping off my condom, I collapsed onto the bed next to her. She breathed deeply and I was instantly tired. A ceiling fan whirred and its chain tapped out the seconds on the dark glass of the lamp and the cool air it pushed down at us made the sweat on my naked skin tingle. Dom spoke quiet words about how she'd seen me around, but like the song playing in the background, their meanings were lost to my satisfaction and fatigue. The fan whirred, and the chain tapped, and Dom whispered, and I fell into an easy, easy sleep. The first time. But not the last time.

The Mod was a venue in a run down building on a street where the other run down buildings had all been bulldozed. Surrounded by homeless people pushing carts and muggers lurking in parking garages, the people who braved downtown Phoenix after dark to see shows at The Mod parked close, walked in packs, and stood near the door when they dared go outside to smoke in the yellow lamplight. Collin parked along the curb, and after killing the engine he looked around and asked, "Think I should leave my windows open?"

"Why?"

"So the fucking bums know there's nothing to steal."

"Your call," I said, hefting my bag straps over my arms. "They might take it as an invitation to sleep in your backseat though."

Collin locked his doors. "One hour, and we're outta here."

It was AZ PM that sent me to cover the Underground Empire show. Their staff photographer was sick and the editor was familiar enough with my work to trust that I could handle a simple assignment. He said it was mine if I wanted it. A cash gig.

The opening act was a hardcore band called Esther. At the front of the crowd, young men were shoving and jumping into each other and they pumped their fists in the air as they screamed along with the music. In between songs, the singer caught her breath and thanked the crowd and said that they were going to play one more. Her speaking voice was soft. It was hard to believe that she'd been the person seamlessly alternating between satin chorus in perfect pitch and lyrics yowled with the timbre and fury of a mother lion. She smiled as her fans told her they loved her. Said thank you meekly. I found her in my viewfinder and snapped away. As her band played their final song, I caught angles that included them all, but were always centered on her. With closed eyes she sang that *we'll burn for what we've done*, and with fists thrusting at the air above, her fans sang back, *but we'll burn alive.*

Underground Empire took the stage and I moved back and forth across the room shooting the muscular guitar player, the drummer with erratic curly hair, and the small woman who sawed at an electric cello. A local band on a national tour, AZ PM was giving them a two page spread, and after they'd played a few songs I was confident I had enough to satisfy the editor, so I slipped to the back of the room where the bands displayed their merch. Behind a stack of folded T-Shirts and CD cases, the singer from Esther sat rocking her head in time with the music. I squatted next to her and told her I had photographed her band. She pointed to her ear and mouthed that she couldn't hear me. I spun my camera in front of me and lifted it. Pointed at her, then to the door, then to her again.

Outside the venue, skinny teenagers kept their backs to the building and smoked. Walking side by side with the singer, I offered her my hand and explained who I worked for. She told me her name. Quinn. On the far side of the building we stood on a bed of dirt and broken glass. I had her pose against the brick. She tilted her head and her long brown hair fell across one of her eyes. As my flashed popped, I told her the magazine would maybe use a shot or two, but that I was happy to give her everything else.

The building reverberated with sound. I changed lenses, requiring that I stand closer to her. The more she changed her pose, the more I noticed the features of her body. Fit but not too skinny. Wide hips hidden under the pleats of her skirt. Shapely calves hidden under black knee socks. Probably big tits hidden under her black hoodie. As I fired off the shutter, she tried not to smile, but did so on reflex and I made sure to capture it. Her eyes were green, but I wouldn't know that until the next day when I reviewed the photos one by one.

When I lowered my camera, I took out my phone. "How do you prefer for me to get you all this? Do you want to text me an email address?"

"That could work." She typed her number into my phone. I saved it as *Quinn Esther*. I texted her back.

Riley. Photo Guy.

"Great show, by the way. You're a captivating performer." She looked at her shoes. When she lifted her head she pushed her hair behind her left ear and thanked me. I told her that I liked her voice. That it was interesting how different she sounded when she spoke. Up the road someone yelled and a bottle shattered on the street. The yelling grew angrier and the screaming silhouette of a man ran into the glow of a street-lamp and another silhouette pursued him screaming curses and threats.

"We should get back in," she said.

I walked alongside her and before we were in earshot of the teenagers with their cigarettes, fans of hers I didn't want to risk embarrassing her in front of, I stopped and said, "You know, if you want, I could meet you in person and give you everything on a flash drive."

The corner of her mouth went up. "Oh, you could?"

"I know a good breakfast place. That is, if you like break-fast. Do you like breakfast?"

She smiled. "Yes, I like breakfast."

"Can I call you then? About breakfast?"

She made a face as she sized me up, one eye half closed, lips pursed. Shaking her head she sighed, and said, "Sure." She turned and made for the door and I watched her go the whole way. Skirt shifting from side to side. Hair swishing across her back as she disappeared into the sound.

I packed my gear. Michelle texted to tell me that she was at an after party. Collin said we should go. I agreed and we drove to a Circle K to buy beer and we cracked our first cans as the car merged onto the expressway.

Smoking a cigarette, my hand surfed the wind outside my open window, and as we exited the I-10 onto the 60 our car was high above the land and I was high with it, driving toward another house and another party, a night like any other every other night. From that place in the air, the valley sparkled and shined and seemed like a not so unreasonable thing. Everything is so beautiful from far away. Like a painting you view from a line on a gallery floor because it dissolves into nothing when you step too close. The music was turned up loud and a song on the radio cautioned that I control myself, that I take only what I need from it, confirming that there was in fact an it to be taken from, and at that moment, the twinkling ruby lights on South Mountain blinked with the beat of the music and it was as though every clock had fallen into sync, like that was the absolute center of the palindrome of time and we were hanging in the exact second between the moment the universe began and the moment when it would end.

Then we fell back toward the land. I let loose the stub of my cigarette and the red ember shot upward, tumbling and turning behind our car as it sped us into the mouth of a night we'd lived before and that we'd live again. Three beers deep, we arrived at a flat block house constructed in nineteen-sixty-who-gives-a-shit, that since erection had housed several different families, several different sets of now grown children and now dead parents, and as I crossed its threshold, was home to three young men. Aspiring musicians. College dropouts. Brethren in our unenviable order taking their turn to offer backyard and bathroom where we could all go through the motions. Consume and be consumed. First alcohol, to quiet reason and silence the ledger keepers, to blind them so that tomorrow their pages might be blank. Then cocaine, to speed the blood and call into question Einstein's laws, slowing all the world, freezing in place the constellations that dared to turn

above our hurried flesh, numb and ringing. And always, cigarettes, to pace the breathing and plant the seed of death in case
anyone might question our faith, our dedication to the sacred
now and our rabid disdain for the thought that one day we
might grow old. Dom arrived at some blurry hour. Drunk, but
not nearly as far gone as me. As dawn approached, we fled the
scene. She ran a red light driving us to her house and then
clipped the curb as she pulled into her driveway. I have little
memory of any of it, but I know that in the darkness of her
room, I closed my eyes and thought of Quinn.

Thea had been given two passes to the Tempe Music Festival by the drummer from Dear and the Headlights. As we drank two dollar you-call-its at The Vine, she told this to Collin and me, and in a deep state of drunkenness we spoke into existence a plan whereby Michelle and Thea, once inside the festival, would cut off their bracelets and pass them to us through the fence. The next morning, Collin woke me by digging his toe into my ribs. "Get up," he said, standing over me where I'd passed out on the bathroom floor. Conscious, and with the power of my hangover fully realized, I lamented having promised anyone that I would do anything. I showered. Stiffened up with coffee. Looked at my phone and thought of lies I might text to Michelle about why I couldn't come. Why I couldn't make good on words I'd spoken. But Collin was excited and loud and I finally accepted a slug of whiskey from his bottle and that there was no getting out of today.

The sun high overhead, we walked along the temporary fence that ringed the park. Scouted for an unguarded length where the girls could meet us on the other side. Behind a stretch of Porta-Potties that blocked us from view, I opened my phone and began sending Michelle a text. Collin looked left and right then stabbed the tip of his shoe into the fence and scrambled to the top bar.

"What about the plan?" I whispered.

"Fuck the plan, just climb." He kept his chest low, and grasping the links on the far side he fell head first toward the ground, spinning his body right before touching down and landing on his feet. Without looking back to see if I followed, he rounded the row of toilets and disappeared. I checked to make sure no one was watching. Climbed carefully. Tried to not shake the fence and inadvertently send a wave of motion down the length of it. Cresting the top, I couldn't throw myself over like a cat burglar the way Collin had, so I did my best to keep my shoulders hunched and my head down. As my first leg lifted over to the far side, the tidal pool in my mind's eye started to churn. I moved fast, bringing my trailing leg over the bar and climbing down just as my stomach began to clench. Touching earth, I straightened my shirt and took a deep breath, regretting it instantly as the stench of the chemical toilets passed over my tongue.

"You alright?" Collin asked when I found him on the other side.

"Yeah. Just a bit woozy."

"Let's get a beer. That'll make you feel better."

"Let's find the girls first."

"Text them from the beer line," he said.

I did, and when Michelle and Thea found us some minutes later, we all weaved through the patchwork crowd to get as close to the stage as possible. Thea was already tipsy. Collin asked if she'd gone to bed or if she was still faded from the night before.

"No, I slept," she said.

"Where's Walker?" I asked her.

"Have you been drinking all day?" Collin asked at the same time.

"He's at work," she said with a burp. She banged her chest with her fist, then said to Collin, "No, I didn't have a beer until we got here." She sipped from her cup and wiped her mouth with her wrist. "I just get fucked up kinda fast."

"You're a lightweight," Collin joked.

"Cause I'm an Indian," she said.

"Oh, no shit?" Collin said. "That's cool."

She shrugged, "It's whatever."

My Chemical Romance took the stage and the crowd cheered. We stamped to the music when it demanded it. Swayed like drops in the sea when the tempo slowed. Collin and I took turns retreating to the beer tent and then returning with six cups, three pinched in the fingers of each hand. We were drunk by the time the band finished their set. Standing in a tight circle as we waited for the next act, Thea told us about her adoption by Mormon parents. Her childhood in Anthem.

"Did you ever meet your biological parents?" I asked her.

She scrunched her face. "My dad died before I was born. He was shot."

"For real?" Collin asked?

"Yeah, fucking, nine times in the face." She slurred the words fucking and face.

"That's gnarly." I said. "What about your mom?"

Her left eye lid was lower than her right. "Nah. She was an addict."

"Hey! Me too!" Collin said, gently punching Thea's shoulder. "Want to hear something fucked up? My mom didn't know she was pregnant with me until the eighth month because she was drunk the whole time."

"How is that even possible?" Michelle asked. "Did she think it was just a coincidence that she was gaining weight while missing, like, eight periods in a row?"

"She wasn't actually unaware. She was in denial." Collin crumpled his empty cup and dropped it on the ground and passed his full beer from his left hand to his right. "She was a nasty alcoholic and didn't want to quit drinking."

"That's so fucked up!" Thea yelled, leaning into Collin.

"What if you were born all, like, messed up?" I asked him.

Collin slapped his chest. "Dude. Look at me. I am messed up."

"No, like, what if you were born with your heart outside of your body, or like, with no bones or some shit."

"No bones?" Michelle laughed.

"That stuff happens!" I insisted.

"Jelly baby!" Michelle said, wriggling her arms and laughing harder.

"She probably hoped she'd have a miscarriage." Collin

said. "She was seventeen and banging some bricklayer from Staten Island. I can't imagine she actually wanted to be a mom."

"To not being wanted!" Thea said loudly. She raised her plastic cup high. Collin touched the rim of his cup to hers and they each took a swallow.

"You guys are dark." Michelle shook my arm, "How about you Ry? How did your parents screw you up? Did they lock you in a closet or put you in baby food commercials or something?"

"No. Nothing like that." I looked to the stage where crew members in black clothes dragged cables and moved equipment. "My mom was just, absent. You know?" My tone must have been too sincere because Collin and Thea both stopped laughing and Michelle looked at me with sad eyes. "My mom left my dad when she fell in love with some other guy. Then dad took a job in Pittsburgh. And mom, she just wasn't there."

"She left you to fend for yourself?" Michelle asked.

"I had to lift frozen burritos from the corner bodega," Collin said. "When my mom found out I was stealing she told me to always take one for her too."

"That's fucking hilarious," Thea said.

"My mom always did the basics of parenting," I said. "I never went without shoes or toothpaste or anything. She just wasn't around much. And when she was around, it was like she wasn't. Like her attention was far away. I'm sure she loved us, my sister and me. But it always felt like she loved Kip more. Like there wasn't enough room in her heart for us."

"Wait." Thea held up her hand like she was stopping traffic. She sounded angry. "The guy's name was fucking Kip?"

I cracked a smile. "Yeah."

"What kind of bullshit name is Kip?" she asked, wrinkling her face and hitting Collin with the back of her hand.

Michelle was still looking at me with soft eyes. "That sucks," she said. "I'm sorry."

She touched my arm, and I said, "But here I am, so it all worked out, right?" and I raised my cup and Collin and Thea raised theirs with a cheer. We touched the plastic rims and tipped beer into our faces until our cups were dry and then we dropped them onto the pile gathering at our feet. The crowd roared. A shirtless and well muscled man in a shimmering red and black suit walked to the center of the stage. Tall and broad with skin that looked golden under the ellipsoidal lanterns beaming from above, he bowed.

"I love this guy!" Thea yelled into my ear.

"Who is he?" I asked, recognizing him at once.

"*XRXS!*" She struggled with the annunciation of what she'd said and to my ear her words were a smear of consonants. He took his place behind turntables and the crowd roared again as an electronic squeal and the thud of bass came deafening from the stacks on either side of the stage. Thea threw her hands into the air and screamed, stumbling into Collin who happily helped to right her. Circles of white light scanned over the crowd. The sky was red behind the stage and the water in the lake was red with it. In the west the sun had vanished behind the mountains leaving only their peaks visible against the swipe of crimson behind them, dark circus tents in the coming night. The crowd danced with abandon, arms above heads like they were flagging rescue from an invisible searcher in the sky. Collin pushed his way through the tumult of bodies and returned some time later with more beer for Thea and I. On three LCD monitors fixed to the trusses, *XRXS's* face was intense as he scratched at his turntables and made precision adjustments to the sliders and knobs on the pedals and boards before him. Under our feet the ground rumbled like some triassic creature buried in the rock had woken and was desperately hammering away at the stone egg of the world.

XRXS didn't play songs so much as a continuous piece built of samples from across the broad history of recorded music, track layered on track, all overlapping each other with the constancy of rolling water, beats finding beats, melodies always exciting in their coming then quickly forgotten for those that usurped them. There was no rest for the thousands of sweating dancers who slowed and hurried with the alternating tempo, puppets on strings who jerked and flailed according to the dictate of the rhythm. In the middle of his set, *XRXS* danced his way to the front of the stage, his legs and arms and neck and hands all aware of the notes to come, all moving in crisp alignment with them as they blared from the amps. A dervish with the footwork of a boxer, he spun and popped his shoulders in time with the bass kick, the glimmer of his sequined jacket sleeves bolstering his hypnotic allure. On the massive hanging screens, the cameras followed in close up as he whirled his way to stage right and reached for the dimly lit hand of a woman who'd been watching the show from the corner darkness. Michelle's face was bright with the flicker of the screens as we turned to each other in disbelief. The crowd wailed approval as *XRXS* pulled his red haired partner to the footlights where his hips and feet circled and stepped in an expert tango and the gorgeous tattooed woman he danced around improvised an expert response. Her arms serpentine. Her hips fluid.

"What the fuck?" Michelle mouthed to me.

Thea gripped my shirt and screamed, "It's Ashli!"

After replacing Ashli where he'd found her at stage right, *XRXS* returned to his equipment. The music came louder. Night had fully arrived and behind the stage the bulbs running the Mill Avenue bridge flicked on along with their rippling twins on the surface of the lake. Above us in the velvet blue, a string of passenger planes crossed the sky from right to left. Embryonic stars in the east that came apace at five hundred miles per hour until they were fully formed over the

Papago Mountains, landing gear lowered and ready to touch down, their engine noise no match for the music that animated us to exhaustion as the air cooled. When the show was over, we followed the ambling crowd through the exit gates. Drunk and unwilling to let the night end, we walked the avenue. Thea said *XRXS* must be Ashli's new boyfriend. I confirmed that he'd been her date at her birthday party. Michelle wondered how the two could have met. Thea asked if I was hiding anything and I promised that I wasn't. Ashli hadn't contacted me in weeks. Hadn't been at the bars or parties. Thea leaned against a wall to complain that her feet hurt. Collin let her climb onto his back. She insisted I carry Michelle and that we have a race, so I stopped and bent and Michelle hiked her long skirt that her knees could pinch my waist. I looped my arms under her hamstrings and we set off down the brick sidewalk, dodging around the other pedestrians. Collin ran faster than me but the bounce of his step shifted Thea's weight to one side and together they fell into a laughing puddle of splayed limbs.

"Are you alright?" Michelle asked over my shoulder as I slowed to a walk and stood next to where they lay spraddled and huffing. They both were caught in a fit of laughter. Their eyes closed. Their palms and knees scraped but the pain of it suspended. Waiting until morning. I lowered Michelle and we helped our friends to their feet. Heading south again, Michelle put her arm in mine. A street preacher spoke through a PA system, waving a blue bible and warning us of our sin. We mocked him. Thea showed him both of her middle fingers. Collin slapped the bible from his hand. Onlookers laughed and pointed at the preacher as he hurried to collect his book and we went away merrily and lined up outside the nearest bar.

———

Quinn arrived before me. When I stepped off the bus, she was reading a menu at a table for two. In my pocket I had a flash drive with the photos I'd taken of her band. She saw me approaching and waved. The iron chair scraped against the pavement as I pulled it out to take my seat. I folded my sunglasses and set them on the table and pointed to the white mug in front of her, "They have the best coffee in town."

"I haven't taken a sip yet," she said. "He just poured it."

I set the flash drive on the white tablecloth and slid it towards Quinn. "As promised."

"Thank you," she said, taking the drive and turning it in her fingers before tucking it in her pocket.

"Sorry it took so long for me to call," I told her. "I wanted to make sure everything looked really good, so I spent a lot of time working on the color and tone in Lightroom."

"You didn't have to do all that."

"The magazine is going to run one of your whole band and one of your portraits."

"Really? Wow. That's exciting." She sipped from her mug and made a sound of pleasure.

I sat back. "Good, huh? They won't tell anyone the brand either. They keep it secret so people come here to drink it."

"Really?"

"Yeah, watch." I flagged the waiter and he came to our table. Pointing at Quinn's mug, I asked, "What brand of coffee is that?"

He stiffened and said, "I'm sorry, sir, it's a store secret. All I can tell you is that we import it directly from Guatemala."

I flashed my eyes at Quinn. The waiter asked if we knew what we wanted for breakfast and Quinn apologized and said she hadn't decided yet. I ordered my own coffee and the big waffle with extra butter and Quinn said to bring her the same.

The waiter took our menus and in the silence after he walked away, Quinn said, "I think it's neat that you ride the bus."

I chuckled. "Everyone here thinks it's quaint and that still makes me laugh."

She rocked her head. "It's kind of a superficial place."

I held my thumb and forefinger a half inch apart.

"How long have you been here?" she asked.

I looked at the sky as I ran the calculation and then back to her. "About a year now. You?"

"I was born here," she said. "We moved away when I was little, but then came back not long after."

She was asking me how I got into photography when the waiter brought our plates and topped our coffee. Quinn made fun of me as I meticulously filled each nook in my waffle with butter, then chewing her first bite, she stabbed the air with her fork and said, "Yes. This was the right choice." The sun warmed the patio as it rose higher in the sky. In between bites I asked Quinn about her life. She worked as a substitute teacher. She shared an apartment in Scottsdale with her best friend. She'd been singing in the band since high school. She graduated from ASU and had applied to grad schools hoping to get a masters in art history. The waiter cleared our syrup covered plates and Quinn leaned over her folded arms. "So. Riley. What about you? You're a photographer. What else?"

Her posture and the low cut of her shirt made her large tits look even bigger. I fought to keep my eyes on her face. "I work at a bar. That's about it."

"Well. Good breakfast. Take care." She slapped the table with her hands and pushed herself back as if to leave.

I laughed and found the smile in her eyes. "Oh, you want the real stuff. OK. Are you sure?"

"Well, I do now." She rested her chin on her interwoven fingers.

"Real stuff, let's see, let's see." I took in the manicured fronds of the palm trees that lined the sidewalk. The sky and its promised blue. Finally, I started in, "I grew up in Chicago. I came here a year ago hoping to make it as a skateboarder, but on my very first night I was a little overly eager and I took a bad fall and cracked my head open and my career was over before it started. Now I work at a tequila bar and I drink too much and I take party photos, not so much because the money is any good but because it helps me pretend that there's a greater point to going out every night and doing the same thing over and over. Deep down, I know this is all because I have no idea what to do with my life. All I know is that going home isn't an option. I'm sure this is horrible stuff to tell somebody I'm trying to impress, but it's the truth, and I like you, and I like your green eyes and the way one corner of your mouth goes up a little higher than the other when you smile, yeah, like that, so I don't want to do that thing people do where they only show others the good parts of themselves. So even if that means confessing that I'm kind of lost right now, it's the truth and telling you the truth feels good."

I shut up and watched her face for tells. She laid her hands on the table. "Wow. OK. That was a lot."

"You asked for it."

"I did, didn't I?" She tilted her head. Focused on my face. Asked, "Why is going home not an option?" And because I sipped my coffee and thought before I spoke, she said, "That bad?" I laughed and she said, "What is it? Arrest warrants?"

"Way worse."

"*Ooh*, worse than that? Let's see. You testified against the mob and now there's a hit out on you?"

"I'm dumb, but not that dumb."

"I know," she said, her hands held out, her fingers bursting open as she said, "Ex-girlfriend."

"If only."

"What, then?"

I reached for my sunglasses and began unconsciously spinning them on the table. With every rotation, the sun would appear and then vanish in the lenses, and like staring into a film projector, I watched it flicker as I continued the spinning, unable to help but nod along to my coalescing thoughts. To smile lightly as I spoke them into being. "You know what I like about this place?"

"What?"

"No one here ever asks me what I plan to do with my life. They only ever ask what I plan to do tonight."

"I think that's what I hate about it the most," she said.

"But you're from here. For me, there is no one in this place who ever heard me declare my dreams out loud." I opened my arms, "Here I am exactly what I said I would be. If I'm a barback or a line cook or a valet parker, so be it. I'm just a guy making a buck like anyone else. There is no one around who can point and say, 'Poor Riley. Remember when he thought his future would be one thing and then it turned out to be something else? Something so much smaller. So much more pathetic.' Here, there are no dashed hopes. No what-could-have-beens."

"Why do you care what anyone else thinks?"

"I'm not sure I can help it. I'm not sure any of us can. What other people think, even if they never say a word about it, will always reflect the truth back at us. And beyond the people I knew, it's the city itself. Every stair set I ever jumped down. Every handrail. I landed my first kickflip in an alley off of Jackson and LaSalle. I was fourteen and alone and I remember it so clearly. How excited I was. There is nowhere in that city where some ghost of who I used to be can't find me."

"So you're just going to hide here?"

I held my arms open wide. "In my desert oasis. If I have to be nothing, why not be nothing in a place where the sun always shines? Where even time itself struggles to find you?"

"Wherever you go, there you are," she said.

"John Lennon?"

"Buckaroo Banzai."

"You lost me."

"It's a movie I used to watch as a kid."

"Want to watch it together?"

She tossed her head back to let out a big laugh. Her hair followed and it was the first time I saw the scars. She saw me see them and her smile left. A sadness she couldn't restrain replaced the shine in her eyes.

"Show me," I said.

She studied me. Looking for some assurance. Some goodness. I shifted in my seat and softened my posture. Softened everything about myself so she could inspect me. So her gaze could tiptoe over my being like fingers combing through hair for nits. I swept back the hair covering the long pink scar that ran along my skull, still tender to the touch. "This is the big one," I said. "I'm sure I have others, but this is the one that took me out."

Quinn pushed her chair back. Let her hoodie fall from her shoulder and removed her arm. She turned her head to the side and drew up her long hair in her hands. The right side of her body had been heavily burned. The tip of her right ear was missing. Skin from the rear of her neck to the crest of her shoulder and wrapping the length of her arm was pink and abraded, marbled with ripples like a shoreline after cross cutting waves have receded into the sea. "Our house burned down when I was five," she said, still holding her hair up.

"Jesus."

"I hid in a closet. A fireman saved me. My parents were killed." She lowered her hair.

"I'm sorry," I said. "That's awful."

"It's OK. My uncle took me in and raised me. He's the one who showed me Buckaroo Banzai."

"You're proving me right, you know?"

"About what?"

"Not going home."

Quinn never stayed out late. Only when I worked a day shift could we get together. Go out for dinner or talk over a drink. And she only ever had one. At nine PM she would be moving to her car. You could set a watch to her.

"Stay longer," I'd plead, her window rolled down, my hands on the door frame.

"I can't, I need to be up at five thirty," she'd say.

"Fuck those little shits," I'd joke. "You know they don't want to learn."

"But I want to get paid," she'd say smiling.

"I'll pay you."

"Oh yeah, for what?"

Replacing my hands with my forearms, I'd stoop low to lean into her window. "What have you got?" And we would kiss, her soft hands on my sandpaper cheeks. Then she would break away and turn the key in the ignition. "I gotta go," she'd say, turning down the stereo.

"I wish you wouldn't."

"Call me."

"Of course."

Then she would pull away and I would watch her taillights go, and when she was gone, she lasted. For a little while anyway. Until the silence in my apartment started to ring in my ears so that when Collin pushed through the door asking where we were going, or when Michelle texted to ask if I needed a ride, what of Quinn held me in place began to slip. Then the night and its fountain of alcohol would lighten my head and my heart would forget. Carried along by singing voices and stamping feet, it was easy to shut one door so that another could open. The me that wanted to belong to Quinn was boxed up and saved for morning while the me that needed to not be alone was loosed on the night. A cur sent sniffing in the shadows.

Fridays I had to close the bar. Sundays she had band practice. So on Saturdays, I was always hers. Because she rose early out of habit, I cursed my alarm and dragged myself into the shower to wash away whatever clung to me from the night before just in time to tap dance down the apartment steps where she always turned down the music as I buckled myself into her passenger seat, and off we'd go. She showed me everything the valley had to offer. The desert botanical gardens where every alien plant was named and tagged. The bodegas with the fresh baked pastries where my limited Spanish made the silver toothed ladies at the counter smile for its childish sound in their ears. The flat trails at the base of the Superstitions where we stayed low and safe in the shady washes. "There's gold in those mountains," I told her, one blinding morning.

"I'm pretty sure that's just a myth," she said.

"Some people believe it."

"Yeah, and they die up there searching. It's a shame you can't deal with heights, or else we could hike Camelback. It's got the best view in Phoenix."

"I'm looking at the best view in Phoenix," I told her.

She called me a dork and kissed me quickly and walked ahead, telling me to come on.

Quinn knew of a camera store in downtown Mesa that had been in the same location since the nineteen sixties. Closed when we arrived with a cage pulled across the glass, we peered through the window before walking on to find a cafe for lunch where she talked to me about the future, which she hoped, for her, was antiquity. "Do you want to work in a museum?" I asked.

"Only if I had to. I'd rather work in the field." She was fascinated by the ancient world. Roman frescoes buried in

Galilee that she imagined herself stooped over brushing away centuries worth of dust and sand. When she fell into visions of her future, describing faraway places and all there was to be discovered, she spoke with so much purpose and certainty that it felt as though she was speaking to fate itself. Telling and not asking as to what lay ahead. Her faith diminished me. Made me feel like more dust to be cleared away.

"What about photography?" She'd ask when the conversation turned to me. "You seem to like it. And you're good at it." She had ambition and discipline and was willing to believe that I possessed them too. If not their developed form, at least their seed.

"Yeah. I'm not sure there's a living in it."

"Even if you focus on skateboarding?"

"Especially if I focus on skateboarding."

She mentioned community college. Just a few classes. I already had a degree but I could improve my skill with a camera. Learn the new software. I acted like I was considering it. "It's a thought," I'd say.

With her hand in mine, we walked the bricks of Gilbert, of Chandler, and in the bright span of day I loved her. Back in my apartment, the blinds stole half the light of the setting sun and what remained cut slashes across my bed and her waiting body. She and I would kiss and touch and begin to undress but never have sex. My hands crawled over her like spiders, walking her body where it was so wonderfully taught, dragging along where it was so wonderfully soft. Still covered in her underwear and socks, she made me sick with desire. Desperate for more of her, she would leave me, time and again. Never questioning who I really was. Unaware of who I would become after she'd driven away and midnight sent a crack through time just wide enough for me to slip through, to the place where Dom's body joined mine on a dance floor or a dirty couch, and her words, smothered and smashed by music, were lost in the black ocean of my inebriated mind.

I'm sure Dom and I spoke. I'm sure I was charming. I just don't remember much of it. Only the voice in my head the mornings after. Whether I'd had Dom in the pink glow of her bedroom on the edge of passing out, or in the bathroom of The Gemini on a cocaine high that stripped me to my most simian impulses, or my God, the time I pressed her against the wall in the storeroom of The Rogue when she'd worn that tight silver dress to Shake, and grinding against me as we danced she had my dick hard and my mind tormented beyond even rudimentary thinking. With a lust that verged on anger, I'd yanked her by the hand through the crowd, past the bar and into the liquor closet where she gripped the steel shelf and I pulled her panties aside and spit on my hand so I could slide into her, and if anyone heard the chiming of bottles rattling against themselves with each glorious thrust, I wouldn't have stopped. I couldn't have.

And no matter the night's infraction, I'd wake to my internal attorney drafting silent arguments in my defense. Reciting them with swagger. Reminding the jury that no promises had been made. No oaths violated. Implied commitments were inadmissible and just because Quinn might believe one thing to be true, until she spoke her requirements and my own lips confirmed them, all we had were our individual perceptions of our obligations to the other. That was no contract. I wasn't lying, I just wasn't offering every truth. And since I wasn't pressing her on the every detail of her comings and goings, how, fair ladies and gentlemen of the jury, could I stand accused of hypocrisy? My tongue diving into Dom's vodka stained mouth, my fingers deep in her pants working to get her wet, day after day my counsel was there to bury my conscience under words until it ceased to raise objections. Until it hadn't so much been tamed as conditioned. So that as Dom moaned into a pillow before I spun her around and dragged her up to lock eyes as I finished on her face, I could take everything the moment promised without muddying it

under the weight of guilt. I would say no to Dom when
Quinn said yes to me. That was the deal I made with no one
but myself. I was engaged in no particular evil. This is what
people did. Everyone my age. So I believed. In this place. Alive.
Young.

Lights were stretched from palm tree to palm tree, crisscrossing the length of the street like shoelaces. Walking under them they formed hourglasses against the sky. Several blocks were closed to car traffic for Cinco de Mayo and the whole of Old Town was staged for a day's long party. Drunks wearing plastic beads circled north and then south and then north again, buying beer and tequila shots as they went. Saladas was one of the few Mexican bars on the strip, and tents were raised in the driveway to accommodate extra cash registers and long metal tubs heaped over with ice and bottled beer. Behind the main bar where Collin was stationed with Parson, they stirred margaritas in a plastic trash can with a wooden oar. We sold so much alcohol on Cinco that Rich had to come to our registers multiple times throughout the day to cart off the cash and run it to the bank. It was the one day of the year that we could steal with total abandon, and Collin told me that I'd be a fool to not walk with at least three months rent. By mid afternoon, the pocket of my jeans was so thick with folded bills that I had to sneak to Collin's car to stash them under the seat.

I was able to get Caleb a job for the day working as a barback. He was stationed with me under the tent, and throughout the afternoon we sipped cold bottles of Sol to fight back the heat. As the sun began to set, we switched to Tequila. When someone would order shots of plata shaken over ice, I would over pour the tumbler so Caleb and I could split the excess after money had changed hands and the customer had walked away. When the sky turned purple the lights clicked on and the crowd grew younger. The middle aged men in polo shirts and their wives with botoxed lips had fatigued and filtered home, while those in their twenties came fresh and loud and eager. A group that included Dom and several other girls with tattoos and heavily painted eyes had their ID's checked and they lined up at the main bar. After she'd already bought a drink, Dom spotted me under the tent.

"Hey," she said, pushing a curl of black hair from her eyes.

"Hey," I said back to her.

"When do you get off?"

"Closing this fucker down," I told her.

"What time is that?"

"Midnight. But then I have to clean and cash out."

A man behind Dom in line was growing impatient but I ignored him.

"Will you come out tonight?" she asked.

"Where is everyone going?"

"It's Saturday."

"I know. I guess I meant after."

"Not sure yet."

She didn't say anything else so I asked if she needed a drink. She looked at the drink already in her hand, swallowed it in one long gulp, then dropped her cup and said sure. I poured reposado over ice in a plastic cup and squeezed a handful of limes into it. I handed it to her and she lingered there to take the first sip. The next customer shoved his way forward with bills folded between his knuckles and began reciting his order. I watched Dom's ass move side to side as she walked away, and she must have known that I was watching because each movement was bigger than it needed to be.

In the street in front of the bar, bodies that tried to walk forward were cordoned on all sides by bodies content to stay in place. Music blared from every bar and the competing songs all merged into an angry cacophony. A woman bent over the railing of the patio and threw up onto the sidewalk. The people in the crowd closest to where it fell cried out in disgust or laughed and pointed in mockery at the puker herself. Her friends carried her off and the pile of sick remained and was scattered by the shoes of those who didn't know to look down as they went.

Caleb came to and from the tent, leaving with garbage bags full of empty cups and bottles and returning with boxes of beer and plastic tubs piled high with ice. "Dude," he said, returning from such a trip. "Dom is fucking wasted."

"So?"

"So, Collin told me to tell you to get her out of here."

"Why?"

"He said she was dancing on the bar and Rich went to get the bouncer but when he got back she was gone."

"So what's the problem?"

"Collin said she locked herself in the bathroom and now there's a long line of women who can't get in."

"I fail to see how this is my problem."

"I don't know man, she screamed at Collin when he tried to get her out, so he told me to tell you to deal with it. So I'm telling you."

I swore. Handed Caleb the bar key from my back pocket. Said, "Cover me."

He didn't want to take what I was trying to give him and he held his arms back saying, "I don't know how to bartend."

"You know how to drink, don't you? It's not much different." I set the bar key and my butt towel on the table top and tore off a long piece of blank receipt paper. On one side I wrote *shots*, and on the other I wrote *beer*. "No matter what people order, tell them it's five bucks. Take cash only. Make a tally for everything you sell and hand me the cash when I get back."

He tried to say something about how he didn't want to do what I was asking, but I cut him off, promising that I'd be fast, and then I walked quickly up the patio steps and into the bar. Passing Collin, his eyes were wide and white, telling me without telling me that I needed to deal with Dom, fast. In the mop closet I grabbed the restroom key. The line outside the lady's room was relieved when I pushed past them, but they collectively groaned as I went inside and shut the door behind me again.

Dom was sitting on the floor against a wall. She opened her eyes halfway and seeing me, she smiled. "Riley!" There was a puddle of piss on the tile and a trail of drips led to where she sat, her legs spread, her arms reaching for me.

"We gotta get you out of here." I tried to help Dom to her feet, but she was dead weight.

The door opened and a woman stepped halfway in. Seeing Dom and the dark yellow puddle, she yelled, "Oh gross! She pissed all over the floor!"

"It wasn't me!" Dom yelled back. I tried to heft her again, and she started laughing. "Yeah, it was me."

The woman walked in a wide arc around the piss and shut herself into a stall. Another woman started to enter but stopped at the sight of me crouching behind Dom and lifting her from under her arms.

"Did she piss?" the new woman asked.

"No!" Dom insisted, as I got her to her feet, draping her arm over my shoulders.

"Yeah you did!" the first woman yelled from her stall, her own urine now streaming into the bowl.

"Fucking, bitch." Dom slumped as she cursed.

"Fuck you, bitch!" the woman in the stall screamed back.

The second woman backed out and the door fell closed as I worked to steer Dom around her puddle. Her ears pricked up at the song that was playing and she started shaking her hips to the beat. I gripped her body more tightly to keep her upright, but she slipped loose as she popped her hips to Justin Timberlake telling us that he was bringing sexy back. She steadied herself on the sink and with that added support, began tossing her head playfully, her black hair whipping side to side. In the mirror, her uneven eyes found mine. My shoulders fell.

"Come on, Dom." I put my hands on her waist to direct her towards the door, but she held the sink and pressed her ass against me. In the mirror, her bursting cleavage and her teeth biting her lower lip were a bludgeon against reason. She let out a breath. Smiled a tiger's smile. My pulse was in my ears. Beating with the music. She made figure eights with her ass against my tightening pants and I knew that I was about to do what I shouldn't do but the wanting was so strong that it closed the curtain on my thinking self shouting its warnings, and with one long step, I was at the door turning the bolt, and with one more step I was back behind Dom as she steadied herself on one arm while with the other she pulled her dress up over her hips. She wasn't wearing underwear and my mind was bereft of higher things like language or choosing or regret and my belt hit the floor with a *clank*. When the woman in the stall flushed and opened the door, I was tonguing Dom from behind to get her wet.

"For fuck's sake!" The woman screamed and slammed the stall door shut, hiding behind it. I should have cared. I should have been terrified that I was going to lose my job. But there was no I to hold to account. There was only that pounding music and the salt smell of Dom's pussy and her half moan, half growl as she hammered her ass back against my thighs. A piece of rigid flesh against which she could exhaust herself. My mind dialed down to the exclusion of all but one sensation. A slave to her painted eyelids and wide mouth in the mirror. Her face a spectacular misery of both sin and salvation.

"You two are fucking nasty!" the woman in the stall yelled, and Dom's lips curled into an evil smile. Insults and curses and declarations of how just plain wrong we were fell like high praise amidst the music and Dom's demands for more and harder, faster, until her body trembled and tightened and my eyes rolled back in my skull as I came into her.

Then time started again. With my pants up I helped Dom pull her dress down and took her by the hand. She moved sleepily. Told me I was bad. That she liked it. I unlocked the door and the woman in the stall swore at us one last time. Dom cackled madly and we slipped past the line of women waiting to use the bathroom and into the sticky crowd. With an arm around her ribs, I was the structure that held Dom upright. Together we moved out the door and my legs followed her wayward finger pointing to the rear lot where she'd parked. I placed her in the backseat of her car. Her arms were around my head and she tried to pull me on top of her and I had to push her away to free myself from her determined grip. She muttered something. Her eyes closed. Semen ran down her inner thigh. I looked at it with pride. A signature on a painting. She was immediately asleep and I slammed shut the door.

I ran back to the tent and to Caleb. He had filled a pitcher with cash and demanded to know what had taken me so long.

"Don't worry about it. I'll explain later."

Caleb squinted. "Dude, your breath smells like pussy."

"Really?" I held my cupped hand in front of my mouth and exhaled. "Well, shit." I *snicked* the cap off a bottle of Sol and swished the beer in my mouth. After swallowing, I swished another mouthful.

"Did you just fuck her?"

"Any better?" I breathed out.

Caleb waved the air away from his face. "Now it's just pussy and beer."

I retook my place at the counter and tended to the line of customers. The bar was full until closing. At midnight the bouncers moved like a line of riot police, starting inside and slowly marching toward the patio and the sidewalk to force the crowd into the street. Caleb and I were drunk as we collapsed the tent and carried unsold beer back to the walk-in cooler. Rich was drunk as he counted down my drawer and signed me out. Collin was drunk when he met me in the parking lot where we both changed our shirts.

"How'd you do?" He asked over the roof of the car. "Get three months?"

"And then some."

"Told you." He rolled deodorant under his arms. "What happened with Dom?"

I was rolling a cigarette. "She was wasted. She's probably still passed out in her backseat."

"Where's she parked?"

I set my cigarette on my lip. "Back lot." I clicked my lighter. "Why?"

"Maybe we should check on her."

I breathed out smoke. "She'll be fine."

Collin drove us south to The Rogue. He rolled over a curb and rear ended a car as he tried to parallel park, so he backed out and drove further down the road and found a different parking spot. Checking his front fender, he wiped away the touch of white paint that marked his guilt. We cut the line at the door and Clint thumbed us in. Faye poured us tall shots of whiskey and cracked us each a can of beer. Collin went in search of customers and I didn't see him again that night. At the back table, different people at different times asked where my camera was and I screamed past their ears that I had come straight from work. They nodded or shrugged or scrunched their eyebrows and then went back to sitting and watching and drinking and saying things into each other's ears that no one else could hear. All people whose names I knew. All strangers just the same. Ashli wasn't there and Dom wasn't there and I thought of Quinn and how she was asleep in her bed and I felt very alone until Michelle came smiling through the crowd.

"Hey loser!" She yelled at me as she pulled me into a firm hug. Later she drove me to the after party where we smoked and complained about how boring it was and made fun of people under our breath. Their clothes. Their hair. Their clumsy attempts to hit on someone that were obvious and pathetic even at a distance. On the road home Michelle rolled down her window and sang into the wind. In the parking lot of my apartment she asked me if I could make it up the stairs alright.

"I think I can manage." I dropped my keys and she offered to help me get inside. "I'll be fine," I told her.

"Are you sure?"

"I'm sure."

"You're sure?"

"Yeah, I'm sure."

Quinn's uncle had a cabin in the mountains near Payson. He invited us to come stay for a weekend, saying he wanted to meet me and that it would be a good way to escape the hellish heat of the valley, which sounded great. Quinn and I had been spending more time together since school let out. She taught remedial reading three days a week, but only until noon, and though I would have spent every day with her, she made it clear that she needed space. For her other friends. For her music. So when she would have me, I was with her, and when she would not, I made do with Collin. With Michelle. With the bars and parties and Dom. Ashli had reappeared in town but only in two dimensions. Her Suicide Girl profile had gotten her work as a model for American Apparel, first in black and white quarter page print ads, then in full color. Ten feet high and three times as long, stretching across the windows of the Mill Avenue store. Laying prone. Wearing their brand of tights. Her forearm hiding her nipples. A few nights before leaving town with Quinn, I drank at the Palo Verde Lounge fending off questions about it.

"Did you see it?" Thea asked.

"I did." I told her.

"People are saying it's in other cities, too. Like Chicago and L.A."

"She, so, owes you," Michelle said.

"Wait, did you shoot that?" Thea asked?

I told her I didn't.

"But she wouldn't be taking off as like, the new, hot, it girl if it hadn't been for Riley," Michelle explained. "He has done all her stuff up till now."

"Your girlfriend's here," Thea said, noticing Dom across the room.

"She isn't his girlfriend," Michelle said for me.

"She's not?"

I shook my head while looking over shoulders and between limbs to where Dom sat with a crowd of girls. Sensing my eyes searching for her, she looked away. Feigned indifference. Our usual game. "Are you and Quinn official?" Michelle asked. I told her I wasn't sure and she said that probably meant no.

In the rear lot, I smoked a cigarette as I readied my camera. Dom took the seat next to me. Said hey. I screwed a lens onto the camera body and asked her how she'd been. Fine. I stood up and pointed the lens at her. Pulled the focus ring. She canted her head, feeding me her jawbone. How about you? I released the shutter. Watched the screen for the result. Same. I spun a dial to open the aperture and pointed again. She looked up and away. Almost a smile as the red exit sign cast a pink gloss on her skin. She said we should hang out sometime. I released the shutter. Turned the camera to share the result with her. Asked her what she thought of the picture. I'll send it to you. I took one last drag off my cigarette and dropped it to the blacktop, letting the ember smoke itself out. Back in the bar I shot away. Elbowed my way into the tight gaps between people and interrupted their conversations. Leaving the bar that night, I passed Dom near the exit and told her to take it easy. What magical words. What else were we doing if not taking it easy? Like we were nothing but air breezing into open windows before breezing right back out again. Easy didn't have to apologize or explain. Didn't have to say things like, "It's over." Didn't consider that we could feel anything for each other beyond mute lust. Easy was so damn easy. That was the beauty of it. Easy took itself.

And so it was that as Quinn's car wound the path through the desert east of Mesa, slowly gaining in elevation, I was able to feel weightless. Innocent. Out my window, the Four Peaks were like two sets of tits pointed skyward and that thought made me smile.

The road to Payson bent in wide arcs as it lifted us into the mountains, a steel guard rail the only boundary between our speeding car and a sheer plummet into waterless ravines of broken stone far below. For miles, Saguaro grew tall and straight from the barren ground, their limbs bent at human angles like they were hostages at gunpoint, the sum of them looking a forgotten tribe in a final, failed migration up and out of the valley, refugees fleeing a forsaken city in a time when God no longer had a taste for salt.

"I got accepted into my grad program," she said.

I was watching the sky in the rearview mirror.

"Did you hear me?"

"Yeah. Sorry. That's really great. Congratulations."

"Thank you. I only found out yesterday. I thought it was important to tell you at the start of our trip."

I didn't grasp what she meant.

"I'll be leaving at the end of August."

The car was climbing higher into the sky and to the east the first clouds were visible. Gray lint against the blue, far beyond the red mountains.

"Are you upset?"

I shook my head. Smiled. "Of course not. I always knew you might leave."

"But now it's real."

"Yeah, but it's what you wanted."

"I don't want it to ruin the weekend."

"Why would it?"

She thought for a moment and said, "OK. Good," and taking my hand in hers added, "We're going to have fun."

The motor gave all it had to keep pace with traffic as we climbed. A green carpet of pine covered the mountain faces ahead of us. Cresting a peak, the nose of the car leveled, then dipped, pointing back to the Earth. Dropping a thousand feet, we hooked left then right, the car gaining speed despite

Quinn's foot steady on the brake. I pretended we were in a crashing plane.

"Are you OK?" she asked me.

"Yeah, why?"

"You're just being quiet."

"It's just a lot to think about."

"I know. I thought about waiting to tell you until Sunday, but that felt wrong. Like hiding it from you."

"Maybe I should come with you."

"To New York?"

"If that's OK."

She was quiet for a second. "Would you do that?"

"I don't know. I only just thought of it. I think I would. I'm not doing anything important here."

"Let's think about it," she said, her face and voice equally measured.

The car strained against the next climb.

"I like you Quinn," I said, meaning it very much.

"I like you too, Riley."

At the end of a long gravel driveway flanked by tall pines, her uncle's cabin was nicer than I had imagined it would be. The structure had a western aesthetic but everything inside was new. The stone counters. The steel appliances. The big TV. Only the patterned rugs with their stripes and diamonds laid over the deep brown pinewood floor told of the south-western setting. Out the back door, a hot tub sat shaded by a pergola that was hung with white privacy drapes. Across from it a grill was set into a stone counter, and four chairs faced each other that could be warmed by a ceramic chiminea. When we arrived, I followed Quinn into the smaller of the two bedrooms. Having set our bags down, I pushed her backward onto the bed and we kissed, grinding our bodies together. I slid her pants off and she let me go down on her for the first time. Her body shuddered as she made short gasps. When she came she arched her hips and her thigh muscles tensed and she pushed my head away. I kissed her stomach and she laid still until her breathing slowed.

An hour later we were in the living room playing Scrabble on the coffee table when the sound of gravel crunching under tires grew out of the silence and then stopped. Quinn smiled and we rose to greet her uncle in the driveway. She went to him as he stepped out of his car and they embraced. Balding, and not much taller than her, he kissed Quinn on her forehead before he turned to me. "You must be Riley," he said, his eyes tight and scrutinizing behind his glasses, as if I might not in fact, be Riley.

"Yes sir." I shook his waiting hand.

"None of this sir, stuff. It's Morty. Why don't you kids help me with the groceries."

There were only three bags. I carried them inside. In the kitchen, Quinn began putting the food in the refrigerator.

"Leave the fish out. It has to thaw," Morty said, heading into his bedroom. Passing the coffee table, he looked down and asked, "Who got haboob?"

"That would be me," Quinn said, proudly.

"She's kicking my butt," I said.

Morty grinned, "I haven't beaten her at that game since she was eleven." He disappeared into his room and returned a few minutes later wearing a heavy cardigan sweater with a thick collar and wood buttons running the lapel. On his feet he wore slippers that *skiffed* over the floor where it wasn't covered by a rug. He sat down in a leather chair. Shifted. Sighed with delight and said, "I set the air on. Let me know if either of you get cold." To me he said, "Sit. Sit."

I obeyed and sat on the couch but left the cushion nearest Morty's elbow open for Quinn.

"I like getting comfortable when I'm up here, so I wear my big sweater." He rubbed his hands down his chest and belly, then added, "But I'll start to sweat if I don't put the air on."

He looked to the kitchen where his niece was wiping a counter and said, "Quinnie Bear, leave all that. Come visit."

"Does anyone want a glass of wine?" She asked.

I did want one but didn't want to be the first to say so.

"What time is it?" Morty asked himself. He adjusted his glasses as he consulted his wristwatch. "Gosh, it's only four." He let his sleeve fall over the watch and said to Quinn, "You know, why not?" To me he whispered, "We're here for a good time, right? We can be a bit naughty." Then he tossed his head to Quinn and said, "Why don't you grab the Berkshire?"

"We brought a bottle with us," she told him.

"Oh, wonderful. What did you bring?"

"Something called Templar," I said.

"A malbec?"

"A pinot noir, I think."

"Good. Let's try that."

Quinn took wine glasses from the cabinet and they rang on the stone counter. She fed the screw into the cork but struggled to pull it from the bottle.

"Don't break it," Morty said. "Riley, why don't you help her out."

I went to rise but Quinn scowled at her uncle and said, "I can get it," her voice straining as she pulled again, failing a second time to remove the cork.

"He's a bartender!" Morty said. "You are a bartender, aren't you son?"

"I am. But we don't serve wine."

"No? That's too bad. You look strong though. Why don't you go help her out."

"She's pretty strong too," I said, looking to Quinn. Her face was red and she had the bottle gripped between her thighs as she hauled on the wine key. The cork popped free and I said, "See, she didn't need me."

She laid the wine key on the counter and shook the pain from her fingers. After pouring three glasses, she handed one to her uncle and one to me. With her own glass she took the open seat I'd left for her on the couch and she drew her legs up so that both of her knees pointed to Morty. He raised his wine glass and said, "To new friends." We raised our glasses in turn and then sipped. With his eyes closed, Morty moved the wine in his mouth and swallowed. Deciding that he liked it well enough, he opened his eyes and took a larger mouthful.

"Quinnie Bear has told me a lot about you, Riley. She says you're very sharp. That you graduated from, where was it, the University of Chicago?"

"I'm from Chicago, but I went to DePaul. The University of Chicago wouldn't want me. That place is for geniuses."

"DePaul is still a good school, though. Very good. And what did you study there?"

"Criminal justice."

"Criminal justice, very good. Why did you choose that? Are you hoping to go on to law school? Maybe be a defense attorney, or..." He left the question open ended.

"A lawyer? God no. I only went to college because that's what everyone said I was supposed to do. I think I picked criminal justice because I needed to pick something but had no idea what I wanted to be. My dad was a cop, so I guess it made sense to me. It seemed as good as anything else."

"Is your father a police officer there in Chicago?"

"Well, he's dead now. But he was in Pittsburgh before that."

"I'm sorry to hear that, son. I really am. Did he die in the line of duty?"

Quinn had her hand on mine. She already knew the story. "Car accident," I said to Morty. "A trucker crashed into him on the highway."

Morty put his hand over his heart and closed his eyes for a second. He made a humming sound and said, "Awful. Just awful." Then he asked, "Were you close with your father?"

"Not particularly. But I loved him. My mother left him when I was still very young and he finally moved away."

"Your mother raised you, then?"

"If you could call it that."

He made the humming sound again then swirled the wine in his glass, choosing his next words carefully. "Was she not, might we say, always up to the challenges of parenting?"

Quinn's hand squeezed mine. "We don't have to talk about this," she said.

I looked at her worried face. "It's OK. Really, I don't mind."

"She's right, son. We can change the subject."

I sipped my wine and set the glass down on the coffee table. Opening my hands, I was about to speak, but thought for a moment longer, then said, "My mother got pregnant with my sister when she was young, and so she married my dad probably because she thought she had to. I was born two years later. Then when I was maybe four or five, she met a man she actually loved. They had an affair and she told my dad she was leaving. I think for her, that was when she felt like her life finally began. When it finally became hers. After that, she was there, but not there. Like we were part of something that was dead for her." Nothing I was saying was new to my mind, but I'd never said any of it out loud before. Not to another person. And they didn't interject, so I kept on. "If I'm being honest. Really honest. I couldn't say whether my mother loved me or not."

"That's awful," Quinn said.

"She loves you," Morty insisted. Setting down his wine, he folded his hands over his stomach and said, "It's probably impossible for her not to love you. At some level anyway. Parents cannot help but love their children, even if some of them are very bad at actualizing that love."

"Maybe," I said.

Morty was looking at Quinn. "Quinnie Bear is the best

thing that ever happened to me, and only because of the worst thing. When my brother and sister-in-law died in that fire, I was crushed. Totally crushed. Aaron, my brother, was my best friend in the world. We grew up in Queens, and we were attached at the hip. I was ten when my father took a job here in Arizona. Aaron was thirteen. And being the new kids, Jewish new kids, no less, we got into a fair number of scrapes." His face lightened and he rested it on his hand. "Some brothers, they get into it with each other, you know? They fight over this thing and that. Not so with me and Aaron. Not once. He looked after me like keeping me safe was his only charge in life. And I looked up to him like he was the truth of the world. If Aaron spoke, his words may as well have been the word of God. There could never be a fight between us because I couldn't conceive to disagree with him, and he couldn't conceive to hurt me. When he got married and moved to the Bay with Quinn's mother, I was heartbroken. I didn't tell him so because I was happy for him, and I didn't want him to stay here just for me. In fact, I was considering moving there, to California, to be near him, because I was so lonely without him." He picked up his glass and aerated the wine. "Then the fire happened. They called it the Tunnel Fire, and, well, you know what happened next. I'm sure Quinnie has told you all about it."

"She has."

He reached out to Quinn and set his fingers on her forearm. "This isn't upsetting you, is it?"

She shook her head.

He kept his hand on her arm and said to me, "Well, long story short, Quinnie survived against all the odds. I don't know how much she has told you, how much detail, but she was in a closet in her room that somehow created a kind of air pocket, a protected place where the fire didn't go. The Fire Marshal explained the science of it to me. He said that these things, as counterintuitive as they might seem, that they happen. And maybe that's true. But I didn't need science. I knew it was God's will. That's what I believe in my heart to this day. That God saved her."

He was looking at Quinn as he said this but she was looking at her legs, smoothing her pants with her hand, as though the idea of being one of God's miracles was too ridiculous to consider, or perhaps, too much to bear. She didn't look up again until Morty went on speaking.

"I think it makes her bashful when I say these things, but I saw the house after it was destroyed. The whole block. So many beautiful homes reduced to charcoal and ash. Knowing that a little girl survived such complete devastation, I cannot think of it any other way. It was the hand of the divine that saved her. That passed her to me. And since that day I have cared for her as if she were my own daughter. I consider it my purpose in life. A task given to me by God himself." He looked at his niece and then drank the last of his wine and set the glass back on the table. Pointing a finger at me, he laughed and said, "So you better treat her right!"

"He treats me just fine," Quinn insisted.

"I'll do my best," I said."

Morty was smiling. "I know you will, son."

His eyes were on me in a gentle way, but I still felt accused so I looked around at the cabin walls. "This place is nice."

"Thank you," Morty said, settling back into his chair. "It wasn't so much to look at when I first bought it, but I have been working on it, slowly but surely, and now it's not too bad." He scanned the room. "If nothing else, it's comfortable. Which is what's important. When I come up here, I want to be able to relax."

"How often do you come?"

"I try to make it up once a month if I can. I have to get out of the valley. If I don't, I go crazy."

"Here we go," Quinn said.

"What?" Morty asked.

"You don't like Phoenix?" I asked him.

"He does," Quinn answered. "He just likes to complain."

"I do like it," Morty interjected, "Parts of it anyway. The mountains are beautiful. The weather can be great when it's not one hundred and ten degrees. But the culture down there, that's what begins to bother me."

Quinn rolled her eyes and sighed.

"What? It's true. It's a very superficial place. People there are very self absorbed and they care more about showing off how much money they have than about being a decent person, and after a while it gets to be too much, all the vanity. It keeps people out of touch with the real world."

"It is the real world," Quinn said. "How could it not be?"

"Because they don't have a winter!" Morty said, tossing his hands into the air and sitting forward in his chair.

"So?"

"So they don't have an accurate yardstick with which to measure time! Everything is always the same. Every day. Every week. Months slide by and people don't even notice."

"They have winter," Quinn said.

"Not a real one, not like back east. Not like in Chicago." He looked to me for support.

Quinn became animated herself. Her gestures were those of her uncle. "A lot of places don't have cold winters! What about Florida? Or California? Or Texas? Are those places not the real world?"

Morty waved his hand. "It's not the same," he said. He held out his glass. "This was good. Son, do you mind refilling this for me?"

"Sure." I rose to take his glass.

"Just a half," he said. "And fill yours, too."

"I'm good, actually. Babe?"

"I'll take a half," Quinn said, handing me her glass.

I was in the kitchen pouring wine when Morty started in again. "There's something about Phoenix. It could be the mountains, or the air pollution, or all the palm trees that shouldn't be there, I have to think about it, but there's an element that separates it from those other places."

"The palm trees aren't supposed to be there?" I asked, walking back into the living room.

"No!" Morty said with both humor and despair. He thanked me as I handed him his glass and when I was sitting again, my body close to Quinn's, he continued, "And neither are millions of people! It's a desert for Pete's sake. A death trap! Maybe that's what really boggles me, being down there. Everywhere you go, it's just strip mall on top of strip mall in between housing developments that are all indistinguishable from one another. All of it like it up and fell from outer space!" He raised his hands and dropped them like he was smashing an unbaked ball of dough on a surface before him. Then he sat back, exhausted by the topic. "The palm trees were all shipped in and planted along the roads to dress the place up like a paradise," he said, calmer now. "But what really grows there, what's native, is the ocotillo. The cholla. The nopal. Plants that will slice you open if you get too close. That's the real desert. Rattlesnakes. Scorpions." He pointed a finger at me while resting his head on his other fist. "Let me tell you son, the desert is a place God designed to test man. Moses. The Israelites."

"I never thought about that," I said.

"And what did we do with it?" He was animated again. "With God's grand proving grounds? We paved it over and made a mini-mall!"

Quinn rolled her head. "You are so dramatic."

"Do you think people even have that kind of power?" I asked him. "To do something outside of God's will?"

"Yeah, maybe God wanted us to make a mini-mall," Quinn joked. "Maybe God got bored of rattlesnakes and scorpions."

Morty scoffed. "And what? Wanted sushi restaurants and liquor stores?"

"Maybe!" Quinn said.

"Or maybe the test has changed."

Morty tapped the air in front of him with his finger. Looked at me with an expression both pleased and serious. "Very good, son. Very good." He sat forward and sipped his wine. "I like him, Quinnie Bear. He's a thinker." With another gulp, he patted his knee and stood. "Let's get started on the dinner. I'm famished."

On the redwood deck Morty grilled cuts of pink salmon. With his tongs he pointed to the trees surrounding his cabin and told me the names of their kinds. Quinn brought out a wooden bowl with a salad that was topped with crumbles of feta cheese and olives. Morty squeezed lemon wedges over the salmon filets and then dressed them with thin sprigs of dill. As we ate, he told Quinn and I of the hawks he would watch from the deck that flew in high circles and of the owls that called out in the night to no response. He opened a second bottle of wine at the table and filled his glass and Quinn's. I told him I didn't need any more, but he insisted, so I let him fill my glass halfway but I only took small sips from it, enjoying my clear head and the clear air. Morty asked how I liked the meal and I told him it was probably the best food I had eaten in years, certainly since moving to Arizona. I explained that I took a lot of my meals at work and Quinn added that, when together, we always ate out. Morty teased that she should be a good woman and cook for me and she threw a crouton at him and we all laughed.

As the sun went down, Morty talked about his childhood. About his almost marriage to a woman who went on a pilgrimage to Israel and then never came back. He asked Quinn about her band and told her more than once how beautiful her voice was. He asked if I had seen her perform and I told him of course. Several times. He asked if I didn't think she had a beautiful voice and I told him I thought she had a beautiful everything. He said he was so proud that she should get accepted to NYU. That if not for his job he would follow her back to New York. With the second bottle of wine drained, he looked at his watch and said that he had gotten up early and now needed sleep. He told us to make use of the hot tub. Said it was a good place to watch the stars. Before retiring to bed, he removed its heavy cover and explained how to operate the controls. "It's one hundred and two degrees," he said, dipping his hand into the water and then shaking it free of drops.

In our room we changed into swimsuits. Quinn said she would get towels and meet me outside. The night air was cool against my chest and a beautiful sting of pain sung in my body as I lowered myself into the steaming water. In seconds, I was perfectly comfortable and missing that first pain of the heat. Quinn slid the glass door shut behind her and laid towels over the railing next to the hot tub. She was wearing a red two piece bathing suit and her hair was held up with a clip. She breathed out as she dipped her first and then second leg into the water. Lowering herself until the water line was at her collar bones, she exhaled again. Closed her eyes. I spread my arms and let them rest on the edge of the hot tub behind me. My head fell back. Through the beams of the pergola overhead, the black sky was dotted with thousands of stars and it was the first time I had seen them in years. Quinn pulled her body onto mine and I held her around the waist and we kissed. It was Quinn who removed my swimsuit and raised herself onto me. She moved up and down to find the place where it brought her the most pleasure and I lost myself watching her large breasts rising and falling in front of my face. Not wanting to finish too quickly, I looked again at the stars and to the sway of the black pine tops against the sky. She moaned with her movements and held me by the shoulders. As the pleasure of it swelled in her, I felt her tighten around me, and then with her mouth open her eyes met mine and we looked into each other and her orgasm brought me to one as well.

"Fuck," I said, not expecting the height of the euphoria. We both breathed out long breaths and she laid her chest against mine. Her heart was beating quickly. I held her face and kissed her and meant it more than any kiss I'd ever given anyone. I dragged the tips of my fingers down her scarred flesh. She kept her eyes closed in the steam and let me trace a path from her butchered ear down her rippled neck, over every bump and fissure of discolored skin. At her clavicle, I lifted my hand to her chin and kissed her mouth again.

A light wind blew and the white curtains hanging from the corners of the pergola whimpled in its flow. Pinon sap rode the breeze and was strong in contrast to the constancy of chlorine rising from the water, but there was something else, too. Something hidden between them. I wrapped my arms fully around the hourglass of Quinn's waist and pulled her body to mine. Still inside her and not wanting to leave, I let my forehead touch hers. Warm under the water and cool above, the wind shook the pine boughs and they rushed against themselves. The steam floating around us moved in circles, wide at the surface of the water and tightening as it coiled upward. Hurricanes of vapor that made giants of us. She pushed the hair from my eyes and we saw each other.

"I love you, Quinn."

Rain came in the night and was gone by morning. I didn't hear it as I slept, but knew that it had come. Had passed over us as we dreamed, naked, her body fitting into mine. In the gray dawn she crept from the room without waking me and when finally a band of light warmed my eyes I opened them to find that I'd been hugging her pillow. Breathing the smell her hair left behind. I checked my phone and was embarrassed to find that it was almost 9:30, so I showered quickly and dressed and went to find Quinn and Morty.

On the sunlit deck they each sat with a cup of coffee. Him bent over a folded newspaper with a pencil in hand, her tilting her head to read a crossword clue from across the table. She said good morning. Without looking up Morty told me that mugs were in the cabinet above the coffee maker. Returning with my own coffee in hand, I took the seat next to Quinn. Desperate for a cigarette but wanting to impress her uncle more, I resisted going to the car for my makings and instead sat with the craving as it begged and bargained. Morty laid his pencil on the table and held his reading glasses a foot beyond his face to read the print on my sweatshirt.

"What's Antihero?" He asked.

"It's a skateboard company."

"Oh. Is that something you enjoy? Skateboarding?"

"It is."

"Are you any good at it?"

"Used to be."

"I told you Uncle," Quinn said. "He was almost professional before he got hurt."

"Is that true?" He asked.

"Well, not quite. But I was on the path, you might say."

"That's right. Quinnie Bear did tell me. What was it, you fell on your head and now you have motion sickness?"

"It's like vertigo. When I skate, the world starts spinning."

"The world is spinning."

"Uncle." Quinn reprimanded him with a look.

"I'm sorry," he said. "I should be more sensitive."

"It's fine."

"Is that the only thing, then? The only problem you have since the slam? That's what they call it right? When you fall? Slamming?"

"Slamming works."

"Because a head injury, that can be serious business. Serious business. Do you see a doctor?"

"They wanted me to come back and see the neuro team for more follow ups, but I didn't have health insurance so I never went."

"Oh, son, you should go."

I shrugged. "Maybe. I think I'm fine though. Aside from the vertigo thing." He was looking me up and down and I began to wonder if I was actually fine. Like maybe he saw something I couldn't.

"There are all sorts of conditions that can be associated with a traumatic brain injury," he said.

"Uncle, leave him be. He knows."

"It's OK," I said. I put my hand on her hand and took a drink of my coffee.

Morty went on, "I don't want to interfere in your business, it's just concerning. When people have a serious injury to the brain, the downstream effects can be things you wouldn't expect. Depression. Mood swings. Diminished executive function. Even suicidality. It's very serious business."

"Yeah. They mentioned all that when I came out of the coma."

"You were in a coma!" He sat back with his hand over his heart.

"Medically induced because of the swelling."

"Oh God, son. You need to see your doctor."

"Let's change the subject, now," Quinn pleaded.

"OK," Morty said with his hands up. "I'm sorry. I don't mean to pry. I just get concerned, that's all."

"I'm fine," I assured him. "The funny thing is, I honestly never think about it now."

Morty folded his reading glasses and set them on the newspaper next to his pencil. He crossed his arms against the morning chill and asked me, "Do you miss skateboarding? If you were trying to do it professionally, I imagine it was something that you loved."

The answer should have been automatic. It wasn't. In finding the right words, I stared away through the furry pine boughs to the blurred ridges in the distance and then to the gray nothing in the haze beyond, nodding a little as I thought. It was such an easy question. But every time I almost spoke, I considered it longer. No one had asked me this. No one had cared enough to know. I chuckled a bit and Morty was patient waiting for that chuckle to become speech.

"I dream about it," I said, returning to their faces. "When I dream at all. What hurts is knowing that it's all still inside of me. The skill. Trapped in my muscles." Beneath the table, Quinn touched my leg like she might feel that caged ability, and I looked at her as I said, "There is nothing else in the world like it. The way you can float over the ground and how with time your body grows attuned to it so that it's almost easier than walking. It's like cheating in a weird way. Like you are doing something you were never meant to do, feeling the world in a way that humans weren't supposed to feel it." I hovered my hand over the table, clearing invisible obstacles.

"Being able to flow over transitions, whipping through the pockets of a bowl then sitting on a long grind, and doing it all without thinking, carried by instinct..." I was trying to use words to explain what could only be felt, so I moved on. "It probably sounds silly, but when you're really into it, when skating is your life, you don't see the world the same way any more. Everywhere you go, there is a part of your mind scanning whatever is in front of you asking, 'Can I skate that?' And you end up knowing the names of stair sets and handrails and ledges around the world and you know the names of people who have done the best tricks on them. It's like living in another version of reality. We're here with everyone else, but we're experiencing it in a whole different way. A more exciting way."

Morty made a deep sound in his throat and said, "You have your own map."

I waited for him to say more.

"The world is just the world, but as a people, we agree on names for the terrain before us so we can all be in the same world together. So my west is your west. And you and your friends, the other skateboarders, you have your own map. One only shared by the few initiated, which makes it exciting."

"I guess, yeah."

"A man can't have a map unto himself or else he'd be called crazy. Sharing it with one other person alone, is also not enough. Two people can be mutually insane when weighed against the rest of the world and their claims. But there are enough of you sharing your map to create an argument. To bind the world in a story and bring its parts together into a coherent whole. That's the foundation of every religion." He took a beat then added, "And cult."

Quinn rolled her eyes, "Skateboarding is not a cult."

"Honestly, it kind of is," I said to her. "We have our slang. Our clothes. There isn't some grand leader to obey, other than the feeling itself. When you're skating and you land something, you feel this charge go through you. And when you're with other people, they feel it too. You all build this stoked energy together. Amping each other up. And it feels like something real is happening. Like the minute that you're living in is stretching out. That it has to if it's going to contain all of the love, and the pain, and the hype, and everyone there is just feeding it, and feeding off of it, and you feel like brothers. Like you're all in it together. Fighting the same battle or discovering the same truth." I stopped myself. Though I was smiling with my whole face I knew I was about to cry, so instead I forced a laugh and pushed my hands through my hair to hide my eyes just long enough to blink back the tears. "I'm sure it sounds stupid to you because from the outside most people see a skateboard as a kid's toy. But when you really learn how to use it…"

"It's thrilling," Morty said. "And you get addicted to the adrenaline."

I rocked my head as I weighed his words. "Not exactly. I know that's what people think, but it's not quite it."

"How would you say it?"

"It's like disappearing into your body. Living as pure sensation."

"Like an acid trip."

Quinn hit her uncle on the arm with the back of her hand.

Morty flinched and turned his palms to the sky. "What, you think I wasn't young once? I came of age in the seventies! They were a wild time. Talk about feeding off each other's energies." He tugged at his lapel, "You think when I was seventeen I wore this sweater and did crossword puzzles?"

We laughed with him, then in the silence that followed I said, "I think I miss my friends the most." I was looking away again. To the static out beyond the mountains where my eyes could no longer construct solid lines or discern colors. To the boundary of my perception. "I bought a camera so there would be a reason to keep me around. But when I go out to take skate photos, I'm not part of it. Not from the inside. Everyone is nice enough. They're glad to have me there. But I'm a tourist. They do the doing and I'm behind glass. Watching."

"And it's not the same," Morty said.

"And it's not the same," I said.

We talked and drank coffee until the day warmed. Morty asked Quinn about her plans for moving to New York. Having been born in Queens, he was very excited for her. He asked her about her band and if she planned to continue with her musical aspirations when she was away and she said that she was unsure. There were many things that she was unsure about and Morty told her that was a wonderful thing, to have so much life before her, so many open doors. He asked if we were going to try and make our relationship work over the distance and I told him that I was considering moving to New York as well. I said I didn't want to be a distraction to Quinn, but that she was the best thing I had going on in my life and that there were plenty of bars in New York City so I was sure I could find a job and that if it meant being with her, I'd happily leave Arizona. Morty said that we both had a lot to think about. Quinn lifted her hand, taking mine with it, saying, "It's up to you," and I looked her in the eyes and knew that I had already made up my mind.

At noon, Morty led us on a hike. It was hot under the sun at its peak but the path was easy and flat. The ground was strewn with pebbles and dry pine needles so our feet alternatively crunched and scuffed. Morty talked most of the way. Pasyon still had large stands of virgin Ponderosa Pine. Wild horse herds roamed the land, too. Stopping on the trail, he pointed to a clearing where a local had seen a mountain lion, and he stopped again to point out the Mogollon Rim high in the distance and he told us its name. I walked close to Quinn but dropped back to bring up large balls of phlegm and to spit them in the duff. I knew they could hear me coughing and I was trying to be polite but couldn't help that my lungs were now two days free of cigarette smoke and were strained by healing and elevation. After stopping to hack and spit a third time, I rejoined them where they waited and Morty said, "You sound like a smoker."

"Trying to quit," I said.

"That's good, son. It's an awful habit."

"I know."

When we returned to the cabin, Morty took a shower and packed his things. He insisted on going to temple and so he would be making the drive back into Phoenix and leaving us to enjoy the cabin alone. In the driveway he held Quinn tightly and kissed her on the forehead. He told her how proud of her he was and she thanked him, telling him that she loved him. When he released her I stepped forward with my hand extended but he said, "Bah!" and pushed my hand aside and pulled me into a hug. "It was very nice to meet you, Riley." He patted my back and without understanding why I felt a choke crawling in my throat so I stepped away and forced myself to cough something up. "Good luck, quitting smoking," he said, as I spit something large onto the ground behind a tree. I returned to where he and Quinn stood and I said "Thank you. For everything. It was an honor to meet you."

"Help yourselves to anything in the house," he told us, as he sat down into the driver's seat of his car. With the motor running, he rolled down the window. "Let's do this again. In the valley next time."

"Absolutely," I said.

"I love you," Quinn told him.

"I love you too, Quinnie Bear. Be safe on your drive out tomorrow."

"We will."

She waved as his car reversed slowly into a three point turn. When his brake lights were around the bend and hidden by the pine trees, she took my hand and we returned to the cabin. That night we grilled burgers for dinner. We found a bottle of malbec in Morty's collection that had a Ram's head on the label and we drank it slowly. On the couch, Quinn laid her legs across my lap and I spread a blanket over them and we watched a VHS copy of *The Adventures of Buckaroo Banzai Across the Eighth Dimension*. When it was over we had sex that felt like making love. We took our time. Made it last. Kissing and touching and exploring the nuances of each other's bodies. I wanted to know what made her feel good. Her orgasms excited me and so I made sure not to finish until she did. It felt good to tell her that I loved her, and so when afterwards she was lying naked in the piebald moonlight I told her again, and she smiled but didn't say it back. I laid on my side next to her with my head propped on my hand and I combed her hair with my fingers. Admiring her body. Loving her smell. Her silence made me eager to speak. To make poetry and promises. To confess. But I knew better.

When Quinn slept I watched summer lightning flash on the ceiling, flickering a false daylight that was swallowed by the black as quickly as it had come. Coyotes howled somewhere, first one and then many, but they quieted when a low roll of thunder told of a storm across the distant ranges. My fingers feathered the arm Quinn had draped over my chest and I committed myself to be good to her. Actually good. I'd spoken my love in the throes of sweat and skin only to find in the following calm that I'd meant it. I did love her. And more than anything, I wanted to believe that love was real. That it took up space inside of us and that I could love her still when morning came, thousands of times over. I wanted to believe that night's passions could survive the scrutiny of the day for all the days to come. That even as seasons turned and years vanished, with the onslaught of new dawn after new dawn, two people could, by their love, hold each other steady. Come wind. Come storm. Come hell's own chariots and lances.

I wanted to believe that ecstasy wasn't the end of our story. That the flutter of excitement inherent to new relationships wasn't all we had, but rather that we could genuinely welcome the epilogue. The pages after the happily ever after. Because the sun was going to rise. That was the one true thing I knew. I had learned it and learned it hard. Living only for the prestige of expanding moments, scratching for meaning in the gutters of frozen seconds only to wake eager to wash myself clean of night's merry proceedings, sick with a gut full of poison and a head full of loathing, despising the mirror, preferring the camera. A life spent desperate for the veil of the coming dark and the shadow it provided was a forever sort of thing. Always running. Chasing my tail. It was exhausting. But now I knew I could have something better. I could be something better. I put my arm over Quinn and wrapped my leg around hers. From the open window, cold air pushed against the curtains so they gently expanded and collapsed like a pair of working lungs. Pine sap was on the air, and two days free of smoking, my sense of smell was repaired enough to catch a hint of something else stowed away on the breeze. Something all its own. Creosote. An ancient oil shed by the oldest living thing for miles in any direction, portending rain before the first drops even fell. That was the best night of my life, I think. Me as my best me. So full of belief. High on the idea of purpose. Watching the lightning as Quinn slept. Dreaming a better life with my eyes still open. But like I said, the sun always rises.

PART TWO

For the living know that they will die, but the dead know nothing, and they have no more reward, for their remembrance is forgotten.

— ECCLESIASTES 9:5

Quinn was up before the alarm. I woke alone, and for a moment I laid listening to the noise she was making in the kitchen. She was whisking something in a bowl and humming and it made me excited for the day. I stripped the bed and put the sheets in the wash. We ate French Toast and showered and drank a last cup of coffee on the deck as we waited for the bedding to dry. With the cabin as we found it, I loaded our bags into the trunk and Quinn turned the deadbolt in the door behind us. She drove slowly down the winding driveway, a cloud of dust fogging in our wake, and as her turn signal ticked at the edge of the highway, I said, "I wish we could have stayed longer. I should have taken the afternoon off."

"We can always come back."

Leaving Payson, we were something new. Something we hadn't been when we'd arrived. The space between us seemed smaller in the way it does when you have seen another person at their most domestic. Brushing their teeth. Drying after a shower. Picking dirty underwear off the floor. She was real and the scarf of boiled skin she wore on her neck made sure I couldn't forget. I focused on it where it escaped her curtain of hair as we waited at a stoplight and Quinn cycled through albums on her iPod. "What?" She asked, feeling my gaze.

"You're beautiful," I said.

"Someone is happy to finally get laid."

"It's true," I told her. "That you're beautiful."

She blushed and asked, "What do you want to hear?"

"Play your album."

"Oh God," she scoffed. "Playing your own album is so lame."

"I like hearing you sing."

"Here," she said, spinning the dial on the iPod. "I'll sing to this. It'll be way less embarrassing."

She played the new Death Cab for Cutie Album. Quinn had perfect pitch and hit every one of Ben Gibbard's high notes with ease. A sieve of vulnerable optimism, through her, even the most maudlin of lyrics sparked with joy. She sang and I listened to her sing, her voice an expression of her naked soul that made me love her even more, and there, deep in the mountains, falling against red cliffs of cracked and broken stone, I found myself thinking about the question her uncle had asked me the day before. Between jagged bluff and dry arroyo, with Quinn hauntingly singing that the seasons have changed and so have we, I realized I'd never cried about it. About how fate had hobbled me in the most inventive way, robbing me of my one passion. I thought of how, at that moment, standing against the wall of my room, my skateboard waited still, and I realized that part of me yet clung to hope. Believed that one day I would ride again. That by force of will and patience all would be set right, and my time in Arizona as a brain damaged man would prove nothing more than a foot-note to the greater story of who I would be. A hilarious detour. An oft told anecdote after I returned to prior form and path.

But returning to Quinn's scars, a truth I already knew was immediately made clear to me. Tragedy is the ordering prin-ciple of the universe and it was only a matter of time before it learned your name. Discovered precisely what it was you dared to love. And it would find you. Hand deliver what comic circumstance might best stamp out your most human of beliefs - that you're a special case. I reached for Quinn's hand. Lifted it to my lips and kissed her fingers. Released it, and decided that when I got home, I would give my skateboard away.

As we descended through the Tonto National Forest, the bits of cloud hanging about the mountains like scraps of crepe thinned until they vanished altogether. Saguaro again stood erect in the sunlight, first by ones and twos, and then as we rounded a rocky bend, by the hundreds. Nearing the valley, the day was hot, and by the time Lake Saguaro crept into view before us we needed the air conditioner blowing at full strength to keep from sweating. Veering west, Red Mountain greeted our arrival, its signature butte standing like an erect nipple, a red breast at full salute to welcome us home. In east Mesa, we left the Bee Line Highway and took side streets until we could descend into the wide, walled trench of the 202. In that manicured canal the concrete overpasses were the color of terracotta and the builders had dressed them each with images of coiled snakes and skulking coyotes, forgeries of what the first inhabitants of the Sonora left behind on pottery shards and painted cave walls. Finding a signal again, my phone buzzed in my pocket. I looked at it. One new message. From Dom.

Im pregnant

I clapped the phone shut. The highway rose above the local roads and the walls fell away revealing the desert on both sides of us. The high-rises of Tempe were in the windshield and the sun was high and bright. I was quiet for too long. Or I was the wrong kind of quiet. The kind that alarms the people nearest you. Quinn stopped singing.

"What is it?"

"Nothing."

"Is everything OK?"

"Yeah," I said with a big fake smile.

"OK. You just seem off, and I thought maybe you got some bad news."

"No. It was just Caleb asking when I would be back in town." I had lied to Quinn before, but only by omission. By implication. Now my words were false and I hated Dom for it. This lie would lead to more lies and the only weapon against them was the truth. But the truth was dynamite. It couldn't clear away my deception and leave both of us intact. I knew Quinn deserved it. I knew it was owed to her. But I wanted my time. My ride home from my perfect weekend. We were minutes from my apartment and I suddenly knew those were going to be the last minutes in my life in which Quinn thought well of me. In which she thought my love was a thing worth having. The phone vibrated again. I shifted in my seat and buried it in my pocket. Quinn noticed me ignoring the new message. Before she could say anything I asked if she had a pair of sunglasses in the car.

"Check this," she said, tapping the arm rest.

I opened it and removed her white rimmed sunglasses and put them on. I had to speak. Quiet would only invite questions about the worry I was now leaking into the bliss that both of us had so effortlessly created only moments before. I would tell small truths.

"Wish I didn't have to go to work," I said.

"Me too. We could have stayed another day."

"I had a great time."

"So did I."

"I really care about you, Quinn."

"I really care about you, too." She wasn't automatic. She said it thoughtfully. That made it hurt more.

"I have never cared about anyone the way I care about you."

"Do you mean that?"

"I do."

"Did you mean it when you said you would consider moving to New York?"

"I did."

"I think you should. I think we'll have fun there."

"I can't imagine anything better."

She took the exit and headed north to my apartment. I watched her as she drove, and when my watching finally made her self conscious she asked why I was staring at her, and I told her it was because she was beautiful, and that I was so, so, so glad that I'd met her. In the parking lot she got out of the car to kiss me, and I held her face with both of my hands because I knew it was the last time we would ever kiss. And it was. The pain of it twisted my insides, so I smiled all the brighter to make certain I sent her off knowing that our time together had been perfect. That there was nothing to question. Not today. From the balcony, I listened as the sound of her radio faded into the din of traffic, and I watched the sun glinting off her car as she steered it onto the road. In a chair outside my apartment, I rolled a cigarette. My phone vibrated in my pocket. I ignored it. Smoking. Staring. Seething.

We were the only ones sitting outside. The day was more than hot, the sun directly overhead and somehow larger than usual. A black iron pipe ran the perimeter of the patio and every twelve inches along its length it spouted a jet of mist down toward the tables, but before the droplets of water could land on our bodies and cool our skin, they were swallowed by the dry air. It was like sitting at the center of a perpetually dying cloud. Something desperate to be that could not find form.

"How did this happen?"

"We fucked."

"Yeah, but aren't you on the pill or something?"

She laughed and I asked her why.

"It's just funny that you're finally asking me that."

"But aren't you?"

"Yes."

"Then what happened?"

"I don't know what to tell you. It's not one hundred percent."

A waiter came to our table. He asked if we were doing lunch or just drinks. I said drinks but Dom asked to see a menu, so the waiter froze. Dom said he should come back in a minute, and he walked away. We watched ourselves watch each other in our dark lenses. I was twinned on her face, a version of myself staring back at me both from her left and right eyes, my own sunglasses doing the same for her. And like that, we sat, dividing like cells down into the deep trench of infinity as the misters went on hissing, cradling us with impotent fog. Finally she said, "I'm thinking of keeping it."

I tried and failed to keep my feelings from my face.

"I know that's probably not what you wanted to hear."

"It's not what I expected," I told her.

"It could work."

"What could work?" I asked, finding myself in her sunglasses again.

"Raising a baby. Being parents."

"I'm with someone." I said it as reflex. Words not meant to be cruel, but to beg. To sandbag the flow of her thoughts so her imagination wouldn't go wide. Wouldn't envision and then come to adore a future that included me. But it came out wrong. Like a conqueror planting a flag. In her ears I'd claimed territory that she believed was in contention and now she was wounded. On the back foot and feeling the sting, she looked away. To seek a compass reading in the blooming mist. I couldn't back down, but I could be kind. Soften my voice. Speak with great care and intention. Like I was setting a bone. I tried, anyway. "We've been seeing each other for a while now. It's starting to get serious."

"OK," she said, refusing to look at me.

"I didn't mean it like..." The waiter was back at the side of our table asking if we wanted something to drink. Dom put on a smile. She asked for a rum and diet. I gave her a hard look that she felt despite the layers of dark glass between us and she responded with a look of her own fired back in my direction.

"And for you?" The waiter asked.

"I'll have water."

"He'll have the same as me," Dom said, her smile full of teeth now. "And make them doubles, please."

The waiter was about to go when I stopped him. "No diet for me," I conceded. "Regular." I was looking at Dom. "Use good rum, too. Not well."

When the waiter was gone, Dom crossed her arms and asked, "Who is she?"

"Just a girl."

"Does just-a-girl have a name?"

"Why do you care?"

"Why do you care if I know her name?"

"I don't."

"Is it Michelle?"

I scoffed. "What? No. God, no."

"Is it someone I know?"

"I doubt it. She's not..." I looked up as I searched for words.

"Not what?"

"Like us," I said, gesturing rapidly to implicate both of our bodies, to make sure she knew I was not accusing her of anything that I myself wasn't also guilty of. "She isn't in the party scene."

"How did you meet?"

"Taking pictures. I went to one of her shows." Dom waited for more. "She's a singer in a band," I said.

"How cool of her." Dom smiled like a straight razor, shaking her head to make sure that it cut.

The waiter set down our drinks and retreated to the shade of the restaurant. Both glasses were quick to sweat, beads of moisture running down their sides to the wooden table where they evaporated on contact. I didn't touch my drink because I didn't want Dom to touch hers. "Dom, I'm confused."

"Clearly." She was on the attack. A doberman at the end of a chain.

"I thought we were just..."

"Just what? Fucking?"

"Having fun."

"Well at least I'm that."

"What?"

"Fun," she said, reaching for her drink. When her hand was on it, her voice cracked, "You always run away. Every morning. You never stayed. Not once. Why not?"

"Dom."

"Why not!"

People inside the restaurant turned to watch us. Judged our volume and tone from the safety of the shade. I tamped the air with my palms. Through my shirt the sun was baking the skin on my back. My dark hair was hot on my head and the hiss of the fuming misters was like a creeping worm in my ears slowly inching towards my brain. I wanted my drink for the wetness of it. For the cold of it to run against the inside of my parched throat. But I knew that if I drank, then Dom would drink, and even though I was terrified of going through with it, of her going through with it and making me a dad, I was more terrified for that little thing. That tiny being who was trying to be. That bundle of proteins animated with the electricity of life building itself out of her body, that greatest of miracles so common to the world we have come to find it an absolute bore. It wasn't anything, but it wasn't nothing either. Evolving too fast to be named, pure potential that wouldn't stand still while we talked about it, while we came to terms, while we hashed out who did what or who said what or who felt what and why any of it was right or wrong. It knew its place even if we didn't. It knew its function, assembly line and product all at once. Moving. Becoming. I wiped my forehead then tapped my fingers on the table like a pianist at both the high and low ends as I told her, "It's what I thought I was supposed to do."

She waited for me to say more.

"I thought that's what all of this was."

"All of what?"

"This!" I said, sitting back with my arms open to condemn the world around us. I gestured to the palm trees and the string lights and the empty cocktail tables that tonight would be full, my hands up and open as if I expected pyrotechnics to burst from them as I stated my case. "This place. This town. All of us using it like a fucking theme park. Like an island in the middle of the ocean far from everyone that says you have to be something other than what you are. Where every day can just be what it is. A day. A little bottle of time to drink up in the hope that you might feel something good. Bottles we line up, one after another, that don't have to add up to anything. Allowed to stand alone.

Not telling a story or meaning anything or teaching anything. And I thought that you understood that. That we all did."

Dom's hand hadn't left her drink. The corners of the ice cubes had all been rounded by melting. She very slowly circled the glass and watched the ice trapped in the motion of the liquid. "OK." she said. "That's all you ever wanted. Meaningless fun." She raised her head. Sat forward. "Then explain something to me."

"What?"

"Just-a-girl. Why is she different?"

She had me. It was a damn good question and I didn't have an answer. I thought of Quinn and all of the reasons I loved her and I made sure not to speak any of them. To constrain my face against even hinting at my feelings for her. "I don't know," I said. "She took me by surprise."

"Is she pretty?"

"Yes."

"Prettier than me?"

"No."

Dom looked at me as though I had told her an obvious lie.

"She isn't. I mean, of course she's pretty, but if I'm being one hundred percent honest, if you two stood side by side, I think most people would say you're better looking than her. You're very attractive, Dom."

"OK, great. So it's not that I'm ugly, I'm just, what exactly? Annoying? Dumb? I mean clearly if it isn't my looks, then there must be something about my personality that you find totally off putting."

"Stop it."

"Stop what?"

"Making it about a comparison between you two. She isn't better and you aren't worse. You're just different."

"I bet you don't run away from her when the sun comes up."

"I haven't had many chances."

Dom sat back, her mouth wide with knowing. "Oh. So that's it. I fuck and she doesn't."

"Dom."

"She is the quirky, cool band girl who won't put out, and I'm the come dump you can use in the meantime."

"Jesus, Dom."

"Fuck you and Jesus. It's true and you know it." She lifted her drink, the ice cubes so diminished by the sun that they were silent against the glass. She wanted a sip but she wanted to hurt me more. "You're such a piece of shit, you know that? Telling me the things you do and then running off and saying them to another girl. That's so slimy."

Both of me threw up my hands in her glasses. "What things?"

"Don't play dumb, Riley. You know exactly what I'm talking about." Her drink was back on the table, the liquid rounding at the meniscus but not a drop spilling over. "Your whole charming man routine."

I had to take a breath. To think. To crawl back through the scraps of memory my brain hadn't thrown overboard during the toss of stormy nights as I'd walked swaying through flicker and flash and smoke and sound. I knew that Dom and I had had conversations, but the words they were built from hadn't stayed with me, only the feeling. There would have been pleasantries. Attempts at humor, both endearing and mean. Self deprecation to counterbalance the cruelty. Then words that led to the bedroom, because always there must be. Like wine with meat, I would have paired compliments and questions with the soft touch and suggestive eye that carry two people away from the pack and into the sanctuary of dark quarters. Certainly I had stepped to this familiar dance, but only in the depths of my stupor, as rote recitation. A pathetic, slurring call and response.

"Dom, I know this is going to sound bad, but all of those nights, I was wasted. We both were."

"So it was all lies?"

"I don't know."

"What do you mean you don't know?"

"I don't remember."

"Riley," she said, her voice walking a taut line between agony and rage, "You told me you loved me."

And in an instant, I was in her bed. Her black hair fanning over the pillow behind her head. Fingernails deep in my skin. Panting. Our flesh in motion. Meat leading mind. Those words pass my lips but they are not for her. Not her as an upright and feeling, first, middle, and last name that goes about the bipedal world making plans, wielding decisions like scissors so the future can be pasted on a wall and contained. But rather, for her as a foaming beast. Atavistic and carnal. Ninety eight point six degrees of pumping animal blood that doesn't count the hours or the days but runs on all fours and howls at the rising moon.

My back was hot. My hair was hot. The misters were so loud. With my finger I wiped a line of sweat from my glass. "You said it too." I wanted it to be an accusation. It came as confession.

"Yeah. I did." She cursed herself for crying and turned away so I could only see one side of her face. Dabbing hidden tears from beneath her sunglasses with the tip of her ring finger, she let out a deep breath. "I'm keeping the baby," she said.

I was in her one lens, pleading, "Dom."

She pushed her chair back and it scraped on the concrete. "You don't have to be a part of it if you don't want to. But think about it, Riley. Think long and hard. This is real. This is forever. And it's happening whether you want it to or not."

"Dom, I'm sorry."

"You're only sorry for yourself." She began walking away

but stopped after only a few steps to turn and say, "Oh, and tell your roommate to stop stalking me at work. It's never going to happen." She slapped at the billowing mist that was blocking her exit. A rainbow that glistened before her shattered as she stepped through it. She was swallowed by the fog. I drank both of our drinks. Plus two more.

Ashli was back in town. Michelle said that I should tell her to fuck off. Or at least demand that she pay me. "She's using you," she said, which of course I knew. I just didn't care.

"Thanks for driving."

"Yeah, yeah. She knows I'm coming right?"

"I told her. She said you could hang out by the pool or whatever."

"How good of her."

Driving east on the 60 towards Superior, we rolled the windows down to vent our cigarette smoke and then quickly raised them again to trap the cold air pumping from the dash. "So what's the deal with this house?" Michelle asked. "Do they live together?"

"I think it belongs to *XRXS*, but I don't think he lives there."

"It's so far away."

"I guess it's worth it if she doesn't pay rent."

In Gold Canyon we turned north off the highway onto a road that led to the Superstition Mountains. Enormous before us, the steep rock faces were speckled with green. Saguaro and cholla and yucca and sage, all but flecks of color at a distance. The jagged mountains peaked high in the blue air above the arterial grid of houses built on the plain skirting their craggy base. Leaving the subdivisions behind, the paved road was a snaking trail that forked off into many unnamed gravel paths. As we closed in on the mountain's foot, large homes set back from the road had expansive yards inside their own block and stone walls, marking them as a thing apart from the boundless desert in which they were seated. Within these walls, land-scapers had placed boulders with intention and cut the ground into gullies and swales so that when the summer monsoons came, as always they would, the rip and tear of all that horrible water could be sent on a predictable course. Chaos safely channeled.

Checking addresses against mailboxes as we went, at last we came to a black iron gate that kept us from the long driveway behind it. "Do you have the code?" Michelle asked. I opened my phone and read off a series of numbers that Ashli had texted me, and Michelle punched them on the keypad outside her window. After the final number, a dial tone sounded and the gate chain began winding on its crank. When the gate had fully drawn inward, we drove on. Up the ever ascending white concrete driveway that curved around a stout foothill and ended in a car park that fed into five garages. Dwarfing the garages, an all too large white adobe house, capped with a sloping roof of Spanish tiles, its many windows fitted with black sun screens. A walled courtyard in front of the house was elegantly Mediterranean, adorned with hand painted floor tiles and a porcelain fountain standing center, bubbling and flowing. Heavy cedar timbers jutted from the face of the house and formed a pergola over one corner of the courtyard, sheltering two rattan couches that faced each other from either side of a gas fireplace.

"This place is insane," Michelle said.

"Kinda small, though."

Opening the car door was like opening a blast furnace. A dry wave of heat immediately swarmed all of the space surrounding my body, and finding nothing to drink, it began clawing at my skin. My eyes. Seeking water from deep within me. Walking up to the house, the heat came down from the yellow sun. Up from the white concrete. From left and right and all possible curves as it radiated every available molecule of air. I rang the bell desperate to get inside.

Ashli answered the door wearing a long, silk robe. "Welcome!" she said, one leg peeking from the part in the fabric. She stepped out of the way so we could enter then closed the door behind us and the house was immediately cold and dark.

She leaned in to hug me, but quickly backed off, "Oh, you're so sweaty!"

"It's fucking hot."

She gave Michelle a practiced hug that Michelle mirrored perfectly, their bodies almost coming together but then pushing away at the final second like two magnets of the same polarity. "Nice place," Michelle said, looking at the high ceiling.

"Isn't it grand?" Ashli turned and swept her hand like a gameshow girl. There was barely any furniture. Nothing hanging on the walls. Michelle gave me a look so I would know that she was annoyed and we followed Ashli into the kitchen. She pulled glasses from a cabinet. "You don't drink, right?" she said to Michelle without looking at her. Michelle said no. "Didn't think so." Ashli pressed one glass into the ice dispenser on the face of the freezer and then another. Setting the glasses on the counter, she glided on her bare feet to a standing liquor cabinet and crouched to scan the bottles on its lower shelves. "Where's your friend?" She asked.

Michelle checked my face to see if I knew who Ashli was talking about. I didn't. "What friend?" She asked.

Ashli was hidden behind the cabinet so she spoke loudly. "The girl who's always following you. The Asian girl."

"You mean Thea?" Michelle asked.

"I guess."

"I don't know. Probably with her fiancé if I had to guess. And she's not Asian." Michelle gave me a disgusted look.

"Fiancé? Oh, the poor thing." Glass bottles knocked against each other as Ashli made her selection.

"So. Does this place belong to your boyfriend?" I asked, searching for a new topic.

"Boyfriend?" Ashli laughed, appearing again from behind the bar. "I imagine you mean Kamran."

"Is that his real name?"

"You don't think his parents named him *XRXS* do you?"

Before I could say anything, she came with a black bottle in her hand and asked, "You like rum, don't you? Of course you do. You've got to try this. It's to die for." Her robe floated on the air as she returned to the counter where she'd left the glasses.

"So you and *XRXS* aren't together?" I asked.

"Kamran." She reiterated. "And how to answer? I mean, we're together when we're together."

"But he's letting you live here," Michelle said.

Ashli poured each glass full with the brown, almost black rum. "Try this," she said, handing me a glass.

We *clinked* our glasses together and drank. The rum was damn good. Smooth molasses with only a hint of alcohol and absolutely no bite. I made a noise of delight. "This is fantastic."

"It better be for five hundred dollars a bottle."

Michelle's mouth fell open.

"Relax, I didn't buy it," Ashli said. "This is all Seth's booze." She sipped again, then held up her finger knowing we'd ask. "Seth is Kamran's money guy. This is his house. He's a big real estate investor. Did you know you can buy a house, and then after a few months, you can turn around and sell it for thousands more? Seth's been making millions doing it. He owns property all over Arizona. Vegas too."

"So how long can you stay here?" Michelle asked.

"Maybe six months. Maybe a year. Who knows? All I care about is that Seth pays for it." She drained the rum from her glass. "Are you ready?"

"Where are we doing this?" I asked.

"Oh, I have a spot on one of the trails."

"Wait, what?"

"It's a swimsuit shoot. I told you that."

"I thought you said we'd do it by the pool."

"Yes. A natural pool. By the mountain."

"It's one hundred and ten degrees."

"You'll be fine," Ashli insisted. "Come on, get your things."

"Bring water," Michelle said.

Ashli gulped the rest of her drink. "I think there's some in the garage." She tossed the ice from her glass into the sink. To Michelle, she asked, "What size are you? I'm twenty five inches in the waist. You're about that, right?"

"Yeah, why?"

"Stand up," Ashli said, taking Michelle's hands. Michelle rose from her chair. "I'm a bit taller than you. I definitely have bigger hips and boobs. But some of it might fit you."

"Some of what?"

"There is a closet full of clothes. Stuff Seth sends me that I couldn't possibly ever wear."

"Why does he send you clothes?" Michelle asked.

"Because he has more money than he knows what to do with and he's trying to be a dear." Ashli looked at me, "I'm going to take her upstairs." To Michelle, she said, "There's a closet full of shit. You can take anything you want." To me again, she said, "I'll be back in a minute."

Ashli pulled Michelle by the hand away and up the stairs. When they were out of view I went to the five hundred dollar bottle and poured myself another glass of rum. I sipped it over the kitchen sink where I could see through the heavily screened window. The day on the other side of the glass looked bright and hot and it was.

—————

Ashli didn't wear shoes. She kept to the path, but walking behind her I felt the gravel crunching under me was angular and sharp. And she walked fast. Always upright and rolling her feet heel to toe, never hopping or making an effort to avoid anything before her. Lifting her robe a few inches so it wouldn't drag as she went, she looked dainty. A fire haired Geisha inexplicably crossing the desert.

On either side of the trail, pockets of cholla grew to the height of a child, their dense yellow spines so faint they appeared as white fluff until you got close and their warning became apparent. The land was at a slow rise, and with the sun on me as I strained under the weight of my pack, sweat ran from every pore. My shirt was heavy with it, and what dripped from my hairline fell into my eyes which I couldn't wipe for the jugs in my hands, so I suffered it. Tried to blink it away. The heat stole the moisture from the sweat, leaving my skin sticky with a glaze of oil and salt.

We climbed high into the foothills and the path was beset with boulders, some lying flat and stacked like stairs, and others, huge and daunting, were like the backs of great tortoises who slept hidden beneath the sand. Ashli surmounted these with ease, hiking her robe and climbing the smooth, round surfaces like she was ascending steps cut specifically for her. A few paces behind, I could see on the rock where her feet left a trail of blood. Specks of it from the ball and heel and big toe. I had to move over and between boulders with care, finding my footing with intention. Feeling dizzy from the sun and the second rum I shouldn't have drunk, I finally let Ashli's red hair disappear around a standing column of stone and I stopped to take deep, guzzling swallows of the water. It was warm and tasted of plastic. With the cap replaced, I walked on.

Near the foot of the mountain, saguaros crowded the trail, ancient and tall, as big around as oak trees. The walking path ended in a canyon between two high rock walls. Cut by rainwater, the ground was flat and pocked with many pools, some wide and shallow and dry, others narrow and deep and holding water still despite the season. Ashli stood at the deepest pool, dipping her feet in it and dragging them side to side. Blood drifted in the flow like smoke leaving a flame. On the rock faces there were carvings made by ancient migrants in that land. Etched into the walls, stone age men with lances and bows hunted stags with crowns of branching antlers. I lowered my bag and rested against one such wall that was entirely shaded, but hot all the same. I drank from a jug and sucked breath when I lowered it.

"Are you going to survive?" Ashli asked, watching her own foot move in the water.

"Hope so," I said, replacing the cap on the jug.

"Here," she said, letting her robe fall from her shoulders and handing it to me. She was wearing a black and white polka dot bikini. The way her hair was tied up in a black bandana with the knot in front made her look like a pin-up girl, her image fit to be painted on the hull of the Enola Gay if not for the tattoos wrapping her arms and legs and chest. Noticing a particularly vibrant tattoo on her thigh, I asked, "Is that new?"

She turned her hip out to present her leg to me. "This?" she said, her buttock firm, her hand sliding down her leg to the bright ink. The tattoo was a crowing rooster, comb and wattles bloody red, plumage a sheen of blues and greens, standing before three mountain peaks, themselves foregrounding the setting sun. The bird's tail feather was long, arcing up and then looping down, wrapping her thigh. "I got it in L.A." She said. "Marlon Quito did it for free. You can see in the talon where he hid his signature. Do you like it?"

My eye wandered from the rooster to the shape of her ass, then up her body to her shadowed eyes. She was holding a pose and I hated that I thought she looked incredible. That I wanted to keep staring. That if she pushed me up against the hot stone and kissed me I would have ignored the sear and forgotten about Dom and Quinn and anyone else she asked me to forsake. I hated that there wasn't a command she could give that I wasn't likely to obey. "It's cool," I said.

She returned to the pool and explained where she would sit to begin the series. I got to work clamping a gold foil bounce to a stand. I stepped left and right, looking through my viewfinder, then making slight adjustments to that great gold coin that shone with Ashli's reflection, rimming her neck and cheek with the perfect glimmer of light. Standing, crouching, pressing into the rock, I took photos of her from multiple angles for every pose she gave. Throughout the whole affair I was expected to bring my camera to wherever she sat or kneeled or lied and to scroll through what I had just shot of the previous action. If what I showed her met her standard, we could move on. If not, we went back so she could make infinitesimal adjustments to how she pointed her chin or directed her eyes. Her mouth had to be perfectly agape. To look wanting. Needing. Possible.

If she thought that she looked oafish or sleepy, we reshot the pose. When she unclasped her top and held it against her breasts with the straps falling, it was a performance she wanted to repeat. Again. Then again. Reclasping it and resetting her eyes. Perfecting the reveal. We were both bathed in sunlight, but only I was sweating. I took my sopping shirt off and laid it over a rock while she lowered herself into the pool. With a prime lens, I moved in close. She put her fingernail to her red lips. Smiled. Looked at me over her shoulder. With her hands together to form a cup, she raised water from the pool and poured it down her chest, the individual trickles of water finding their preferred routes over the curve of her tits, the cold of it raising goosebumps on her pale skin, hardening her nipples. She only needed forty photos for her set. We shot hundreds, ending with a sequence in which she removed her bottoms, held them in her teeth, and laid in every manner of suggestion.

We were losing light in the canyon as the sun fell into the west. The heat fatigued me and my camera was heavy in my hands. Sensing my winnowed enthusiasm, she asked, "What, I don't do it for you anymore?"

"What?"

"You look bored."

"I'm hot. Aren't you?"

"I don't know, am I?" She was kneeling and she pressed her tits together with her arms so they grew, reaching towards me.

"What are you doing?"

"Teasing you."

"Why?"

"Because it's fun for me."

I hated Ashli Rose. I hated her because I wanted her. Because I was helpless not to. Because she was born perfect and had never known the ache of desire, an ailment too foreign to pity because it was beyond her experience and therefore her comprehending. Whatever she wanted, she could have, and so wanting came to bore her, which magnified her rot. Made her dangerous. A beautiful snare who didn't pretend to be anything but. Rather advertised it. Proclaimed with pride that she was venom. And didn't you want some? One delicious taste. For one terrible second I wanted to drown her in that pool. I imagined my hand gripping the round base of her skull, my fingers knotted in her red curls as I held her under, laughing as her demon screams were muffled by her choking, her painted toes kicking at the stone. But even my rage failed against the length of her eyelashes. The cut of her hip. In my imaginings, I was no longer holding her under water but holding her waist, fucking her like a dog. A damn stupid dog. Panting and proud. And then I began to cry. Ashli was aghast. "Riley? What are you doing?"

I moved to a boulder and sat. My body was too dry for tears. Choking and sobbing, I made a cavern of my arms to hide myself, but the heaving of my shoulders gave me away. Ashli gathered her robe and scolded me. "Riley, stop it. You're freaking me out." She pulled her robe over her arms and cinched it, scanning the canyon as if she hoped someone would come to her aid. "Riley, seriously. You need to stop. If you don't, I'm going to leave you here. I don't want to walk back alone, but you're not giving me much choice." She picked up her polka dot bottoms and stepped into them, shifting side to side as she pulled them over her hips. "I'm going," she said.

I breathed out a long, deflating breath and pinched the corners of my eyes with my thumbs. "I'm sorry," I said. "I'm just really stressed out right now."

She watched me for a moment, looked away to the trail and the broad desert, then sighed and sat next to me. She removed the bandana from her head, setting it on her lap so she could untie the knot. The sun peeked into the canyon between two jutting rocks high on the western wall and colored Ashli with a slash of golden light. "Whatever could be stressing you out?" She asked, incredulous and without sympathy.

I shouldn't have told her. That's obvious to me now. But all things are obvious when you see them completed. In that moment, I was drained. Weak. Desperate for someone to tell me what to do. So I told her about Dom and the pregnancy and how I was scared and not ready and how I was with Quinn and that things between us were good and that if Dom had the baby, I would lose her forever. As I told her these things, she nodded along, said *"Uh-huh,"* and took to scratching at the rock wall next to her with a small stone. I was so consumed by my telling that I paid no mind to her movements or to the *scritch scritch* sound of rock on rock. It was only when I stopped speaking that I turned to find that as I had poured out my heart, she had been defacing a thousand year old petroglyph. A simple stick figure of a hunter, etched by an Indian hand so many centuries ago, Ashli had given an enormous erection. Little squirts firing from its tip.

"Why did you do that?" I asked, confusion at once displacing my despondency.

"I thought he needed a dick. What, you don't like it?"

"You ruined it."

"Don't be so prude, Riley. Even you have a dick."

"I'm not being prude. That's not..." I had to stop. To tune myself to her particular insanity. "It's not the dick that bothers me. It's that you destroyed something ancient."

"Or maybe, I made it better."

"You shouldn't have done that."

"Why not?"

"For future people."

"What future people?"

I had no answer that would satisfy her, and her bemusement had me questioning my own indignation. She pushed my shoulder and laughed. "Riley, you're hilarious. Look, he's even blowing a load!" She pointed to her etching and laughed again, and looking at it I started laughing too. She threw her carving stone into the pool across from where we sat and it hit the water with a *plunk*. "Come on," she said, rising to her feet, extending both of her hands to help me up. My shirt was dry where I had left it lying in the sun and I pulled it over my head. Looking again at Ashli's destruction of that old thing made by a long dead man, I felt a certainty calling from beneath the part of my being that has the ability to make words. There was something true at the bottom of me that Ashli understood, and that she wasn't afraid of. That she didn't pretend not to know the way the rest of us do when we walk about the world, the shame of our genitals hidden away, the purpose of our movements buried under invented motives and costumes that we gleefully pitch when the door closes and the lights go out. She knew what I was. She knew what I was not.

"I don't want to be a father," I said, as much to the stone wall as to Ashli.

"And she doesn't want to be a mother!" Ashli said with confidence.

"You don't think so?"

"Fuck no! Ry, listen, I've known Dominique for a long time. She has never had her shit together, and she certainly doesn't have it together now. She has only been clean for, what, a year?"

"What do you mean, clean?"

"Shit, Ry, you didn't know? Girl used to be deep into heroin. Like, bad. Back when she was with Troy, she used to have to do blow just to get out of bed in the morning."

"I never knew that."

"It's true. When Troy went to jail, her supply was cut off and she went into rehab."

"Did he go to jail for dealing?"

"No! For beating the hell out of Dom. You didn't know this?" I shook my head. "Yeah, he smacked the shit out of her behind Cabaret one night. Cops rolled up on them while he was doing it. Good thing too, because she would never have pressed charges."

"It wasn't the first time?"

"Oh, God no! He's a total psycho. I don't know if she was more hooked on him or the smack. That girl used to be gutter, for real. You know why they never let her dance at the club?"

"Why?"

"Because she was a cutter. She has those gross scars on her thigh." I went inward to flip back through my memories of Dom's body. Ashli brought me back, saying, "You should fuck with the lights on every once in a while."

"She never told me any of this."

"Why would she?"

"But she's clean now?"

"I think so. I mean, she drinks, but who doesn't?" For the first time since knowing her, Ashli looked me in the face like we were almost equals. "Listen, if you want me to talk to her, I will." She pulled up her hair and tied the bandana around it, knotting it in the front.

"You'd do that for me?"

"I'd do it for her! I mean, can you even imagine? A baby? *Elch!* How awful!"

I thanked her. She said whatever and told me to clean up my shit, so I began gathering my gear and packing it away. As I collapsed the tripod and folded the bounce, I told Ashli how Quinn was moving to New York and how I was planning on following her there. How my life in the valley had been fun, but directionless, and how I thought a change could be good for me. She asked if I would seriously leave and I said yes, but the baby could ruin everything. With my pack hoisted onto my back, I grabbed the water jugs. "I really appreciate you talking to Dom for me. Already, I feel a lot better."

"Come on," Ashli said. "I want to get back so we can review everything we shot."

And with that, Ashli was back on the trail, barefoot and tall, her curls up and bouncing. The sun was in the west and the day was still morbidly hot. I soaked through my shirt a second time and drank the entire second gallon of water before her house was in sight. Ashli never asked for a drop.

The world was dark when the gates closed behind Michelle's car. The black surrounding us was total but for the triangle of white light cast by the high beams. Carving a hole in the night, the lights revealed the curves in the road and the short signs that pointed us towards the highway only when we were upon them. We were silent passing the hidden mansions, and didn't speak as the world brightened around the subdivisions. When we made the sixty and our faces were clear to each other in halogen light, Michelle finally said, "He was weird."

"Weird how?" While I'd been out photographing Ashli, Michelle had been trying on a dress, when Seth let himself into the house. She hadn't heard his steps until he was right outside the bedroom where she'd stripped her clothes, and as the door opened, she held satin quick to her chest.

"Oh," he'd said, expecting to find Ashli. "Who are you?"

"I'm Ashli's friend," she'd explained.

"That dress would be lovely on you. It's Versace," he'd told her with a smile.

"That's pretty creepy," I said, handing Michelle a cigarette and then spreading a pinch of tobacco in a fresh paper for myself.

"Ya think?"

Driving west, Michelle moved into the left lane and fed the car gas. Pools of yellow light lit our faces and then abandoned us to the black, a slow flicker bringing us to life then snuffing us out as we passed under lamp after lamp. I rolled my window down to vent my smoke. On a mountain face, white letters and an arrow pointed the way home.

"Why didn't you just say no?" I asked.

Michelle blew out smoke. "You don't know what it's like being a woman, Riley. Being alone with a strange man is terrifying."

"So you modeled clothes for him the whole time?"

"Not the whole time. Eventually he said he was hungry and he offered to make me something to eat."

"What did he make?"

"He grilled me a steak."

"Seriously? Why didn't I get a steak?"

"Because you took your sweet frickin' time outside!" She took a drag.

"How was it?"

She exhaled and looked me in the eye. "Best damn steak I ever ate." She laughed her usual, cheery laugh. "Creep can cook."

When Ashli and I had returned to the house, I was exhausted. Seeing her step into the living room, Seth had taken her by the waist, but she'd slipped from his arms and introduced me. He squeezed my hand hard when we shook, then Ashli took my other arm, telling Seth that we still had work to do. In the kitchen she filled two glasses with ice and grabbed the black rum bottle, then led me away to an empty bedroom, locking the door behind us. On the carpeted floor, I opened my laptop. Ashli laid prone with her crossed feet swaying, so I laid next to her. Sipping rum with the glow of my laptop screen lighting her eyes, all of the pictures I'd left open in Photoshop materialized.

"Is that you?" she asked.

"Yeah." The picture on the screen was several years old. In it, I was half way down an eight stair handrail, standing on a backside smith grind.

"I didn't know you could skate," she said, looking at me like maybe I was a person after all, and I must have looked back at her with sadness or disgust because seeing my face, she begged, "What?"

"How did you not know that?"

She pushed away an errant curl of hair and squinted at me. "How would I have?"

Studying her in that blue light, I realized she was right. "I don't know. I guess I just assumed you would have heard somehow. Anyway, it doesn't matter. I can't do it any more."

She looked at the picture. "You were good."

"Yeah. I was. But I got injured."

"You could have been something."

"Probably."

"And now?" It was open ended. For me to answer. I dragged my finger over the trackpad and closed the picture. The ice in her glass rattled as she took a sip. "Who's that?"

Having closed the photo of myself, a picture of Quinn was now center screen. In it, Quinn was laughing. Her eyes closed. Her head back. She looked beautiful. "That's Quinn."

"Why is her neck all fucked up like that?"

"She was burned in a fire." I closed the picture.

"*Hm*. Bummer." She sipped again.

I loaded the photos we took that afternoon onto the laptop. Ashli kept our glasses full and watched with rapt attention as I made tiny adjustments to sliders, altering the colors and contrast of everything she said was worth keeping. She wanted to try every permutation of highlight, saturation, and curve. While comparing images against themselves, music had come on downstairs.

"And what was that music he was playing?" I asked Michelle, the red ember of my cigarette dancing with the movement of my hand.

She gripped the wheel and turned to me wide eyed. "Right? It was in German or Russian or something. And he knew every word!"

"That's kind of cool."

Michelle finished her cigarette and stuffed the butt out her cracked window. "I danced with him," she said, almost ashamed.

"Why?"

"I don't know! He was charming in a classy, but kind of scary way. It's so hard to explain."

I took the last drag my cigarette had to offer. Blew the smoke. "You think he's banging Ashli?"

"Oh, one hundred percent!" Michelle said, looking at me like I was offensively naive. "Are you kidding me? They are so, fucking."

I rolled my window down further to toss my cigarette then rolled it up again. The night was still hot. The sun being gone from the world did nothing to cool the paved over desert. I adjusted the vent in front of me so the air conditioning would blow directly on my face. "I wonder why she isn't into *XRXS* anymore."

"Because Seth is way more rich!" Michelle shifted in her seat like the obviousness of what she was saying needed to escape through more than just her words. "She'll fuck him and take what she can from him until she meets some other, even richer asshole that she can sink her teeth into. She does it for sport."

"At least you got some free clothes out of it."

"Free? I paid for those, alright? By having to entertain Seth while you and Ashli took forever." She glared at me as she said the word forever, stretching it out so I'd feel the intended accusation.

"Sorry. A Versace dress, though."

We were between street lamps and she shook her head in the darkness. "That whole situation was fucking weird."

But I was glad we'd gone. A weight was lifted from me. And because I was verging on drunk from both rum and the curious nature of the day, and because I trusted her and she trusted me, I told Michelle so. I told her that Dominique was pregnant and that Ashli had promised to talk to her on my behalf, and that I had been terrified about it until now. I thought Michelle would share in my relief, but she was quiet until I prodded her for a response.

"Does Quinn know?" she asked.

Hearing her shift in tone, I shifted my own. "No."

"Riley…" But she didn't say anything else. Only shook her head.

"I know. OK? I know."

The road beneath us climbed into the air. Funneled us onto the expressway and we were a car among cars again. Michelle cut over to the left lane and drove faster. All around the lights of Mesa beat back the darkness.

"It's funny how you learn from someone by not wanting to be like them." Parson was spinning his bar key on his finger, catching it every few turns and then spinning it again.

The Prospector was hunched forward. In long sleeves and pants despite the pernicious heat, the awning over the bar shaded him as he stirred his Bloody Mary. "In the beginning, I did want to be like him," he said without looking up. "I thought he was really something. He read a lot and could argue convincingly on almost any topic. And he was brave. I thought those things mattered. But as time went on, I realized he wasn't so much brave as he was just, angry."

After tapping my employee number on the computer screen, the printer sent out a strip of white paper with the exact minute and second printed on it. I tore the paper off and crumpled it and dropped it in the trash. "Who are we talking about?" I asked, joining Parson in leaning against the bar.

Parson said, "David's friend passed away," his trademark gravel an octave lower in deference to the dead.

"Oh man, I'm sorry."

The Prospector waved away my words. "Nothing to be sorry about. It was cancer. He knew it was coming."

"That's good I guess. Knowing. It gives you a chance to plan your end. Make your peace and such."

He snorted and stirred his drink with the celery stick. "You'd think that, wouldn't you?"

"What was his name?" I asked.

"Eric. Eric McDaniel. But we all called him Mac."

"How long were you friends?"

"Gosh. I've known Mac the better part of my life. More than fifty years." The dirty pints and stemware in the well had piled up, so as I listened to The Prospector, I washed them in a sink full of hot soapy water, then dunked them in rinse and sanitizer, then stacked them on a rubber mat to dry. His eyes followed my working hands as he spoke. "We met back during the Vietnam era. He was against it. I was against it. Eventually we went to a big protest together. A march. Someone in the crowd threw a Coke bottle at a police officer and then all hell broke loose. We got our skulls thumped pretty good and we spent a few days in jail."

"Seems like those were wild times," I said, twisting two pint glasses on the scrub brush in the sink.

The Prospector waved his hand again. "It was all bullshit."

"How so?"

His mouth chewed and his gray mustache circled as he prepared his thoughts. "When you're young, doing that kind of thing, screaming at buildings, screaming at police, it makes you feel like a serious person. Like someone who cares about serious things. Like you're living a life that matters."

I dried my hands. "But didn't that matter? Didn't protests stop the war?"

"Maybe. Or maybe the NVA killing American soldiers stopped the war. I don't know the answers to such things. I do know that most of the guys I hung around with who went to the rallies and shouted the slogans, they were just there for the pussy. The free love, as they called it."

"Is that why you were there?"

He sipped his drink and stabbed the ice with his straw. "I don't know that either. Maybe? I look back on my life now, and I'm more confused than ever. I don't know what motivated me to make the choices I made, and I damn sure couldn't speak to those of other people. It's all a big mess, to be honest with you. When I was young, I thought I was motivated by justice. As I got a little older..." He didn't know how to land his sentence, so to fill the space he lifted his glass and gave it a shake. "Mind making me another one of these?"

Parson had stepped away to serve other customers so I took The Prospector's glass and set about making him a Bloody Mary.

He took his hat off and leaned back in his chair letting the sun hit his eyes which squinted until his pupils vanished in his leather skin. He watched the bustle of the patio and finally said, "Time did what it does. It marched on. The war was over and the world was still the world. But for Mac, the war didn't end. It couldn't. It was the story he told himself about who he was, so he looked to different fronts. If it wasn't Mai Lai or Agent Orange, then it was Nixon. Reagan. Bhopal. Dow Chemical. Always an enemy was out there waiting to be fought. Eventually, he found his way here. To the valley. He linked up with a group of hardcore environmentalists. They thought the American west was the last pure place in the country and that it needed to be saved from civilization itself."

"How'd they figure to do that?"

He snorted again and returned to the shade as I set his drink before him. "By breaking things. Bulldozers. Power lines. Monkey wrenching is what they called it."

Parson walked back behind the bar and stood next to me. "Where are we?" he asked.

"David's hippie friends wanted to blow shit up."

"Sounds about right."

"Mac asked me to join them," The Prospector said. "That's how I ended up in Arizona."

"No shit," Parson said.

"Yep. It was the eighties. My life back east was a bore. One day Mac calls me up and says to come visit for a week. Guaranteed me I wouldn't want to go back home. And he was right. But it wasn't his campaign to save the west that interested me. It was the west itself. The mountains. The sun. I ended up living in a house with him for a few months while I got the lay of the land, and he and his friends were all fired up about some project, but I just wanted to kick back. Get drunk. Find a nice woman. Then one day the Feds raided the house, and that was that."

"Really?"

"Oh yeah. Terrifying stuff." He sipped from his glass and wiped the red from his mustache before going on. "Had a gun pointed at my head while I was fast asleep. Near pissed the bed."

"What happened?"

"They took me in for questioning. Wanted to know about some plot to take down these high tension wires that ran out to a power plant."

"Did you talk?" Parson asked.

"You're damn right I talked." With his napkin he dabbed the sweat from his forehead. Parson set a fresh napkin on the bar in its place. "I'd already been to jail once, only for a few days, and it was awful. I damn sure wasn't about to go to federal prison for years on years over something I wasn't even involved with. To be honest, I didn't have much to say. I was just a roommate. I bought beer and hung out."

"Was he mad at you?"

"For a time. But eventually, everyone talked. There was no point in not. He ended up doing fifteen years."

"Damn."

"I wrote him letters and I think he appreciated that. When he was released, we got together. But we were never close again. We'd get coffee from time to time." He smoothed his mustache with his fingers and spoke quietly as though his words were revelations to his own mind. "I think he wanted us to be friends. I know he did. He was lonely. But he made it so damn hard. He never climbed down from the watchtower. Never stopped looking at the world through a rifle scope. You'd think all that time in a cell would have birthed in him a zest for the things of living. For joy. So much time had been taken from him, and what he had left, he didn't know how to use. To him the world was a problem to be solved. And when he looked around and saw so many people more concerned with their own gratification than the never ending list of injustices occurring at any given time, he became angry. He was difficult to be around.”

“Sounds like a miserable fuck,” Parson said.

“Of a particular sort,” The Prospector agreed.

Parson reached into the beer cooler and brought out two foggy bottles of Sol. He *snicked* the caps off of them in quick succession and handed one to me. “That time already?” I asked, knocking my bottle against his. The Prospector raised his half full Bloody Mary and Parson and I raised our bottles. We all took deep drinks. I belched and tapped my fist to my chest. Parson moved to the end of the bar to drop menus for a trio of blonde women who were taking seats. Servers weaved between tables levitating pitchers and glass laden trays, and beyond the iron railing at the patio’s edge, cars waited in the center lane for an opening in traffic so they could turn into our parking lot. “We get swept up,” I said, pointing the neck of my beer bottle at the motion of it all. “Your friend was no different.”

The Prospector shook his head. “I think he was a prisoner to the story he invented for himself. Plain as that.”

“Is it possible not to be?”

“We choose our folly. One lovely day at a time.”

———

The day would be hot. To beat the heat, if such a thing was possible, Caleb was going to pick me up early. Sunrise. Fighting off what lingered of the previous night's drunk with a coffee that steamed next to me and a cigarette smoking between my fingers, I typed out my first message to Dom since she'd left me sitting alone at the bar, helpless and imagining so many regrettable futures.

> *I know you hate me. You have every right. I just want to know if you are still going through with it. If so, we need to talk. Again, I'm sorry I hurt you.*

The front board Caleb landed on the ten stair hubba was insane. The sequence I shot captured the height of the concrete wall, the rough texture of the landing zone, the shock absorbed by his knees before he rolled away. He'd spent the better part of the morning trying to get the trick, and had taken a few rough falls. "That's so sick," he said, watching the camera screen as I clicked through the individual pictures of his stunt, one by one. While he changed into a dry shirt, I packed away my camera and checked my phone. Dom had texted me back.

> *Its already taken care of. Youre free. And I do hate you. Or I want to anyway.*

I clapped my phone shut. It was a cage door closing behind me. Driving away from the spot, Caleb could sense the weight leaving my body. He asked me what was up. Out the window and well below where we sped along the 101, deep green alfalfa that didn't belong anywhere near the dirt and rocks of Pima land grew anyway. I smiled and told Caleb that I was leaving. Moving to New York to be with my girlfriend.

"Oh yeah? That's awesome," he said. "I'm probably moving to L.A. when my lease is up."

"No shit?"

"Yeah. To a skate house in Culver City. Some Enjoi dudes live there and they have an open room."

"You're making it," I said.

"Trying. I gotta come check you out when you're set up in NYC. You can take me to the Brooklyn Banks."

"Hell yeah."

It was later that week, or maybe the next, when I ran into Dom in person. I was at Casey's, and it was after midnight because every table on the patio was full. Low on enthusiasm, I made my rounds, moving clique to clique, the night's partiers still eager to be photographed, but my head and heart already on the road east. At a table with a three sided bench, Dom saw me before I saw her. She didn't say anything. I snapped a picture of the group, and when they returned to their conversation, I asked if she would talk to me for a moment. Alone. "Please," I said, when at first she looked away. She snuffed the cigarette she'd been smoking in an ashtray and slid out of the booth and walked ahead of me to a dark corner.

"You smoke now? I asked.

"So?"

I shrugged. "I was just noticing."

"What do you want?"

"To make sure you're OK."

"I'm fine."

"Good. That's good."

"Anything else?"

I looked into her eyes because I wanted to make peace, but she averted, refusing to let me stay fixed on her. "I'm leaving, Dom. I'm going to be moving away soon, and I guess I thought I should tell you."

"With Quinn?" She snapped. She saw me trying to puzzle out how she'd learned that name, and said, "She's on your Myspace, you idiot. Number one friend. I never even made top eight."

"That shit doesn't matter."

"You're really good at deciding what should matter to other people, you know that?"

A hand fell on my shoulder, and when I turned, Troy was already pushing past me, reaching for Dom's hand. She let him take it. "It's Riley right? I don't think we've ever been introduced." He looked me up and down. I was taller than him, but he was wider than me, and I knew he was deciding that he could kick my ass if he needed to. "I know you and Dom had a thing. But she's with me now. So you need to leave her alone. Consider yourself warned."

"He fucking said that to you?" Collin was livid for me when I told him the story the next morning. We were on the balcony, observing our morning ritual. "You should have knocked him the fuck out, right then."

I tapped the ash from my cigarette. "Yeah, right man. I've never been in a fight in my life, and the last thing I need is another head injury."

"He's a bitch. You can take him."

"Do you even know what he looks like?" I asked.

"Like a bitch?"

"Like a bitch who's been to jail. I'm not about to mess with that."

I hadn't told Collin about the baby. The abortion. I probably had a lot of reasons for keeping it from him. Things I told myself that left me intact. Lies about the priority of his feelings over my fear. But the truth was that the baby being dead wasn't enough. I needed the story of the baby to die too. The more people who knew that it was once real, despite being shapeless, unnamed, would make it so that the baby had lived, even if only as gossip, as lore, and that meant it could be born at any moment as words. Spoken alive in spite or in passing. And there was so little time before I would be leaving Arizona forever, and then there would only be one mouth that could break Quinn's heart with the truth of what had been, and that was my own. But that I could conquer. I could carry a lie. One lie. Like an ember in my palm that hurt less and less with the passing of time because its own heat would fail while my callus against it hardened.

Collin decided he hated Troy in that moment, not because he had threatened me, but because he was with Dom. Collin had wanted Dom since laying eyes on her, but I was in the way, and he couldn't hate me for having seen her first. He could have chosen to hate me for using her. For having what he wanted and being so careless with it. So cruel. But then he would have to hate himself because his indifference to women outperformed mine at incredible scale, so instead, he waited for the inevitable morning when I would swear her off forever. He knew those mornings well. Knew mine would come. He needed only to be patient. Had I told him about the baby, the abortion, maybe he could have worked out how to hate me proper. Maybe then his anger would have been divided between Troy and me. His rage diffused by its many targets. Maybe then he would still be alive. But maybe is a false foundation on which to build. It is no mortar and certainly no stone. There is only what was and what is, and what was was a lie, a smile and whiskey in our coffee and the summer heat forcing us back inside where I cradled my secret, and happily dreamed of days to come.

"Is it true?"

"What?" I knew damn well what.

"Did you get a girl pregnant?"

The moment of hesitation was the yes.

Tears gathered in her eyes and she turned away from me. I wondered who could possibly have told her. Ashli didn't know Quinn. Didn't care. It had to be Dom. Quinn straightened her back and pushed the tears from her face with the ball of her hand and I knew better than to ask how she'd found out. "I can't believe you," she said. "I can't."

"Quinn." I reached for her hand, but as soon as my skin was on hers she pulled away.

"Don't," she said, shifting further down my bed to expand the space between us. The light that passed through the slanting blinds cut slashes across the blankets. Across her. Horizontal bands of alternating shadow so that she was half there, half gone. "How could you lie to me about this?" Explanations of pure truth crashed in the back of my throat in such a deluge of half made sentences that I choked, my hands at the ready to help convey whichever sentiment poured forth first, but there I sat, trembling and dumb to the point of near laughter. "What's so funny?" she asked, wounded by the smile that almost formed on my face.

"Nothing. I just have so much I want to tell you, but I'm struggling to figure out how to even begin."

"Who is she?"

"Her name?"

"Yes, her name."

I needed a breath before I could say it. "Dominique."

"How long have you been cheating on me?"

"That's a hard question to answer."

"Why?" Her face was angry. Her voice was hurt.

"Because I knew her before you."

"Was she your girlfriend?"

"No."

"But you slept together?"

"Yes."

"A lot?"

"Yes."

"When was the last time?"

"Early May."

"You're sure?"

"I'm sure."

She squeezed then released the edge of the mattress and stood up from the bed. She went to the window and her back was a shadow in the shape of her. "What else don't I know?" she asked.

"About Dom?"

"About anything."

I had already lost her. There were no words that could unbreak her heart. Anything I might say was made suspect by the lie I had so easily lived. I stood up from the bed because it felt wrong to have even an incidental comfort when her pain was so complete. I knew, and had known, that my love for Quinn was genuine, and I knew there in that room that that love was dying. That I was watching it go. That it was a thing I had had only one day before, and that it was a thing that would be gone tomorrow for every tomorrow to come. We were making an ending, and in that package of minutes I could shape its power over me. Speak well and limit my future torment.

"Quinn, before I met you, I was happy to be lost. I thought that nothing mattered, and that the only way to not be totally destroyed by that idea was to celebrate it. To ride it like I was surfing the outer edge of a hurricane. To cheer the destruction because the destruction is infinite, and total, and the only other choice is to let it take you. That's who I was.

That's who I was being. Even when deep down, it hurt. When the emptiness of it all swallowed me one piece at a time, night after night. I thought that if the world was going to destroy me, the best thing to do was to beat it to the punch. And then I met you. And got to know you. And everything changed."

"Except your behavior."

"I guess a bad person doesn't turn good overnight. Even if they want to."

"I guess not." The chain dangling from the ceiling fan rattled. The rushing air pulsed with the spinning blades. Quinn stared through the window. I went to her side. Her face was striped with sunlight. Her eyes glinting in the gold. "Did she know about me?" she asked.

"No. Not until she told me she was pregnant."

"You're really something."

"I do love you."

She finally looked at me. "I know. And I thought I might love you too." That sentence ripped me in half. The naked truth of it in her now tearless eyes. In the noncommittal way she lifted my hand, not loveless, not cold, but pitying, a formality to put a stamp on her words and to certify them as the new reality between us. Then she let go. She went to leave and I said, "Quinn, wait," and she paused with her hand on the doorknob.

"New York was going to be everything. I would have been different there. Away from this place."

She looked in my direction. For her I would have been a faceless silhouette. She said, "That's not how it works. You would have always been carrying a lie. Keeping it alive."

"Yeah. I would have. If it meant having you."

"But that wouldn't be having me."

She walked out of my room, and with me trailing a few paces behind her, out of my apartment. My feet *panged* on the steps and she said nothing as I tracked her all the way to her car. Her keys jangling as she turned the lock, I said, "One day this will be only a memory. It won't feel like anything at all. You're going to keep moving forward, find someone new, then someone else probably, and every new hurt you feel will pile on until under the weight of it all, you lose this moment completely. But one day, I hope you'll hear a song, or smell the air, and that I'll be right there with you. And I hope you'll remember the best of me. I hope you'll remember that I wasn't all bad."

Shading her eyes from the sun that was so blinding when it perched on the tips of those western mountains, she turned to face me. "No. You weren't. But just enough." She slid onto the seat and tugged the door closed. I didn't move as her engine fired to life and the music on her stereo came loud, filtered through steel and glass. It was something I didn't know. The song. She drove off and I never saw her again except in my dreaming, and even there she is far away. Out of reach. Perfect.

That night I got too drunk and smoked too many cigarettes and felt extra sorry for myself as I scrolled through the names in my phone, thinking of all the girls I knew, wondering which ones might maybe kind of like me, might want to hang out, hook up, save me from the loneliness that with every finished beer grew into its own person sitting next to me, speaking first in whispers and then shouts about how I had nothing, and nobody, and no plans, and no future, and demanding that I explain who I even was. And I had no answers. Only a deep sense of having fallen backward and landed in my own body. My own skin a prison and me knowing that the only key was somebody else. Anybody else. Female. Soft. Warm. With eyes that could look into mine and arms that could wrap my body and a voice that could hush my panic and all of them together say yes, it's true, you are a real boy, now sleep.

The sound of it woke me. Somebody retching in the bathroom. It wasn't Collin. It was too meek. A woman. I got up and walked to the kitchen, my footprints in the spongy carpet vanishing as soon as I'd left them. I was fitting a coffee filter into its plastic base when the toilet flushed and the bathroom sink ran. The door opened and I raised my eyes only enough to glimpse who Collin had brought home without looking too interested. Dom saw me see her, and she froze. I looked at her stupidly, asking myself if I had brought her here, and reading the thoughts from my face she shook her head and went to the couch where she sat to pull on her sneakers. Shifting her heel into her second shoe, she looked up at me annoyed. "What?"

At her feet, a ball of clothes and a pair of heels. Collin's door was closed and I raised an eyebrow as I sorted through my memory of the night before. "Did we...?" I asked both of us.

Dom groaned and scooped her clothes from the floor. "You really are something, you know that Riley?"

"So I've been told." She checked her phone and then folded it shut and stuffed it in the butt pocket of her shorts. "Look, I'm sorry. I drank way too much last night, and if we did something..."

Before I could finish, Dom stopped me. "No Riley. We didn't, despite how many times you called me."

Rounding the counter, I looked at Collin's closed door and then back to Dom and she grimaced and said, "*Ew*! Gross! No." She picked up her heels and pushed past me to leave.

"Dom," I said, following her. "I'm sorry. I didn't mean to insult you. I was just really shocked to see you this morning. And you were throwing up, so I thought you were drunk, and

I know I was drunk..." She was struggling to hold all of her things and to open the door so I turned the deadbolt for her, and securing her bundle with her chin, she yanked the door open and walked out onto the sunbathed balcony. My eyes were blind for a second as I followed behind her. "Dom, can you just wait. Talk to me."

She spun around, dropping a shoe. "About what, Riley?"

"About us." I crouched to pick up her shoe and handed it to her.

"What us?" She asked, setting the shoe back on top of her bundle.

"Not us, but, you know, everything. How are you?"

Her shoulders fell. "Why do you care?"

In the light of the day I could see the fatigue that was on her. And the bruise. She looked so unloved, and I hated her hating me. For so long she had been consistent in wanting me, and I had consumed that want. Subsisted on it. And now she was repulsed by me, or played at being so, but I could see in her that it was curable, that she understood me in a way Quinn never could because Dom and I were of a kind. We shared something that neither of us would ever have chosen, but it was there all the same, and as long as we knew each other we would love and hate each other as if the two emotions were one. We each needed the love of the other so we could declare victory over everything we hated in ourselves. "We should hang out sometime," I said.

She cocked her head. "I'm with someone."

"Troy's a piece of shit."

"And you're not?"

"No."

"Since when?"

"Since right now."

She hugged the bundle of clothes against her body and searched me for tells. "You only want me because you can't have me," and because I didn't disagree fast enough, she made for the stairs. I followed, pleading for her to stop.

"What?" she begged. She was fighting back tears.

"I want to start again."

"That's not possible."

"Says who?"

"Says life, Riley."

"It can be different this time."

She was weighing my words when a car pulled into the parking lot. The glare on the windshield concealed the driver, but I knew who it was.

"Tell Collin I said thanks." Dom descended the stairs and went to where the car idled. She opened the side door and slipped inside. The car drove in a wide half circle, and as it made for the exit I waited to see if she would look back, but her window only threw the light of the sun back at me.

In the apartment, Collin was yawning as he watched the coffee maker. I stood opposite him at the counter that divided the living room and kitchen. His cheek was yellowed. The knuckles of his right hand were ripped. Dried blood filled the wrinkles. "Morning," he said.

Pressing my eyes, I said, "Make all of this make sense."

"What's that?" He walked away to get two mugs from a cabinet then came back and set them down.

"Well, your face and hand for one. But maybe we can start with the more obvious question of why Dom slept here last night."

He tapped his cheek lightly where it was bruised. "Guy swung first, so it's all on him."

"What guy?"

"Her boyfriend."

"Troy?"

"Yeah." The coffee maker gurgled. Collin crossed to the fridge, and reaching deep into it, slid something across a shelf and came out with bottle of Bailey's. He returned explaining,

"We're out of whiskey. Have to use this instead." I waited for him to keep on with his story but instead he leveled his eye with the coffee pot to make sure that the last falling drops had been captured and then he set to pouring two mugs half full of coffee. He unscrewed the cap from the Bailey's and topped both mugs with the liqueur and slid one an inch in my direction. I spun my hand in the air to prod him on with his telling. "There's not much to say," he insisted. "Dude tried to fight me, and it didn't go so good for him."

"Where did this happen?"

"Outside of Cabaret."

"Why were you there?"

"Why shouldn't I be? They got my favorite shit. Titties and beer." His answer was bullshit and I told him so, so he said, "A couple of girls who work there are customers. Anything else you'd like to know, Mom?"

"Why did he try to fight you?"

Collin took a sip of his coffee and flicked his eyebrows in approval of the taste. "This isn't bad," he said. "Kinda gay, but..." He sipped again. Seeing me waiting for him, he lowered his mug and went on, "Look, I happened to step outside when he was picking Dom up after her shift, and I could hear him hollering at her about something so I walked over to make sure she was OK. He told me to mind my fucking business and I said I knew her and so I was making it my business. He thought he could be Billy Badass and he took a swing at me. So I put him on his ass."

"What did Dom do?"

"She screamed at me. Told me to leave him alone. But then he got in his car and drove off without her. Real fucking Romeo."

"Why didn't you take her home?"

"She doesn't have one. She said she's been staying with Troy now, so I told her she could crash the night with us."

"That's real gentlemanly of you."

"What can I say? I'm a stand up guy."

He walked around the counter with his mug in hand and patted my shoulder as he passed behind me on his way to his room. "Don't worry, I didn't fuck her."

"I'm not worried about that," I said to his back.

"Yeah you are," he said, closing his door.

Michelle was angrier about it than I was. She called Ashli a bitch. More than once. I honestly assumed it had to be an oversight. Of course I was invited. Why wouldn't I be? We were friends. Sort of. Anyway, she would need me for photos. "Maybe she forgot," I said.

"Riley, she didn't fucking forget. She's blowing you off. Not even that. Blowing you off would mean she actually thought about it first."

"She thought of you," I said.

Michelle had taken a bite of cheeseburger and held her hand to her mouth until she swallowed. "Honestly, I think that was Seth's idea."

"Why do you say that?"

"It's just a feeling. Ashli has never liked me."

My napkin was crumpled on my plate and I pushed it aside to make room for my tobacco and papers. "She acts like she likes you."

"Riley," Michelle said, her head at a tilt that let me know I was an idiot. "Ashli doesn't like anybody. She likes herself, and to her, everybody else in the world is either there to elevate her, or admire her. You do both." She watched my hands as they worked. "You're making me one, right?"

I licked the paper and pressed it down then handed her the cigarette. "I don't admire her," I said, and began rolling my own.

Michelle dropped her head even lower and frowned. "Please. You're just like everyone else who can't see through the fact that she is a mindless hot girl who thinks that looking good and being wanted is the most important thing in life." She raised her cigarette in the *V* of her fingers and held it upright and waiting. "You want to fuck her. I get it. Every guy does. Shit, almost every girl does. But deep down, you know the truth."

I put my cigarette on my lip and reached across the table to light Michelle's. "And what's that?"

She puffed her cigarette and released a heavy plume. "That she's a worthless bitch!" My head wagged as I weighed her words. I took a drag and exhaled it slowly as Michelle came to life, talking with her hands, her own cigarette leaving a thin wisp of smoke impressing in space the loops and arcs of her gestures. "But because she is absolutely perfect on the outside, you and your little lizard brain can't help but want her. And honestly, the best thing in the world she could do for you is to actually fuck you, because then your ability to think would turn back on for the five seconds it would take for you to see her for what she is, which is nothing. Hair. Makeup. Tits."

"She has a great butt, too."

"She does have a great butt." Michelle laughed and smoked and rested her elbow on the table to hold her cigarette high the way I imagine women probably do in old French movies.

"So you're not going?" I asked her.

"No! Why would I go?"

"Because it's a record release party and there will be celebrities there."

"Riley, I don't care about any of that." She flicked her cigarette so the ash would fall. "I'm thinking about moving."

"You've said that before."

"I mean it this time."

"I almost left," I said.

Even though we were both wearing sunglasses, I could feel that her eyes had found mine. Had locked them in place. She wanted to be serious. "You should come with me."

"Yeah? Where would we go?"

"Someplace cold."

"Alaska?"

"It would do us both some good."

We were quiet for a time. I smoked the last of my cigarette and stubbed the cherry in the ashtray. She did the same. "You're probably right," I said.

The party was at the Gold Canyon house. I planned to get past whoever was checking the guest list by claiming I was a hired photographer. Climbing the driveway, a bass beat grew louder with every step. The cars parked at an angle all the way up were expensive brands. Even in the dark, the wax and chrome had shine. Blocking entrance to the courtyard, two men in black suits stood with their hands crossed in front of their belts. A third held a clipboard and flipped through sheets of paper, asking names. I waited in a short line, and then opening my bag to show my camera to the security team, I said I was there to take pictures. Said I worked for AZ PM and that I was friends with Ashli. The clipboard man wasn't impressed. Said he still needed a name.

"Michelle," I said.

"Michelle?" He looked at me like I'd said something gross.

"It's French. Like Michael."

I gave him Michelle's last name and he flipped a page and slid his finger down the list. Finding her name, he lowered the clipboard and stepped aside. The collected voices of everyone inside fell upon me before I was even through the door. A din of enthusiastic banter set to the steady hammer of music with women's voices rising in bright shards of sentences that all ended in a performance of laughter.

The house had been furnished since my last visit. Everything new and modern and white. Probably rented. People were wedged from wall to wall and there was little room to move, only a thin corridor for coming and going like an undersea current that needed no articulation. Walking through the crowd meant being judged as you passed. By extremes of dress and hair, height of heels and daring fit of suit, tattoos on necks and chests prominently displayed, there was a clear demarcation between the artists, the wannabe artists, the sycophants, and then the business class and their plus-ones, women in short dresses that hugged their hips and breasts while they balanced martini glasses on their thumb and middle fingers, their faces painted so that their cheekbones shone bronze and their darkened eyes sunk back into their skulls.

In the backyard a bar had been set up near the kidney shaped pool which glowed suspiciously blue. White lights were strung from the house to poles stabbed into the hard ground near the rear wall. Stainless steel heaters held caged flames in their heads and people gathered beneath them despite the perfect warmth of the night air. A booth with a hexagonal window of plexiglass separating the DJ from the crowd was bookended on either side by tall, black stacks that pulsated with the drum beats they produced. I sat on a rock in a dark corner at the back of the yard, assembling my camera and watching the crowd like a wolf keeping his distance from man's first fire, equally eager and terrified to be discovered.

I don't know why I'd felt so compelled to be there. To attend a party to which I hadn't been invited and where I clearly did not fit in. At the time, I allayed myself with the idea that no matter what happened, if I at least got a handful of good photos I could sell them to a magazine. That was the lie I told myself. That I was there for a profit. That I had done so much free work for Ashli and this party was how I would make up for it. By stealing images of her famous guests. By taking from her something she never offered to give. And especially by dragging down the quality of her event with my shabby presence. I knew Ashli before all this. Before the clothing ads and the big house and the rockstar boyfriend. I'd made her in a way. She owed me. She fucking owed me.

Stepping back into the light, my camera strap around my neck, I tightened the muscles in my arms against the tremor that ran through them. My heart beat from a place low in my chest, like it had gone to the cellar to weather what was coming. On the patio, I snapped pictures of people standing in pairs. My flash hitting the ripples rolling across the surface of the water made the pool appear momentarily vascular. Alive with voltaic circulation. A man in a black blazer posed with his fingers held like scissors. A group of women angled their heads down and away but kept their eyes on the lens as they bent their knees and held their hips. Two men in button down shirts put their arms around each other, and with their free hands, pointed at one another, like he's the guy, no he's the guy. It was the same litany of poses and expressions that I had photographed and sold time and again. It could have been the same people. No one reading the magazines would ever notice or care. All that mattered was the narrative. We're happy. We're having fun. Be jealous.

When I had made a full round in the yard, I crossed through the open patio door. The living room was packed. More people were still flowing in through the foyer. Bodies lined the stairs. At the top, with her hand propped on the railing and looking down on all of us, was Ashli. She was wearing a reflective, gold body-suit. Her red hair blown out and sprayed to achieve and sustain maximum volume. She held a black square thing high in front of her and struck a pose. The square flashed. She dragged her finger along it. Tapped at it. Held it out again. Higher this time. Struck the same pose. The square flashed. She beckoned a nearby woman who came to her side then again held out the black square. Flash. A suited security man with broad shoulders stood sentry at the top of the stairs. Ashli waved him over. Handed him the square. She posed with the woman again. The security man steadied the square. Flash. He returned it and Ashli dragged her finger over it. It glowed on her face and she smiled brightly. And like that I understood. What she was. What I was. What that damn thing in her hand would make of us all.

Before she could catch sight of me, I pushed through the

crowd and disappeared in the kitchen beneath her feet. A catering company was using the space to stage trays of Hors d'oeuvres, and seeing me, a waiter asked if he could help me with anything. When I said no he brushed me back out into the swing of the party. I escaped to the backyard and waited in line at the bar. When it was my turn to order, I asked for a whiskey on the rocks. A triple. The barman told me he couldn't pour that much. I laid two twenties on the bar top and asked for two doubles then. For me and my friend. He looked through his brow and when I didn't break he sighed and took the bills. He poured the drinks and when he pushed them my way I lifted one and dumped it into the other. "Classy," he said.

I raised the dangerously full glass to him. Said, "Fuck you," and took a swallow. Wincing through the burn, I told him to keep the change. On that large rock deep in the yard where the light couldn't find me, I smoked and drank my whiskey. Gulped rather than sipped and the alcohol took me fast. Stirred my anger. Inflated my sense of betrayal. On my second trip to the bar I repeated my order, laying two twenties again. The bartender didn't blink as he wordlessly poured a glass full of whiskey and pushed it towards me. "Good man," I told him.

Crossing the pool deck, a man standing alone beneath the tin hat of a patio heater pointed at me. "Saladas." I stopped and studied him and though he was vaguely familiar to me I couldn't think of his name or remember where we had met. "Jesse," he said.

I stared at him dumbly.

"X marks the spot," he said.

"Oh shit! The treasure hunter!" He depressed the air between us with a level hand. Looked back over his shoulder. Instantly confused by his presence at the party, I asked, "What are you doing here?"

Half of his face glowed red from the fire in the heater. "Seth invited me," he said. "You?"

"I'm friends with Ashli."

"Who's that?"

"The girl who lives here. Red hair. She's *XRXS*'s girlfriend."

"Yes!" He said. "She was at Saladas too."

I lifted my camera and said, "I'm her photographer."

"I bet your stuff turns out better than whatever she's getting with that phone."

"That thing is a phone?"

"Yeah. Apple makes them. They're like a thousand bucks."

"Why do people want cameras on their phones?"

He snorted, "They don't," then taking in the deck full of party guests he smiled and said, "But they will." He sipped his drink through its tiny straw and I asked him how he knew Seth. Jesse looked behind himself again to make sure no one was listening. "Let's just say, we share a common interest." I looked away to the desert and the dark shadow of the nearby mountains. Jesse tilted his glass toward me. "Exactly."

The music cut out abruptly. The DJ tapped a microphone and then told everyone to head inside for a toast. Jesse and I funneled through the patio door and stood compressed in the swell of people filling the living room, craning their necks to the second floor balcony where *XRXS* was centered. When the crowd hushed, he thanked us all for coming. Flanking him were his honored guests who he looked to as he said their names, reminding all of us below that these people needed no introduction. Andrew and Ben from MGMT. Amar'e Stoudemire from the Phoenix Suns. James Franco from James Fucking Franco.

Each celebrity waved and the crowd applauded and cheered them. *XRXS* thanked his dear friend Seth, whose house we were all trashing. Seth shook his fist in mock anger and the crowd laughed. At *XRXS* right side, Ashli stood tall and perfect in that damn bodysuit. Golden hips. Golden tits. Golden calves. *XRXS* put his hand on the small of her back and said that last but not least, his lovely girlfriend Ashli had been the driving inspiration for his new album, which she'd even helped to name, *AZ MODE US*. Looking down on the applauding crowd, she panned her gaze over our faces, never settling on anyone, satisfied by our number alone and disinterested totally in the specifics of who underfoot was awing or feigning awe. *XRXS* was handed a champagne flute by a waiter and when each member of his entourage was holding one too, they mirrored him in raising them. Those below raised whatever they held and roared when those above drank. I didn't raise my glass, but I did drink. Slowly. Watching Ashli and the other honored guests vanish down a hallway as the music came back. The Talking Heads' *Psycho Killer*. It made me smile.

I should have left, but without asking, my feet walked my body to the stairs and when I searched my mind for the fear that should have halted me, or perhaps the many voices of doubt that may have convinced me that no good could come of my actions, I found only hysterical laughter, the goading of my most sincere and maniac impulses. I took a big swallow of whiskey and set my glass on the tray of a passing waiter. Climbing the stairs, I felt like I was skating again. Like I was throwing my body over a gap. Like there was no certainty in what I was doing, but I was here, so there was nothing but to embrace the danger if for no other reason than I wanted to see what would happen. To revel in the feeling of being midair. Making a plaything of gravity. Of not knowing.

The security man showed both of his palms to me to stop my ascending. I lifted my camera. "Ashli asked me to come up. They need promo shots."

The security man looked down the dark hallway where *XRXS* and the other VIP's had disappeared, then waved me through. Passing several empty rooms, I reached a closed set of double doors and leaned my ear to the thin gap between them.

A thread of dim light escaped from that crack and with it, the sound of voices.

I barged in with my back straight. Camera at the ready. The room was designed to be a master bedroom but had been furnished as a lounge. A line of windows ran the far wall and in the center of them, two glass doors opened onto a balcony. A white leather couch in the shape of a crescent moon had its back to the black windows and on it sat all the honored guests. Fashionable men paired with beautiful women. A white mountain of cocaine atop a square mirror the centerpiece on the long, low table before the couch, the rest of which was a repository of bottles on ice and lipstick stained stemware. Stepping forward in the meager light, every head turned to face me. I spoke so they wouldn't.

"Sorry I'm late. Don't worry though, we can get this fast if everyone plays along." I moved to the men at the far end of the couch, one in thick black glasses, both of them with wild hair curling out in every direction. "Let's get a smile then, eh gents?" They reflexively obeyed and I snapped their picture, the flash an insult to the low light of the room. I could hear people whispering about my being there, so I remained loud to over power their doubt. "OK sweetheart, you know the drill!" I said this to a young woman who was hugged close to an older man in a suit. She tilted her head to a specific angle she'd memorized and the man smiled. I snapped the shot, and again the flash was ugly and unwanted and thrilling.

It was asked if she had told me to come. It was said that she had not. Stepping to my right, the objections to my presence grew in volume. Seth leaned to *XRXS* and I could hear one of them say what the fuck and the other say he didn't know and without seeing her I knew that Ashli was watching me. "Franco! Good to see you! It's been a while! Let's see them pretty pearlies!" I pulled my focus ring and watched James Franco's face give its best smolder before firing off a shot.

"Beautiful!" I said. "One more." The camera flashed. "One more." Flash.

XRXS was angry, but calm. "Enough,"

"You're right," I said, swinging toward him. "Gotta get the man of the night!" Ashli watched me, but said nothing. Gave nothing. Seth told me I needed to leave. I squatted and snapped a shot of *XRXS* and he guarded his face with his hand. "You got a pretty girl there, or is she his girl?" I looked from *XRXS* to Seth. "Well, one of you should give her a squeeze!"

"Enough!" *XRXS* growled, his hand still hiding his face as he stood.

Flash. Flash. Flash. He was on me and I stumbled backwards, tripping on the table, falling over it, knocking away bottles and glasses that clattered and spilled their sparkling contents onto the carpet. Voices were groaning and swearing and hands were swatting the air in my direction. Scrambling to my knees, I pointed to the cocaine that was now spread widely over the table. "Is this community blow?" I asked, then lowered my face to the table and plugged my left nostril and took a huge sniff of the loose powder. "*Whooo!*" A star exploded behind my eyes. A supernova that sent crackling phosphorous to my fingertips and toes. Several hands were grabbing me under my arms, lifting me to my feet. It was asked who I was. It was said that I was nobody. By Ashli. That voice was hers. Still able to manipulate my camera, I took a picture of the cocaine pile. "Can't forget the party favors! The people need to know we're cool!" A sleeved arm crossed my face, turning my head and muffling my words. I was being dragged to the door. A man's voice yelled to get the camera and though I clutched it to my body I was no match for the group of hands that pushed and pulled my head until the strap was lifted from my neck. "Ashli, tell them we're friends!" I yelled it, not because I thought she would help, but because I wanted her to suffer second hand whatever disgust was believed of me.

Bodies shuffled in my field of view as I was passed into the hands and arms of extremely strong men. Between broad shoulders and thick necks, I could make out Ashli's face. She hadn't moved from her place on the couch. She blew me a kiss right as a fist drilled into my gut. My wind left me. I bit down so as not to throw up. Hunching into the pain, another fist that was intended for my jaw landed on the top of my skull. Whoever threw it sucked their teeth and swore. I swore. One man took my armpits as another lifted my ankles. A third followed us down the hall and down the stairs, holding my camera in his massive fist like he was holding an apple. Beneath the throb of music, the watching crowd equally gasped and howled until they all came to consensus on cheering my removal.

In the front yard I was dropped on a bed of gravel and told to get the fuck out. As I staggered to my feet, I watched the goon with my camera struggle to understand it. "Can I have my camera please?"

He scowled at me, "Fuck your camera." He spiked it onto the driveway. Plastic and glass exploded from the shattered flash and the myriad bits skipped away across the pavement and into the gravel.

"Well that wasn't necessary," I said, but before I could get to the camera he raised his leg and brought his heel down on it. The lens separated from the body and spun away like a bottle. The other security men chortled.

"Feel better?" I asked.

He pointed at me, "Beat it, funny guy. Before I do the same thing to your fucking head, you French faggot."

I picked up the camera body, never taking my eyes from the team of security men all watching me, waiting for an excuse to hurt me further. With the broken thing in my arms, I walked backwards, stepping slowly so I wouldn't trip as the driveway descended. I looked up to the balcony. To the open doors where voices floated into the night. No one was standing there. No one was watching me go.

We wake up every morning thinking that the day we're about to live is going to be one kind of way. Like the days before it. One to shuffle in with all the rest. When we look back at our lives and all the things that we've done, there's a sad realization that most days are entirely wiped from our memories. We know those days must have happened or else we wouldn't be where we are, but the substance of them is gone. Of a lifetime of conversations, only sentiments remain. Specificity eroded down to a nub of ambiguity. On inspection, whole years are nothing but a vague sense built out of the moments that lasted. The moments that made a deeper imprint. Occasionally, the truly spectacular, but more often, the deeply embarrassing. The tragic. Then without realizing we invent material to fill the gaps. Words never said and actions never taken to add flourish or valor or meaning where likely there was none. Even my two years working at Saladas. Most of it is gone. Washed away by the repetition of it all.

Opening my eyes at whatever time it was that I opened them on the morning of September fifteenth, two-thousand-and-eight, I didn't think the day I was waking up to would be significant. It wasn't until later, much later, that I even became aware of the date itself, and only because world events that I couldn't have given any less of a damn about decided to unfold in such a way as to make that day matter to far more people than just myself.

When I put my feet to the carpet, it was just a day. Morning light in the window as I picked crust from the corner of my eye with my pinky nail. Scratched my stomach on the way to the bathroom for a piss. Stood bleary eyed in the kitchen waiting on coffee. Then my toes gripping the iron railing of the balcony. My legs pushing my plastic chair at a slight tilt. Me pulling on the day's first cigarette, waiting for the caffeine to do its job, and Collin joining me with a cup of his own, whiskey certainly swirling in the mix, clouds here and there mottling the otherwise blue sky. If he and I spoke, I don't remember what was said. The smell of creosote though, riding in on the wind. That I remember. That I'm sure of.

We both worked the day shift. Nothing stood out. The late summer air was warm and people came and went like the clouds that, passing under the sun, cast shadows about the patio. We made our money and left again as the sky was starting to darken. The first spits of rain hit the windshield as we were driving home. When Collin turned on his wipers, two yellow arches of dust smeared the glass. As heavier drops came faster, the dust caked and then washed away.

I was in my room changing out of my work clothes when the text came in. Later the detective asked me if I checked it right away, and I had to think about it. What does right away mean? My phone was still in the pocket of the jeans I'd left heaped behind the door. If I had to guess, I would think that after I was fully dressed I would have emptied the pockets of those jeans, and seeing the new message, I would have checked it then. But when a detective is staring at you and noting everything you say because it can and will be used against you in a court of law, guessing is dangerous. Who remembers such things? I asked the detective that, and he asked if I thought I checked it within five minutes of having heard the phone chime, and I said probably.

And what did it say? That's what he asked me. And that made me angry because they had my phone and my records and he knew damn well what it said but he wanted me to say it, like maybe I would lie, or maybe by forcing the words to pass my own lips the emotion of it all would weaken my resolve against future lying. I gave him a look like why do you need me to say it, but my looks did nothing to him, and he just sat there waiting, so finally I said what he wanted me to say.

"I'm going to kill myself." That's what the text message said.

"And what did you do when you read that?" the detective asked. But that was much later. What I did, but would never be able to fully explain, was that I stood staring at the words, black digital characters against a dull blue light insultingly ill equipped to convey the magnitude of such a statement, a swell of emotions cascading and colliding up and down the length of me. Anger. Fear. Heartbreak. Like stones in a creek that I was forced to cross, I hopped from one to the next because I was afraid that she meant it, while at the same time I wondered if she was only trying to get my attention, and then I questioned myself for having the audacity to question her and all of that happened in the time it took for the backlight of my phone screen to dim. Did that count? Panic running every nerve in my body from center to extremity and back? Because that was the truth of what I did. Nothing at all. I stood there. Staring. Five words flicking unlabelled switches in the breaker box of my brain until my thumb started moving across the keypad, typing a word.

Don't

It was all I could think to say. She was hurt and I needed to stop the bleeding. Later I could berate her. Scream at her. Ask her a million questions and tell her how awful she was and tell her that of course she needed to live and that she was so fucking stupid for even considering suicide and convince myself, by trying to convince her, that she wasn't really serious. Right? That she wouldn't have really done it. Right? But in the moment, I needed to put pressure on the wound, and that was the best I had. Don't.

Why not?

She responded so quickly. Like she had expected my response. Like she had typed those words in anticipation of mine and only had to press send.

"Collin!"

"Why did you call for your roommate?" The detective asked.

"Collin!"

He was already at my door as I was ripping it open to go find him.

"What?" He was loud. Annoyed, but visibly concerned.

"But why did you call for your roommate, for Collin?" The detective asked again.

"Because I didn't know what else to do. It was so out of nowhere. I'd never had someone tell me they were going to kill themselves before, and I was freaking out."

"Is that the only reason?"

He wanted me to say something specific. He had theories and he needed me to confirm them. I knew what he wanted me to say, and it didn't matter anymore, so I said it. "Collin knew Dom, too."

"And he loved her," the detective said, the certainty of his tone begging me to sign off on what he already believed.

"Yeah. He loved her."

It wouldn't have made sense to explain what she'd texted. In those vital seconds. I handed my phone to Collin so he could read the words himself. So his understanding would match my own in the shortest amount of time.

"And what did Collin say when you showed him her texts?"

"Call her! Right now!" Collin pushed the phone against my chest. "She's reaching out to you for help, you can't fucking text her! Call!" I fumbled with the phone and probably hesitated, not because I didn't want to call her, but because I needed to think about what I would say. Collin yelled again. "Dude! Fucking call her!"

So I did.

She said hello. She sounded, not sad, but numb.

"Dom?" I said it like a question.

She said yeah.

"First thing, you need to be chill, OK? Don't do anything crazy."

She didn't say anything.

With unblinking eyes Collin made sharp gestures that I couldn't decipher so I stepped away from him and moved into the living room. He followed me.

"OK, Dom?" I said.

She breathed, then said OK.

Collin grabbed my shoulder and spun me. He mouthed the words *where is she?*

"Where are you?" I asked.

She breathed. She laughed a little. She asked if I remembered where we first danced together. I had to think where that might be and Collin still hadn't blinked and he moved like my own image in a mirror, his face fixed to mine no matter how I tried to break from it. I was scared to answer Dom incorrectly. Scared that if I named the wrong place, she would know that for me the memory wasn't what it was for her, and that might be enough to push her to act. To escape from Collin I went to the window that faced the Tempe skyline and Dom said you don't remember but in an instant, I did.

"Of course I remember. I'm just confused about how you could be there now."

"Where is she?" Collin whispered. I waved my hand to shut him up because I didn't want Dom to know he was listening.

She said she didn't want to live anymore. She said she thought that would be a good place to die.

"Dom, listen to me. You don't want to die, OK? I know you're hurting right now, but it's temporary. I promise you. Whatever you're going through, it's temporary. It won't last."

She told me I was wrong. Promised me that it was a forever thing.

Maybe she would have said more, but before she could, I said, "I'm coming Dom. OK? Listen to me. I'm coming. I'm leaving right now. But promise me you won't do anything until I get there? OK? Promise me."

The detective asked, "Did she promise you?"

She said OK.

"She said OK."

I grabbed Collin's car keys from the counter. "I'll be there soon," I told her. "I am going to hang up, but it's because I'm on my way, OK? I'm coming. Just stay there." She said ok, and I clapped the phone shut.

"Where is she?" Collin was near hysteric.

"Tempe," I said. "I'm taking your car."

"Like hell you are. Give me my fucking keys."

I knew better than to argue. We left without jackets, only sliding shoes on our feet because we had to. Collin locked the apartment door behind us but never thought to clean up the bags and pills and stacks of cash spread over the coffee table that he'd been sorting and counting before everything started.

"Who drove?" The detective asked. I told him Collin did. The detective told me it was later determined that Collin had had a blood alcohol level that was well above the legal limit. I laughed and the detective gave me a look like I'd better explain what I thought was so funny and I told him that Collin probably lived every day with at least that much alcohol in his blood. We had only just gotten home from work when I received Dom's message. During his shift Collin would have had a few shots and he was working on a glass of whiskey when we left. Then I shut my mouth, afraid I'd said too much.

The detective said, "So Collin drove. Then what?"

It was raining. Hard. Traffic was slow because no one in Phoenix knows how to drive in the rain. The dust and gathered oil on the roads mixing with the falling water doesn't help. It's slick. Makes coming to a stop take longer than usual. But Collin was speeding, changing lanes to pass the slower drivers, which was all the other drivers. After crossing the lake we came to a yellow light and Collin stepped on the gas. I braced my hand on the door frame and winced as we ran the red.

"Were you afraid for your safety?" the detective asked.

"I was afraid for a lot of things."

Collin didn't look for oncoming cars when he turned west onto Rio Salado. I told him to slow down. That we couldn't help Dom if we were dead. The detective wanted to know if we talked about anything else. "That's a good twenty minute drive," he said.

"Not the way Collin was driving," I told him.

"Still enough time to talk," he said.

I lied and said that I didn't remember. That the whole thing was a blur.

The rain was pounding. The wipers were knocking with every pass. Collin was driving recklessly and I was doing my best to not shit my pants, terrified that we were going to end up wrapped around a light pole.

But the detective pushed. "Given the circumstances, that you two were on your way to try to save the life of a mutual friend, how could it be that you said nothing?" He wanted to know if we talked about Troy. If Collin had threatened him. He needed me to say that he did because that would solidify his theory. Fuck his theory. I lied.

"Like I said, it's all a blur."

Collin banged his hand on the steering wheel. "This is all that fucking Troy! He's got her back on that fucking shit and he hits her and for some fucking reason she won't leave him!"

"You don't know that."

"Of course I know it! And you know it too! I'm gonna kill that motherfucker!"

Rain battered the car. In the windshield, oncoming head-lights refracted in a kaleidoscope of spiraling stars as Collin illegally passed a truck, its horn blaring. I swore as he cut back into the right lane at the last second. I only saw that he was crying because I shot him a look when yelling, "Jesus! Dude!" hoping that he would slow down. He wouldn't face me, and seeing him red eyed and trembling, I was hurt by his hurt. By the things he wasn't saying. In his damning of Troy, he was damning all the men who treated Dom like she didn't matter. He was damning Dom too, for not seeing in him everything he could be for her, everything he was so eager to offer. Certainly, he damned himself for being just as bad. For the girls whose names he never cared to remember, whose calls he ignored until they got the message. For how easily he had walked through their sadness. And me? He was damning me above all else. For being the one who got the call. For being the one who, despite everything, Dom actually loved.

We parked across the street. Collin wanted to come up, but I told him no. He tried to insist and for the first and only time I puffed myself up against him, and not because he feared me, but because he knew I was right, he sat back down in the driver's seat, telling me to not fuck it up before slamming shut his door. He kept the car running so his flashers wouldn't kill the battery, those blinking orange lights the only hint through the sheets of rain that his car was even there against the curb.

I crossed the street through the downpour. Hopping onto the brick sidewalk, my foot splashed deep in a puddle. Drops pelted my face and arms as I moved along the fence separating me from the bottom of the tower. Finding the chain that we had so easily slipped under that cold night months ago, I slipped under it once again. With bounding steps I crossed the hills of rubble and packed dirt that were now slick with moving water and found cover inside the building where I stopped to send Dom a text.

Im here. Where are you?

I hoped she wasn't where I knew she was.

30th floor

I tried to be fast. To take the stairs at a trot. Two at a time. But after only a few floors my lungs were like coals in my chest, each breath a bellows to stoke them to searing. I cursed every cigarette I'd ever smoked and at the same time wished I was smoking one that very minute. Every few floors, I had to stop to breathe. Starting the climb again, I would try to move quickly, only to find myself unable to keep any pace faster than a simple walk. Passing floor twenty, I needed to pull at the railing with my right arm as my left pushed against my thigh to assist with the motion of stepping.

"Why do you think she chose that location?" The detective asked.

"Why do you think?" I said back to him.

Opening the metal service door onto the thirtieth floor, I could see that no work had been done since Ashli's party. There were still black *X*'s of tape on the concrete pylons where lights had been strung. A lone champagne cork lying like a conquered chess piece rolled in feeble arcs and then rested before rolling again as fitful gusts pushed it towards the waiting plummet out the eastern wall.

"Dom!" I called out. The wind was horrible. It fed in through the open walls bringing fragments of rain with it, slicking the floor, then rushing back out the far side, whistling as it came and went. In the distance, charcoal clouds pyroclastic in their dark blooming came like mud to black the sky. Serpentine threads of lightning struck the mountains beneath them and thunderclaps were only seconds behind in shaking the building. Shaking me. "Dom!" I called again, walking slowly down the center of the open floor, keeping as much concrete to the left and right of me as I could.

"I'm here," she said, her voice so small in that chasm of space, drowning in the steady *shish* of the rain. Though out in the west the sun must have been in its certain place, the muscular clouds held it beaten and restrained leaving the unmade structure gray and dim. I moved forward, unable to see where she stood until a crack of lightning ripped through the air, the space momentarily a white flash that revealed her location in its fading. The boom and rumble that came immediately after sent me to the nearest pylon where I steadied myself. Dom was standing near the edge of the floor where a plate glass window should have been. She was watching the storm where one day a family would watch the sunset. I walked through the space where their front door would one day be, and stepped carefully through their not yet foyer, their not yet kitchen, until I was as close to her as I could comfortably stand. I had to yell to be heard over the wind and rain. "Dom. Step away from the edge. Come talk to me."

"And what did she do?" The detective asked. This part really interested him. The minute details of what happened up on the thirtieth floor. The conversation. The little movements and gestures. What her face told, if it told anything. He made me explain it more than once, which scared me because I knew he would pounce on any discrepancy, any events told out of order, but memory is so flawed, which I even said, to which he replied that I just needed to do my best, but I was still afraid, so I spoke with care, hammering each successive telling into the shape of the previous, which no doubt tarnished my memory of all that had actually transpired. I wanted the freedom to think it through. To see it in my mind and say what I saw. To add and subtract as it came to me, as I returned to it, as my conscious mind *and* the event itself fought for supremacy in the driving wind.

"What did she do when you asked her to step away from the edge?"

She looked at me and smiled.

"What kind of a smile?"

"The best kind," I told him. "The best smile I ever saw her smile."

Dom's hair was lifting and twisting as the wind streamed through it, a black fire rooted in place and whipping with fury. "Come here," she said, beckoning me with both arms.

"Did you go to her?"

"No."

"Why not?"

"She was too close to the edge."

"And you were afraid you'd fall?"

"Wouldn't you be? Would you want to stand at the edge of a building, thirty floors up, in a monsoon, within arms reach of a woman who was eager to die?" He raised his eyebrows and looked to the ceiling to concede my point, and I added, "And besides. I couldn't."

"Why not?"

"I have vertigo. From a head injury. It's triggered by heights."

"So you get dizzy?"

"Dizzy isn't the half of it. It feels like the planet has decided to play a trick on me by flipping end over end. You know when you get really drunk?"

"I'm Mormon," he said.

"Well, get really drunk sometime and then lie down in a waterbed. That's the feeling. Or as close to it as I can explain."

"So you couldn't get any closer?"

"No," I said.

She was in the not yet family room and she wanted me to be next to her. To join her in staring out at the western horizon, in feeling the storm pressing on her body and wetting her face, in daring the wind to rip and swirl and to yank us from our planted feet and toss us wildly away. But for me the balance of the world was already a thing in question. I already stood at the event horizon between a constancy of up and down and a disintegration of that order. To make it to her side, to where I could have taken her hand and walked her back to safety, I would have to cross that meridian. I would have had to crawl, to drag my belly on the wet cement and gag through my breathing. So I stood in place and called to her. "Dom, please, come talk to me!"

"I have to tell you something," she said, the wind carrying her words to me. Past me. Throwing them like darts.

"OK, but come over here and tell me."

Lightning crackled and turned everything white and in the fading light I could make that, for all the rain that had wetted her face, there was a stream of tears running down her cheeks. When I said this, the detective shifted his head and asked me to explain how I knew that she was crying. How I could tell her tears from the rain. I touched my ear, and said, "I don't know. I guess I've made enough girls cry."

She didn't come to me like I asked. Only looked to the street below then back to me to say, "Our baby is dead." I didn't tell the detective this. Not the first time. Not until there was no point in lying anymore. But it is what she said, and it hurt me to hear it spoken. Years of sadness started to rise in me from the pockets and holes where I'd stuffed it all away, and like beads of mercury spilled out over a steel counter rolling into each other and joining on contact, that sadness grew into one outsized pain that I couldn't stuff back down, that I couldn't deny, that I couldn't drink away, or dance away, or fuck away, or throw the meat of myself onto the asphalt to create new and greater pains to rob that primary hurt of any power, and so I stood there looking at her, knowing that I was going to cry.

"I know," I said. "And I'm sorry."

She shook her shadowed head and said, "No. You don't understand. I never got the abortion."

Despite the loss of equilibrium that I knew would find me, I moved towards her. "What do you mean?"

The storm gave no quarter for the delicacy of our words. Against wind and rain and the crack boom of lightning, like in his disappointment, God had come to witness our confessions and he would not accept anything whispered, she yelled to me, "I couldn't do it." Sheets of rain pushed her back into the building by a step. "I made the appointment, but I couldn't go through with it." She was smiling and weeping and her face was tortured with the pull of her contradictions. She held her stomach with both hands, and said, "I wanted her. I wanted our baby," and with that purging of truth, her back straightened. Thunder rolled and her fists clenched. "But Troy, he found out." Her hand went to her mouth and she began to shake. My eyes burned with the scale of salt honed by icy wind. When her hand fell away her voice cracked, "He knew she wasn't his. That she was yours." She broke into full sobbing, "He wouldn't let me keep her."

Inside me, a second storm of both pity and wrath raged. "Please, Dom!" I screamed into the gale, my shirt whipping and popping like a sail ready to fly from its boom. She looked down to the great fall before her. Sorrow had taken her. Instinct told me to go to her, to comfort her, to beg her forgiveness for my perpetual crimes against her. To draw her away from the death she now so lovingly courted. But my feet were crippled by my broken compass. Stepping forward, I dipped to the side. Fell to a knee and tightened my eyes against the spinning plate they believed of the ground. Lightning and thunder came as one and the storm was on us. Everywhere and total. Lifting. Pushing. Driving.

"I'm sorry," she screamed, I thought to me, but rising to my feet realizing, no, not to me, but to someone who was as unfinished as the room in which we stood, to someone who should have been but who never would be. "I'm sorry! I'm sorry! I'm sorry!" she yelled into the wind, each wailing lament bending her further.

I choked back air and forced myself forward. "Dom, please!" I screamed, leaning and listing against the funhouse floor beneath me. She only wept. I tumbled forward and on hands and knees, I crawled to that deadly place. Reached out, and begged, "Take my hand!" But too far to make contact. To touch. "There is more than this!" I howled it with all the strength of my smoke blacked lungs as the monsoon funneled through the building, pulverizing my words. The rain was sharp against my face, each drop hitting like a chip of glass. I yelled it louder a second time as I struggled to my feet, but words were nothing anymore. The atmosphere was against us. The air now a solid and baleful thing batting back at me any sound I might attempt. I stretched my fingers towards her and the rain was blurring the world so I could see nothing as singular. So there were two of her. Two Dominiques that looked back at me. Two watching me beg her not to jump.

"And what did she say?" The detective asked, so incapable of anything but the structure. The mathematics of how.

I cried when I told him. I cried the first time and the third time and the time in between.

"What did she say?"

She said everything. A whole life lived from beginning to end. A little girl so loved and an old woman so admired standing at opposite ends of a path she would no longer walk, and in the middle of it, a family that she'd wanted, a family she thought she could dream into being, me a husband and she a wife that would have been so good, so damn good, if only, if only, if only. She said that she hated me. She said that she loved me. She said that she hated loving me, and that she wished, oh God how she wished, and dammit, Riley, how did we end up here? If we could do it all again, how would we do it all again? Or would we just do it all again? She said I forgive you and to please, please forgive me, and she said all of it with three little words. Words chewed and spit by the storm so for me they were only a shape, but a shape I knew well. These words, I wanted to keep for myself, but I was made to supply them, to listen to their likeness as it was scratched on a yellow legal pad, and each time I was made to repeat them, I broke. Broke somewhere inside where there is no repair. Goddam, she had such lovely brown eyes. Take it easy. And then the wind changed. And Dom was gone.

The thing about being interrogated, is that I wanted to tell the truth. I wanted everything that had been ricocheting around in my head to find a happy exit through my mouth. But detectives aren't therapists. He wasn't asking me what happened, and when I did what, and why I didn't do something else because he gave a shit about my state of mind. He wanted people to go to jail and I was one of those people, so I couldn't get lost in the feeling of it. I couldn't find catharsis there in that little room with the two way mirror and the camera blinking in the corner. Every time the truth tried to take a running leap off my tongue, I had to swallow it back. Breathe. Think really hard about how badly I was fucking myself or somebody else with my words. I had to recall how I had answered a question the first time. The time after that. When he asked me why I didn't call the police after Dom jumped, I said, "I think I was in shock."

When Dom disappeared over the edge of the building, my body went rigid. Terror hardening me like one of the concrete pylons holding up the ceiling. I watched the empty place where she'd been standing and I waited for her to reappear. To pull herself up and push her hair from her face and say "whew, that was close," or something insignificant like that. Looking on and waiting for her, the rain kept sweeping in with the wind. Threads of lightning streaking horizontally across the sky. Maybe I stood there for a few seconds. Maybe for a whole minute. I couldn't possibly know. I don't remember choosing to turn away and run for the stairs, or what the voice in my head was saying as my legs carried me back to the Earth. In my mind, there is a sharp cut between looking out that wide hole in the face of the building and bursting through the exit door on the ground floor where I stepped into the full force of the downpour. Looking for her body, I had to shield my eyes from the falling water the way I would from the beaming sun. Not seeing her, I rounded the corner. Crossed the gravel. Ducked under the chain. Collin's car was still there on the far side of the street. Hazards blinking. Exhaust pluming. But the driver's door was open.

Collin was on the sidewalk. He was standing over the top half of Dom's body where it lay in a pool of blood and muck that the harsh rain was spreading in the thin gaps between the brick. I went to him. He had a hand covering his mouth. The heat from his body steamed. I said his name but he ignored me and crouched over the remnants of her face which had come unwrapped from her shattered skull like a baseball knocked loose of its stitching. A grotesque misalignment of skin and bone, I could see the holes where her eyes should have been, but not her eyes themselves. Collin hovered a hand near the wide mop of her black hair, but touching it, he recoiled, and stood straight. As he lifted his head, I followed the direction of his gaze and together we found the lower half of Dom where it lay on the opposite side of the chain link fence, itself crumpled where she had crashed onto the top bar. Torn bits of crawling innards gripped the diamond links of fencing, stretching and thinning as gravity and smacking rain animated the viscera, a macabre sea thing being born of a sticky egg, invertebrate and bloody and reaching for the ground. Just beyond, Dom's legs. Knees turned inward. Heels kicked out in a hellish jig. One shattered foot somehow shoeless.

Water streamed from the hair matting his forehead as Collin looked at me. Or through me. Before I could say a word, he turned and made for his car at a solid march. His back iron. Fists ready for war. I watched him drive away without ever having tried to stop him.

"He left you alone in the rain with her body all over the ground? Some friend." The detective didn't like Collin, something about what he represented. So he phrased things like he wanted to turn me against him. "Why do you think he did that?"

I built my answer patiently. Structuring it. "Neither of us had experienced anything like that before. I think both of us were terrified. Confused."

The detective did these little nods when he ran back over my words, like he was checking my answers in real time, not so much for errors, but for realism. Like his internal bullshit detector was fired by pistons that sent him into motion. "So then what?"

"Then what, what?"

"What did you do? Who did you call?"

"Like I said, I didn't call anyone. I ran to Michelle's house."

"Why?"

I found myself in the two-way mirror. "Because I thought she would know what to do."

The monsoon had settled over Tempe, like it had work to do and couldn't blow on away over the mountains until a score had been settled. Lightning came and went in bright ribbons that set the streets afire for how much water stood trapped in them. My shoes were soaked through. My socks sponges. With each pounding step my heel was a pump that drew water in then expelled it beneath the arch of my foot. Michelle lived on Ash Avenue only blocks from Centerpoint Tower. Running to her house would be faster than calling her and explaining what had happened, explaining where I was, asking for a ride. Thunder came violent like artillery shells were landing somewhere in the city, making me flinch when it hit, and the water coursing over my brow flooded my half closed eyes so there was nothing but an impressionist's mess of color before me. The little white man telling me it was safe to cross, the glowing red Circle K and its melting yellow windows, brown and green dapple of curbside trunk and leaf, everything stripped of reliable boundary.

A maniac to any who witnessed it, I ran at full clip down the sidewalk, splashing past the shops, charging headlong toward the strip of bungalows beyond, my shirt clear and clinging to my thin frame, my jeans heavy against the meat of my cycling legs. Beneath my ribs, lactic acid gnawed at my oblique muscles and the aching begged me to stop. To walk the last of the distance. But I ran on and yelled to vent the pain, knowing Michelle's house was close, knowing exactly where Collin was going and exactly what he was going to do. I cut across her lawn and ran to her door, falling against the wood, then beating on it with my forearm. When I heard her feet approach, I let myself fold at the waist to relieve the stabbing in my side.

"Riley? What are you doing here?"

"Dom's dead!" I stood straight to say it, but then bent again, sucking air.

"What? Come in!" She stepped back and opened the door wide.

"No." I gasped. "We need to stop Collin." Gasp. "You need to drive."

"Stop Collin from what? Come inside, you're soaking wet."

"No. Get in the car. We have to go now."

The safe yellow light of her house behind her, Michelle looked out to the dark world seized by a tempest and proved her greatness. That's how I see her to this day. Standing in that doorway. Finding my eyes and making a choice to help a friend. In the absence of context or explanation, only knowing that Riley was wet and pleading, she pulled a jacket from her wall and joined me in the chaos of that moment. Her keys in hand, we trotted to the car, ducking our heads as if that could do anything at all to keep the rain from us. That beautiful woman who was never anything but honest, who loved us all despite our many flaws, reversed her car out into the flooded street, and with wipers stoic in the face of their impossible task, it wasn't until we reached a stoplight that she finally turned to me and asked, "Where are we going?"

"Troy's apartment."

"Where is that?"

"Priest. Just south of Southern."

She leaned close to her steering wheel trying to make sense of the gray blur before her, and in it, find the markings on the road. She didn't drive fast, and though I wished she would, I knew better than to ask.

"Did she OD?" Michelle asked.

"No."

"Then what?"

I took the handle hanging above my window. "She killed herself."

"Fuck! How?"

"She jumped from the top floor of Centerpoint Tower."

"Where Ashli had her birthday party? Why there?"

I shook my head like I didn't know.

"When did this happen?" She lowered her head to try and see through the brief rainbow of dry space her wiper blades made on each pass. "I can't see shit," she said.

"About five minutes before I knocked on your door," I told her.

"Did you call the police?"

"No," I said, as she slowed the car to stop at an intersection.

She could finally look at me. "Why not?"

The stop light was a rosette of refracted red in the windshield, blooming and dancing in the shifting pattern of water just out of reach of the wipers. Watching it I said, "Fuck. Fuck. Fuck. Fuck" to count away the half seconds before it would turn green.

"Riley!"

I looked at her.

"You have to call the police." She said it like I was stupid and my stupidity made her mad. But in my face she saw something that disarmed her. My chattering teeth or bluing lips. Or perhaps some deeper tell, something of the whole picture of me that told of my tenuous grasp on sanity, how of the woven threads that gave me shape, one may have been in Dom's firm grip as she'd spiraled to the Earth, and her having pulled that thread so far, I was now at risk of being unmade. "You saw?" Michelle said. Gentle. Forgiving.

I nodded.

"Oh God, Riley."

The light changed and she turned the car south. "We have to tell somebody."

"Let's get Collin first. Before he makes things worse."

"OK," She said. "OK."

When describing all of this to the detective, I put it on Michelle. That probably makes me a bad person. But when the whole book of you is in the red, what's one more page? "She didn't want to use her phone while driving," I told him. "The conditions were so bad. She could barely see."

"Why didn't you call then? From the passenger seat?" he asked.

"Michelle said to wait until we found Collin. She said it was already too late for Dom. She said that when we got to Troy's, she would call." I told this lie to cover my own ass in what way it could still be covered. In truth, when we pulled into the parking lot of Troy's apartment complex, we were immediately taken by the unfolding emergency right before us, and we never thought about calling the police again.

Michelle parked under one of the flat roofed carports. From where we sat it looked like we were behind a waterfall. The last of the day's light cast the world in gray. Porch lights on the apartment building glowed like gems through the curtain of water that was torrenting off the carport and flooding the asphalt, churning like surf where it fell. And there in that spill of color was one man pinning another to the blacktop. Through the veil of water, the top man's arm was a lasso of pink, whirling and looping. I flew from the car and broke through that wall of water and ran toward Collin as he held Troy in place by his torn and bloody shirt, delivering blows against his face and head. I screamed his name as he raised his fist. Collin looked at me only for a second before returning to task. A woman behind a second floor window was warning that she had called the police. Troy made an *X* of his arms to guard his face from further strikes and he screamed for Collin to get off of him. He tried to roll to his side, but they were in several inches of water, so even if Collin had let him ball up there, he would have been unable to breathe. Flattening Troy again, Collin growled words that I couldn't make, if they were words at all. He was dropping a hammer fist on Troy's right cheek as I arrived at his side.

"Get him off of me!" Troy bellowed through a gap in his forearms.

Collin found that gap with his fist and a spray of blood misted in the rain and Troy's head bounced off the hard ground. A long grumble of thunder shook the world, and taking his shoulders, I screamed to Collin that the police were coming and that we had to go. He cursed and shook me off, quickly readjusting his weight on Troy's abdomen to make certain he couldn't escape. The woman in the window was still yelling, but most of what she said was lost to the static of the rainfall. Something about the police. Something about the white boy on top dragging the other white boy down the stairs. A siren in the distance grew from nothing to sharp clarity.

"We have to go!" I said again, this time with total insistence, this time wrapping my arms around Collins chest like a seatbelt so I could begin pulling him up and away from Troy. My lifting hoisted his arms up, flaring his elbows, preventing him from striking. And in that moment of vulnerability that I was alone in making, Troy reached his right hand to his right hip. There was a flash. A glint that came, then came again. Then again. And again. Collin made a sound like, *Unnh. Unnh. Unnh. Unnh.* Four of them. Fast and trivial. His body stiffened and relaxed with each penetration of the blade like he'd received a series of electric shocks. He pushed himself away from Troy with his legs and together we fell backwards with a splash. I didn't know he had been stabbed until he released his hands from the wounds and they were painted a terrible red that splattered and ran as heavy drops smacked his palms. Troy was quick to his knees, and to standing. On his feet, he staggered to the side in finding his balance, keeping the knife arm straight and the blade between us, his nose and orbital streaming blood. Collin tried to stand, but fell forward onto one arm, the other clutching at his leaking gut. The woman in the window screamed. Michelle screamed. A siren took control of the air, and whatever Collin said and however Troy answered were lost to its wail.

Hunched, Collin coughed and quivered and poured blood into the standing water. Troy watched as I tried and failed to lift Collin, holding my hand fast to the hot opening beneath his ribs. Troy stepped in as though he needed a closer inspection to believe what he himself had just done. Red and blue lights streaked past us outside the fence. The police only needed to round the corner to find the main entrance and then they would be on us, and so Troy ran, throwing away his knife, the water quickly swallowing the splash prints he made as he fled. Collin's body trembled, and then, like a tent coming down when the circus leaves town, he collapsed one limb at a time. Eyes closed. Face half submerged. The cricket on his right hand stained red and drowning in the flow. Bubbles near Collin's mouth were either last breaths, or the roiling froth of rain. I couldn't say.

I sprinted to the carport. Held my hands for one second under the deluge of water pouring from its roof to clean them. I screamed for Michelle to get in the car, and before I even closed my door behind me, she threw the car in drive, and keeping the apartment building between us and the approaching squad car, was able to make the exit unnoticed. We were back on the street, driving away when two more police cars sped past us moving in the opposite direction. Michelle was crying. The sound of it only an echo to my ears because I had nothing left. I was blank. Totally unable to assemble the pieces of reality unfolding before me into a convincing whole. There was rain on the windshield. The sound of the blowing heater. The knock of the wipers landing left and right. A few times I think Michelle yelled between sobs how fucked what just happened was, about how fucked everything was. It's likely she asked me what I thought we should do. She must have. But I didn't say anything. I was somewhere totally off the map.

"Why did you guys leave? If you hadn't done anything wrong, why didn't you stay and explain to the police what happened?" The detective made it sound so obvious. I hated him for that.

"Michelle just started driving. Once the car was moving, what was I supposed to do?" Lies. All lies.

"Did you tell her to stop?"

"Yes. I did." And that was true. I did tell her to stop. I wanted a cigarette and when I said so, she said "Jesus. Me too." I hadn't been carrying my makings, and even if I had, they would have been soaked through, but the detective never thought to question it when I told him that I began rolling us each a cigarette. Maybe he presumed the tobacco was Michelle's. Who knows? The way I told it, Michelle kept on driving despite my suggestion that we go to the police, so I rolled her a cigarette to calm her down. What actually happened was that Michelle stopped at a Circle K and I ran in for a fresh bag of tobacco, and sitting there in the parking lot, I carefully rolled her a cigarette and then made one for myself. We lit up. We sat quietly. We took deep drags listening to the rain as it hit the hood and waited for our hearts to find a sustainable rhythm. You'd have to be a high grade of stupid to tell some ice cold shit like that to a detective, so I didn't, but that's how it happened.

Watching smoke drift to the headliner, my mind walked ahead, probing what was to come, and I realized that it wouldn't be long before the police figured out who Collin was and where he lived. They would enter Troy's apartment and find drugs, and even if he flushed them, he would still explain that Collin was a dealer, and then a call would go out on the radio sending an officer to knock on the door of our apartment. With a warrant in hand, the super would unlock our door, and right as they entered, the first officers on scene would find Collin's neatly arranged bags of Xanax, and Molly, and Adderall, and next to them the ordered stacks of fives, and tens, and twenties, and there would be absolutely no reason at all for them to not try to pin his shit on me.

"We have to get to my apartment."

Michelle rolled her head on the headrest to face me. "Why?"

"I have to flush Collin's shit. He left it out. It's right there in the living room." She was about to talk, but my words trampled hers. "They're going to think it's mine! Do you understand? The apartment is just as much mine as it is his, and when they find his stash and his money, they aren't going to be interested in busting a dead drug dealer."

Her elbow on the door frame, smoke draining out the barely cracked window, her cigarette almost at its end, she closed her eyes. "Fuck, Riley."

"Please, Michelle."

She assessed the waves of rain still falling at a harsh angle, then gave me a stern look. "You're buying me dinner."

"Anywhere you want to go."

She took the last drag off her cigarette. Shoved it through her cracked window. Turned the keys in the ignition and we were off, heading east on University. Michelle lifted the iPod from her cup holder and dropped it on my leg. "Play something," she said.

"What do you want to hear?"

"Anything but my thoughts."

Spinning my thumb on the dial, I felt guilty. Like playing music was dismissive of the moment we were in. Like we didn't deserve the distraction from the box step of agony currently waltzing in our heads. It was well earned and demanded space to move and sway, and here we were desperate to throw a blanket over it. To pretend it wasn't there. There'll be time, I told myself. To stare this madness in the eye. Tonight and for the rest of my life. So I scrolled through her catalog from A to Z and back. I couldn't choose. The day had been made of blood and that blood would forever stain anything it touched. Whatever song I played would hereafter be a cab ride to this moment. I couldn't handle that, so I pressed shuffle. *Chicago* by Sufjan Stevens came on. By the first chorus, Michelle was quietly singing along. I started to feel better. Calmer.

Then the rain picked up. From a downpour to whatever it's called when rain ceases to be a collection of individual drops and instead comes as a great dumping of water, as though an atmospheric river has had its belly sliced open and its contents fall all at once. It was the backside of the storm. The far wall. Water hit the car with such ferocity that we couldn't hear the stereo and Michelle had to scream that she was going to pull over. And she did, finding cover under the 202 expressway. She parked on the shoulder. Switched on her hazards.

Hidden from the rain, the wiper blades began to squeak.

"I'm in deep shit," she said, still gripping the wheel. "I shouldn't have driven off."

I set my hand on her arm so she would look at me. "Blame me," I said. "For everything. Tell them that I tried to drive off in your car. That you only jumped into the passenger seat because you didn't want your car stolen. Say that you tried to call the police and that I took your phone. Whatever they ask, blame me. It's OK."

Michelle shook her head. "I'm not going to lie. It'll only make things worse."

"Well I'm going to. So you might as well." Tears were welling in her eyes. She rested her hand on mine. I told her, "I've fucked over enough people I care about, today. I won't let you go down for this. I won't. All you did was try to help, because you're a good person. Out of all of us, you're the only one. I honestly don't know how you can stand to be around us."

Tears rolled over her cheeks and she turned away to wipe them. She stayed fixed on the world beyond the dry sanctuary of the underpass where water bent every line, where no edge was certain. In that dark cavern the storm was a steady roar, but we could hear our music again.

Michelle was so far away. I tried to call her back, but she wouldn't look at me. She spoke to the air. "I'm the one who told Quinn. About Dom being pregnant."

Then it was my turn to be quiet. To look to the cascade of water veiling us from everything else. To get lost in the refrain playing on the radio.

"I'm sorry," she said.

I had to whisper. Low and coarse so as not to cry. "She was the only thing I had that was real."

Michelle's eyes were red. Tears fell freely from them. She met my whisper with one of her own. "No," she said. "Not the only thing."

And that's the last face of hers I ever saw. Like Dom's, it was trying to confess, trying to accuse, trying to explain and implore and if it could, to rip right open and set free the pure sentiment that its assemblage of skin and bone restrained. But then it was washed with light. Dull at first, and then instantly white. A growling rumble buried the music, and without time to even raise a hand against it, a lifted pickup truck that had come skidding through the intersection ahead, broke through the wall of water, jumped the median, and crashed sidelong into Michelle's car. There was that face of hers, finally unburdened, showered in light and glass, then gone, compressed by a wall of chrome and steel. As she disappeared, I disappeared. Her from the Earth. Me from any sense of it.

I was alive. And in pain. I thumbed away the mucus sealing my eyes and my arms ached with the effort. Blinking rapidly to find clarity, the thumping in my head that had been softened by my dreaming was now acute, making an enemy of the bright and sterile light directly overhead. I tried to sit up, but every muscle from my neck down was inflamed, at once taut and tender, so I gave up and settled back into the bed. I lifted my hands, and still blinking away the blurry coating on my vision, I tried to make sense of the wires and tubes that connected me to the wall. To the bleeping box next to my head. The empty bag above it. There was a blue call button on the guard rail at my side. I pressed it, and waited.

The nurse who came asked me how I felt. I told her mostly awful but I had no idea what was happening so I wasn't sure what to compare it against. As she charted my vital signs, she explained everything. The wreck. The coma. The policeman who insisted he be informed at once when I woke up. If I woke up. I asked her about Michelle.

"The woman in the car with you?"

"Yes."

"She died in the crash." Seeing my eyes squeeze shut, she added, "It was instantaneous. She didn't feel any pain."

Knowing that wasn't true, I bit the inside of my cheek. My eyes still tight.

"The doctor will want to see you as soon as possible," she said. "Is there anything I can get for you right now?"

"Water. Please. My mouth is really dry."

She went to leave the room, but I stopped her.

"Miss. How long have I been asleep?"

"Six days."

I laughed through the rasp in my throat.

"Why is that funny?" She asked.

"I don't know. I guess because I'm predictable."

The first time the detective came to talk to me I was still in the ICU. He left his coat on and sat in a chair next to my bed. The uniformed officer who'd come with him stayed near the door. Before they entered the room, I'd heard my doctor loudly explain that I had only been conscious since the night before, and that my memory was unlikely to be reliable, to which the detective replied that the conversation would be informal. He was just trying to gather some basic facts.

When the questioning began, I played up how dizzy I felt. How bad my headache was. Even when the question he asked was simple, I would take a long time to answer. Yawning in between words. Feigning confusion over who he was referring to and making him repeat names. Since waking up, I'd been terrified of this exact moment, but knowing it was inevitable I had decided to use my damaged state as a way to try and learn what the police were after. I needed to know exactly what I might end up being accused of, and I needed time to manufacture the credibility of my innocence.

"How did you know Ms. Vargas?"

I gave him a glassy stare.

"Dominique," he said.

"We were friends."

"Just friends?"

Another glassy stare.

"What about this Troy Scallon?"

I shook my head. "Who's Troy Scallon?"

"The young man who stabbed your roommate."

I moved my tongue in my mouth like it was searching for something, saying at last, "I didn't really know him. He was just a guy I'd see out sometimes."

"Did you know he sold drugs?"

"He sold drugs?"

The detective gave me a stare of his own. When I didn't

flinch, he clicked his pen. "Mr. Byrne. Collin. Your roommate. Did he sell drugs?"

"Collin was a bartender."

"I'm aware of that."

"Then why did you ask?"

He tilted his head to the side and refused to blink. Sitting closer, he said, "Mr. Bloom, I have three dead bodies and a heck of a lot of narcotics and cash that I need to make sense of. What I don't need, is you playing games with me." Before I could respond he held up his hand to silence me. "Now, Mr. Scallon happens to have a very wealthy father and a very expensive lawyer, so for the time being, I can't get jack diddly out of him, so I was hoping that you would help me to understand the violence that occurred between Mr.'s Scallon and Byrne, and whether or not it revolved around access to certain drug markets. Now, I am happy enough to leave you out of the story, despite the presence of a high volume of schedule one substances and a jackload of cash, which I might add, clearly demonstrates an intention to distribute said schedule one substances, all of which were found in an apartment, the lease of which, bears your name. Do you understand what I'm driving at here? Do you understand what kind of jack you're in? A judge is going to decide if you and Mr. Byrne were partners in the drug trade, and that judge is going to ask me my opinion on the matter. What I tell him will decide whether you spend the rest of your life in prison or not. So."

I gave him the glassy stare. Held it long. "Dude. My brain is busted. I don't even know what day it is."

"You're brain was busted long before that accident, and I don't need you to know what day it is. What I do need to know is how Ms. Vargas fits into all of this. Toxicology was able to ascertain that she had been using heroin and Xanax, one of which we recovered at Mr. Scallon's home and the other, which we recovered from your apartment. Neighbors report that Ms. Vargas was seen entering and exiting both Mr.

Scallon's and your apartment within the last month. Further, a review of security tapes from the gentlemen's club where Ms. Vargas worked shows both Mr. Scallon and Mr. Byrne present on numerous occasions, both interacting with the staff, we believe, selling narcotics, and both interacting with Ms. Vargas. However, Mr. Byrne's presence at the club began before Mr. Scallon's, which grew in frequency leading up to the events in question. Taking all of this into consideration, one might say it appears as though Mr. Byrne was upset that Mr. Scallon was moving in on his turf. Stealing his customers. One might say, it looks like your roommate decided to assault Troy to exact some sort of revenge for this trespass. The question is, what would you say, Mr. Bloom?"

"Can you hand me my water?"

The detective picked up the styrofoam cup next to my bed and even pointed the straw in my direction before passing it to me. I took a sip. Breathed out. Took another. Reaching for the tray, I spoke as the detective took the cup from my hand. "I wish I had answers for you. But you have to understand, I just came out of a coma that I don't remember entering. The last thing I do remember was being at work. And right now, my head is still ringing like a bell, and I'm nauseous because my eyes can't hold focus on anything. Like I said, I don't know Troy. He was just a guy I would see at bars, passing in the night. I couldn't tell you the first thing about him."

"And Ms. Vargas?"

"What about her?"

He sighed and dropped his head. "Do you know what HCG is?"

"No, but I'm sure you're going to tell me."

"It's a hormone present in a woman's blood when she becomes pregnant."

My heart beat faster and the damn machine clipped to my finger bleeped faster with it.

"Did you know that HCG can remain in a woman's

bloodstream for six weeks even after the termination of a pregnancy?"

Bleep. Bleep. Bleep.

"What it can't tell us, is who the father was."

Bleep. Bleep. Bleep.

"Was it Mr. Scallon?"

Bleep. Bleep. Bleep. Bleep.

"Was it Mr. Byrne?"

Bleep. Bleep. Bleep. Bleep. Bleep.

"Or was it someone else?"

Bleep. Bleep. Bleep. Bleep. Bleep. Bleep. Bleep. Bleep. Bleep.

"Well, well."

In the night I was moved to a regular hospital room one floor down. I woke early to find my sister sitting in a chair near the window reading a magazine. Her hair was curled about her shoulders and the sun falling on it highlighted the auburn strands that were otherwise invisible, those bands of red a hint of our mother. On the floor, her Coach purse. On her feet, her Brian Atwood heels. Even though I hadn't moved or made a sound, she knew I was awake. "How ya feeling?"

"Carolyn? What are you doing here?"

She closed her magazine and let it slap on the table next to her. "You almost died, dingus." She crossed the room and settled into the chair at my bedside. "Why wouldn't I be here?"

I tried to sit up, but had to lift my pillow and reset it behind my head. When I still wasn't comfortable, I dug the bed control out from where it was wedged between the guardrail and the mattress and held the button that raised the bed into a sitting position. I grabbed the pillow again and adjusted it behind my neck.

"Hey!" Carolyn said, sitting forward. "Stop avoiding me."

"I'm not avoiding you."

"Yes, you are. You're fucking with the bed so you don't have to talk to me."

I sat still and looked at her. "OK. What would you like to talk about?"

"Jesus Christ, Riley, you really are impossible, you know that?" She scooted her chair closer to the bed so she could rest her arms on the guardrail between us. "Do you know how worried everyone has been about you? You need to talk to your family."

"I've been unconscious for a week."

"Yeah, no duh. Before that, dipshit. You've been in

Arizona for what, two years now? How many times have we talked since you moved here?"

My eyes went to the ceiling as if I had to puzzle out some complex accounting.

"Three, dummy. And each time it was because I called you."

"I'm sorry."

"Shut up," she said gently. She tried to reach over the guardrail to take my hand, but the angle was awkward, so she began jostling it, trying to force it down. "How do you lower this goddamn thing?"

With a wince of pain, I reached forward and released the latch. The guardrail fell with a clatter.

"That's better," she said, taking my hand in both of hers, her rose gold bracelets jangling as her wrists came together. "Riley, I love you. You know that, don't you?"

"Of course I do."

"And mom loves you. Even though she has never been good at showing it." My face wrinkled and before I could offer any argument, she said, "I know. I know. She wasn't a good mom when we were growing up. To either of us. But she had her shit too, from how she was raised." Knowing again that I would contest what she was saying, she held up a finger and added, "And I'm not making excuses for her. I'm not. I'm just saying, she did the best she could. That's all any of us can do. And she does love you. You should call her."

"Phones go both ways."

"You really want to say that to me? Mr. Can't even call on fucking Christmas?" I freed my hand and reached for my water. She grabbed it from the table and passed it to me. I sipped until the cup was empty and handed it back to her. "We'll get you some more," she said, then settled back into her chair and patted my hand. "So, how do you feel? You look like shit."

It was true. Since waking up I could sense that my face was

swollen. It was incredibly sensitive to even the lightest touch. My catheter had been pulled and when I'd first been allowed to walk to the bathroom, I wasn't prepared for just how bad I looked. The airbag had broken my nose. Both of my eyes were ringed with black and purple, and neither would open fully. My cheeks were yellow. Where glass had lacerated my skin I'd been glued and stitched. The top inch of my left ear was cut clean off. "I'm fine," I said.

"Good. Can you walk?"

"Yeah. It hurts, but I can do it. They don't want me leaving this room though."

"Great, let's go smoke a cigarette."

"I can't imagine anything better."

On the fourth floor of the hospital there was a balcony for smokers. White, circle tables with white, circle ashtrays were spaced evenly. We were alone and I followed my sister to a table where she pulled out a chair for herself, sat, and began packing a box of Camels against the ball of her hand. Before leaving my room, I'd gone to the drawer where a nurse had folded my jeans and fished out the pouch of tobacco I'd bought with Michelle. Rolling my cigarette, I thought about her. My sister studied me as she ripped the plastic liner from her Camels and put one in her mouth.

"No filter?" she asked, as I put the cigarette to my lips.

"Nope."

"Harsh."

"You get used to it."

"Those are gonna kill you," she said, blowing smoke and smiling.

"Something has to. Can I borrow that?"

She pushed a Bic across the table. "Grievous bodily harm doesn't seem to work."

I clicked the lighter and puffed. "Not for lack of trying." I slid the lighter back to her. "I thought you quit."

She exhaled. "I'm on vacation."

We smoked and looked out over the valley. Camelback and Piestewa Peak in front of us. Red mountain and downtown Phoenix to the right and left. The green tops of palm trees below us and so much blue sky above. Everything sunbathed. Alight with a bit of shine. Cars moving up and down glinting as they came and went.

"I can see why you like it here," she said.

"And you've only seen the hospital."

"It's prettier than back home."

"Looks can be deceiving."

She tapped her ash into the tray. "So. Who was the girl in the car with you? Was she your girlfriend?"

"Michelle? No. She wasn't my girlfriend. But maybe my best friend."

"I'm sorry," she said. She watched her cigarette burn, letting the air clear of that sadness, then asked, "Are you in trouble?"

I daubed the swollen pouches of flesh under my eyes. "I don't know."

"Were those your drugs?"

"No, they were not my drugs."

"Thank God." She snuffed her butt in the ashtray. Shifted her chair to face mine. "The police told me about your room-mate. How he was stabbed to death. Riley, you need to talk to me. Are you mixed up with bad people?"

I dropped what was left of my cigarette and stepped on it. "We're all bad people."

"Riley, don't fuck around. I need to know if you're in danger."

"I'm not in danger."

I felt her waiting until I would look her in the eye. When I did, she said, "When the police say it's OK, I think you should come home with me. I can buy you a plane ticket. We can have your things shipped."

"I don't have any things."

"Even better."

"Carolyn, I have a life here."

She scrunched her face like what I'd just said might have been the single stupidest thing that she'd ever heard. "A life? You call this a life? Riley, your ear is chopped off for Christ's sake. And how many comas have you been in since coming here?"

"Two."

"Are you hoping for a third? Listen, I understand wanting to get away from home. Honestly, I do. But whatever this is," she looked me up and down, and with her manicured nails pointing at me, moved her hands in circles, "this isn't living. This is dancing with the angel of death." Her bracelets jangled with the movement of her arms and I thought of Michelle. Of the night we met. I chuckled even though it hurt my face to smile. "What's funny?" she asked.

"I just realized that I owe Michelle fifty thousand dollars."

"What?"

"Nothing."

"Please get serious. I want you to come home. You're going to die if you stay here."

"Carolyn, I'd rather kill myself than go back to Chicago."

"Riley!" She slapped my arm. It hurt and she saw that it did and she apologized.

"I'm serious," I said, looking her dead in the face so she would feel my words. "You're probably right, that I need to make some changes. And maybe I need to leave this place entirely, but I'm not going home. I can't imagine anything more depressing."

Carolyn sat back in her chair and crossed her legs, looking away to the mountains in the north. I couldn't see her hands, but by the motion of her arms I knew that she was spinning her wedding ring on her finger. I set to rolling another cigarette, and without raising my head I began to describe what I knew she was seeing. "That's Camelback Mountain.

See how the peak in the center kind of looks like a hump, and then off to the left the lower part looks like the head?"

"It does," she said.

"It's got a hiking trail on it. You can go to the top. It's got the best view in Phoenix."

"You been up there?"

"Nope." I licked the rolling paper and sealed it.

"Who was the other girl?"

For some reason I thought she was talking about Quinn, which confused me. "Quinn? How'd you hear about her?"

"The police told me, dumb dumb."

I cupped the end of my cigarette and lit it, still not understanding.

"They said she had been pregnant."

I blew a stream of smoke. "Oh, that's Dom. I mean, it was Dom."

"Jesus Christ, how many girls out here are you fucking?" Before the question had even crossed the table, her hand was up to prevent me from answering it. "Nevermind! I don't want to know." She took a moment to soften, then asked, "What happened to her baby?"

It was only by my sister's asking that I realized I had no idea what came of my unborn child. Her fate an unfinished sentence. A voice shushed before it could think to make a sound. The melee of that day had taken many lives, and since waking I'd not focused on the one that set the catastrophe in motion. "I don't know," I said, tapping ash from the end of my cigarette. "If I had to guess, a miscarriage. I thought she'd gotten an abortion. Could have been drugs or her boyfriend beating her. All I know is that she said the baby was dead."

"Jesus, Riley, who are these people?"

"No one, now."

"Don't be like that."

"You're right. I'm sorry."

"So who's this Quinn then?"

I had to take a deep breath to talk about her, which hurt my back and my ribs. I exhaled as a groan that bled into words. "She was someone who was very special to me."

"What happened?" I gave my sister a bruised and swollen smile. She nodded. Spun her wedding ring. Brushed nonexistent dirt from her knee, and I knew she was preparing something. "Listen,"she said, "I understand that you don't want to come home. Even though our accounts have gone into the toilet with the crash, we're still OK. We can give you some money if you change your mind." I spit between my feet and Carolyn cringed. "*Ew*, Riley! Gross."

"What crash?" I asked her.

She gave me that look again, like I couldn't possibly be any dumber. "You haven't heard?"

"Heard what? Carolyn, I've been unconscious for a week."

"Jesus, Riley. The stock market crashed. All kinds of banks are going belly up. Real estate everywhere is going under. All kinds of people are having their houses foreclosed on. It's like a new Great Depression. Nobody told you?"

I took a drag. "Huh."

The second time the detective came, my sister refused to leave the room. She told him she was going to call a lawyer and that I wouldn't say a damn word. He assured her that he had no intention of pressing charges against me, and that he just needed to clear up some details concerning the stabbing of my roommate. "The more your brother cooperates with our investigation, the sooner he can put all of this behind him." I told her not to jack with him. She took a chair by the window and pretended to read a magazine while listening to the detective repeat the same questions he'd already asked me. When he stood up to go, he handed me his card and told me to call him as soon as I was discharged.

Carolyn drove me home. There was an eviction notice taped to my door. A second copy was waiting on the kitchen counter. I threw both of them in the trash. The apartment was a mess. It had been tossed by police. In the bedrooms our mattresses stood on their sides and our clothes were left in heaps. The bathroom medicine cabinet was empty, what wasn't seized was piled in the sink. In the kitchen, the silverware was spilled over the floor and every drawer was open. Next to the stove, a small hill of coffee grounds was mounded next to their empty tin. Carolyn stepped carefully around the clutter with her hand over her heart.

"Want some coffee?" I asked.

"I'd love some." She laughed as I swept the grounds with the blade of my hand off the counter and into a paper filter.

We took the coffee on the patio and again she asked me what my plans were. All I could tell her was that I didn't know. "I still have a job."

"Have you called them?"

"No. The police have my phone."

I told her not to worry about my job or the eviction. I

knew a lot of people and surely one of them would let me crash until I found a new place. She took me out to dinner that night and we talked about good things. Memories of growing up that were funny or tender enough to overshadow our common hurts. The time she saved me from drowning when mom wouldn't jump in the pool as I flailed and fell under. The time a boy from junior high called her a slut then kicked me in the stomach when I tried to stand up for her. The last Christmas with dad. Dad's funeral. She insisted we eat dessert, so we shared a piece of cheesecake. The next morning she held me by my shoulders and told me to call her if I needed anything. When I reminded her that I had no phone, she shoved five hundred dollars in my fist and hugged me tight. It hurt, but I let her do it anyway. She left for the airport and I was alone again in a way I was not at all prepared for.

Not knowing what else to do with myself, I cleaned the apartment from top to bottom. Even Collin's room. I folded his pants and replaced them in his drawers. Rehung his shirts. Tipped his mattress back onto the bed frame and made it up with clean sheets. Straightened the framed picture of the New York skyline hanging on his wall. I didn't know what I would do with his things when I moved out. The idea of throwing it all away didn't sit well with me. I figured I'd leave everything in place, how it was when I'd arrived. Someone would put what remained of his life in a dumpster, but it wouldn't be me.

So the place was immaculate when knocking woke me some days later. I thought it was the apartment manager throwing me out. Opening the door, I was ready to explain that I still had a week left on the eviction order, but standing there was a short woman with wide hips and curly black hair. She wore big earrings and heavy eye makeup.

"Is this Collin Byrne's apartment?"

"It was. Can I help you?"

"I'm his sister in law. Or I was. I came to get some of his things."

I was too fresh from sleep and confused by her claim to form a good follow up question.

"Can I come in?" She asked. I backed out of her way and drew open the door. She walked a few steps into the living room. "Which room was his?"

"On the left." She started for it and I said, "He never told me he was married."

She stopped. Looked over her shoulder. "Did he tell you he was a father?"

I shook my head.

She turned to face me. "Why don't you get dressed?"

Her name was Anna. Her twin sister Bella had been married to Collin. Finding a seat on the couch, she asked if I had anything to drink. I glanced at the clock on the stove and looked back to her, but she just sat there waiting, so I went to the cabinet for the last of Collin's whiskey. She said no ice. I poured a slug and handed her the glass. "You gonna let me drink alone?" She had an east coast accent that carried authority. I poured a glass for myself and sat across from her. Realizing that I was already being evicted, I smoked a cigarette inside while she held her whiskey with both hands and stared into it, telling me about her sister.

Bella was always a little off emotionally. Up one day and down the next. Outgoing and full of life, until, like a switch was flipped, she would shut herself away, not wanting to see anybody. She was beautiful and funny and had a sharp wit, but all of that was counterbalanced by a dark side that demanded just as much respect. Maybe more. She would push people away. To those who wouldn't be pushed, she would be mean. Even cruel. Collin was crazy about her. And good to her. Willing to ride the ebb and flow of her mood swings. And he was protective. Sometimes to a fault. She was only nineteen when they'd gotten married. Collin a few years older. The baby was born ten months later. A little boy. Corey. They called him Cricket. Collin was driving a delivery van for a construction company. It didn't pay much, but it was a steady job. The problem was that it placed a high demand on his time, and as much as Bella had loved him, and loved Cricket, she struggled with being a mother. After the baby came, her lows got lower. Lasted longer. At this point in the telling, Anna stopped talking, like walls I couldn't see were closing in on her. Her voice choked and she said, "It still makes me cry. I'm sorry."

"Don't be sorry." I had an urge to move close to her, like decency required that I comfort her, and then I remembered that she was a stranger.

She looked up, as if asking permission to go on from someone above where she sat, but there was only ceiling, so she sighed and returned to me. "Bella killed the baby. She drowned him in the tub when Collin was at work. Then she killed herself. Slit her wrists in the same tub and laid there in the water with their perfect son. Bled to death with little Corey lying on her chest. It was Collin who found them."

Anna sniffled and I went to the bathroom for a roll of toilet paper. She thanked me and tore off a strip to blow her nose and blot her eyes. When she was calm, she said, "After the funerals, Collin drove away. Said he couldn't be anywhere near New York anymore. That was in oh-three. We never heard from him. No calls. But every six months or so, he'd send money."

"Why?"

"For headstones. He wanted Bella and Corey to have good monuments. When they were buried, we could only afford basic markers. We had no idea he was a drug dealer." She swirled the whiskey she hadn't yet touched and tossed her head back, drinking it all in one swallow.

"Can I ask you something?"

"Go ahead."

"Were you and your sister identical twins?"

"Yeah. Why?"

"No reason."

I told Anna that she was free to go through Collin's room. She said there was a specific thing that she was looking for and I reminded her that the police had torn the place apart and taken whatever they thought might be evidence, and she said she wanted to look anyway. To give her space, I waited on the patio, smoking and drinking coffee. I left the door open and could hear her swearing under her breath, disordering the room I had spent so much time setting right. She grunted as she moved something unwieldy. I heard it scrape against the wall. Then plastic cracking and a sound of relief. She thanked God. On the patio she thanked me, a folded piece of paper in her hand. I stood up to ask what it was and she showed me. An original birth certificate for Corey Michael Byrne. It had the smallest footprint in blue ink on the bottom corner. She folded the paper again and walked away. Before she descended the stairs, with her body at a distance and the sun hitting her just right, you could have told me she was Dom. I would have believed you.

When the bruising faded I looked mostly normal again, except for my severed ear. Had I kept my hair long it would have been hidden, but I shaved my head. It felt right. To make a change. Looking in the mirror, I ran my palm over the stubble covering my skull. I dragged my finger over the scar from my fall, then touched the soft flesh that had blossomed where my ear had been cut away. I thought of Quinn. When I was alone, I would flip open my phone and find her name in my list of contacts and dare myself to call her. Could I explain everything that had happened? Could I sound sympathetic? Inevitably, I'd clap the phone shut. I had the power to choose the specifics of how she would hate me, and I resigned myself to the fact that the bastard version of me that she left behind was better than the bastard version of me that would be revealed if she were to hear of everything that had happened since.

On the Saturday night before my coming eviction, I went across the street to The Rogue for Shake. It was my first time going back out, and as pathetic as it sounds, I had these visions in my head of people being happy to see me. Of crowds forming around me wherever I sat. Of having to fend off hundreds of questions and drunken hugs. Of people being happy that I was alive. Or at least, noticing.

At the door, Clint asked for my ID. When I showed it to him, he apologized and said he didn't recognize me without my hair. He shook my hand and thumbed me through the door. Pressing my body against the masses, I worked my way to the end of the bar and stood tall, waiting for Faye to come my way. When she did, she smiled, and ignoring the line of people calling for drinks, she stood across from me and asked, "Where've you been?"

"You didn't hear?" I screamed.

She shook her head.

There was no explanation I could shout over the noise. "I'll tell you later."

"I'm super slammed," she screamed. "Do you want a shot?" I nodded and she poured a plastic cup half full of whiskey and passed it to me along with a can of beer. "Good to see you," she yelled, and then turned back to her work.

The back booth was full. Some of the people sitting in that coveted place high up against the wall, I knew. Some I'd never seen before. Not a one of them spoke to me. They saw me, of course. Judged my clothes, my look, then went on ignoring me. The DJ was playing *Common People* by Pulp, and beneath the cross cutting red and white lights, the dance floor was alive with arms and hair and hips. Watching from afar, I felt a deep need to be part of that frenetic motion. To commit my body to the service. I wanted the holy indifference of too much alcohol and the sweaty pressure of the young and the beautiful moving against me that I'd felt so many times before to come into me again. Deeply I craved not giving a shit about anybody or anything. To be washed of the grip that so many dead fingers had on me. So I drank more. Rocking my head to the music, I went to Faye for another shot and beer. And another. And another. But instead of the ecstatic nihilism I was used to finding in that space, the weightlessness that permitted and applauded my every excess, I found my body growing heavy. Sullen. Mean.

Camera flashes popped from every corner of the bar. People were extending their arms to hold out their iPhones, never smiling, but sucking in their cheeks and staring through their brows. After the flicker of white, they swiped their fingers on the screen to confirm that the picture they had just taken would show the world only what they wanted to be seen. Then they posed again.

At the bar, Faye asked if I was OK. I said something she couldn't hear and after snapping the tab on a can of beer, she moved to the next customer. Alcohol had taken command of my limbs and there was a loathing in my belly that I didn't know what to do with. My heart hurt and I wanted to be held by someone who gave a damn that I even walked the Earth. I wanted to cut the electricity and in the dark silence that followed, to line up everyone in attendance so that one by one, they could come to me where I lie curled on the filthy floor and touch my scarred head and say something about how it was good that I hadn't died. I wanted a sappy mix of birthday party and funeral that could infuse me with enough desire to go on living for another week.

A cheer went up. The song had changed and the dance floor approved. A heavy bass beat was pulsing behind the sharp high notes of a synthesizer. I gulped my beer and wiped away what dribbled down my chin. Crushing my can, I dropped it and pushed forward through the crowd.

Climbing onto the stage, I lost my balance, catching myself on the arm of the nearest person who only laughed as I steadied my feet. My head rocking to the beat, red light swinging back and forth aided in decoupling me from any sense of equilibrium. I threw my arms up and out with no concern for those around me. Whipping my head from side to side as I spun, I struggled to stay standing. Like a scarecrow attempting ballet on the deck of a tossing ship, I seesawed in all directions. At first the people I fell into simply batted me away like a fleshy beachball that had come to them poolside, until spinning with my elbows out, high and sharp, I slammed into a group of dancers. They screamed so I screamed, but the only words to be heard came from the speakers to remind us that what we touched, we didn't feel, and with my back turned a man I'd offended shoved me from behind, sending me to my hands and knees. Laughing into the sound, I sprung back up, my head skyward and blinded by the slashing lights, and with a flailing pirouette the back of my skull went fast into the nose of a girl whose hands flew to her face. The impact sent me tumbling to my knees again. On the wooden floor I rolled onto my back, unable to pull focus on any one thing, my pupils wide open and injured by the swirl of colored light that blinked in the space between the stalky legs of shadowed and foreshortened people standing over me. Something wet fell onto my forehead, and wiping it away I saw that it was blood. The girl whose nose I'd just broken stood over me holding her face. She kicked my mouth with the toe of her boot, and as I covered my head with an arm to avoid further blows, I felt myself begin to float. By collar and belt I was being lifted. Carried off the dance floor. Clint had me like airline baggage and he hauled my gangling flesh through a sea of people who parted before him, all of them recoiling as one would from a clawing leper begging alms.

He didn't throw me onto the asphalt. Perhaps that was a kindness he thought he owed me. Instead, he walked me past the cars where people stood smoking and gawking to the side-walk where he put me on my feet and with a shove, yelled, "Go the fuck home!" I tripped over my own feet and fell to my forearms. Rolling to my side, I gave him a thumbs up. Said, "Thanks Clint," and brushed the grit from my palms. Like a marionette moving against the wind, I crossed the street, and when I'd made the far side of the road I collapsed in the grass. Lying there, I squinted and squeezed my eyes to give shape to the glowing red sign announcing the name of the bar. To the line of people awaiting entrance into the fury of red and white light alternating in the open doorway. Fire in the mouth of a concrete kiln. The pulse and drone of the music mixed with the din of pretend happy voices, and I hated them to the person.

"I picked up the check."

"Good for you." The Prospector pointed a plastic spear at me, then pulled an olive from it with his teeth.

"How much did you get in the end?" Parson asked. "After the lawyer's cut?"

"Their insurance is on the hook for the medical bills, but aside from that, I walked with a hundred thousand, cash money."

"Was it true? Did he cut through the bullshit?" The Prospector was asking about my lawyer, Rami, who had billboard and bus ads all over the valley, and in them he was always holding some sharp implement, machete or samurai sword or chainsaw, promising to cut through legal BS to get you money fast.

"I guess so," I said. "I mean, they settled out of court. So that's cool."

Parson was spinning his bar key. "What are you going to do with the money, besides giving some to me for letting you live in my house?"

"Something smart I hope," The Prospector said. "Especially with this economy."

I had been back to work for about a month. Despite the market crash, the bar had remained busy. Every time I showed up for a shift, I expected no one to come. That finally some sense would have been knocked into the local population and that they'd all start stuffing money in their mattresses instead of spending it on pitchers of margaritas. But that never happened. With the summer gone, the afternoons were pleasant and mild, and reliably they brought people who'd left work early to our patio where they ordered buckets of bottled beer or sipped from glasses rimmed with salt, and if they had any problems at all, they let the orange sky of evening convince them that they didn't. Sunday mornings were as busy as ever, and The Prospector was always in his chair when I clocked in.

"You should buy a house," Parson said. "With all the fore-closures, you could probably get something pretty nice."

"Keep waiting," The Prospector advised, peeling strands from his celery. "The market hasn't bottomed yet."

I didn't want a house. Especially not in the valley. The truth was that when I was handed the settlement check, I felt terrible. Those zeros and the opportunity they represented hadn't come from nowhere. The lawyer had been my sister's suggestion, and suing for compensation had seemed like the right thing to do, but now, check in hand, it only stirred the many guilts that stalked the halls of my late night mind. Made me long for those first nights lying on the floor of Collin's apartment when I had so little. When I had everything.

Parson walked away to tend to a customer and I rested my arms on the bar top. Tracing a path between tiles with my finger, I told The Prospector, "I'm thinking about moving, actually."

"Oh yeah? Where to?"

"Haven't gotten that far."

"Not too many places nicer than this one."

"I think I've had my fill of nice."

The Prospector smoothed his mustache then folded his hands. "I understand," he said. "After all you've been through, I'm sure this place feels cursed."

"I don't blame the place."

"Then what's the point in running off?"

I chuckled. "No matter where you go, there you are."

I didn't last much longer at Saladas. It felt different now. Being there. Being anywhere, really. I put in my notice and on my last Sunday shift, knowing I'd never see him again, I shook The Prospector's hand. Told him I always appreciated his stories. When he paid his tab and stood up to leave, I asked him what he would do if he were me. He was confused by the question and asked, "with the money?"

"With my life," I said.

He took off his hat and the sun sent his eyes shrinking back into his wrinkles. He ran his fingers through his fine gray hair and looked about the patio as if the question was one he'd long considered and that the answer was there in the movement of the day. Then, smiling, he replaced his hat on his head, wished me luck, and walked away.

When I told the detective I wanted to leave town, he said I could if I would submit for a deposition. One last round of questions with a camera rolling and a lawyer present. They didn't want me. They wanted Troy, and I was happy to oblige. At the end, he signed a paper that allowed me to reclaim my phone, laptop, and broken camera from property. They'd copied everything. The officer who passed me the plastic tub with my belongings smirked. I knew why.

The truck I bought cost five thousand dollars. It had a camper shell, and looking at the Craigslist ad where I'd found it, I imagined myself parked far out in the desert. Intentionally lost. A sleeping bag rolled out in the bed, my head on the tailgate so I could fall asleep watching the stars, their slow turning teaching me something about the way of things. Me actually learning it. Driving high up onto the interchange that connected me to the 60 East, I knew that I had chosen the Superstition Mountains as a testing ground for this camping fantasy because I could make a stop along the way.

In Gold Canyon, I passed the subdivisions and kept on towards the government land, winding the roads lined with more expensive and isolated houses. I stopped at that last driveway. The one with the black gate. A realtor had stabbed the hard ground with a wooden post, and hanging idle from it was a for sale sign that, despite the breeze, was as dead as the flag on the moon. I drove up to the gate and flipped open my old phone. Clicking back through messages, I found the four digit code that had been sent to me months prior. Punching it on the number pad, each key toned like a telephone, but after pressing the final number, nothing happened. A camera lens bounced my image back at me in fisheye, and I tried the code again. After the last number, a dial tone, but nothing. No movement of the gate. The panel had an intercom button. I hovered my finger over it for a second before pressing it. The box clicked, but I didn't know what to say, so I released the button. Static hissed on the speaker. I pressed the button again, and said to the box that I had been there before. That I was friends with Ashli. More static.

I reversed the truck out of the driveway and parked on the gravel shoulder. Looked up and down the road. Walked to the short adobe wall that enclosed the property and with a vaulting jump, was able to mount it. While on top, I checked once more that no one was watching me, and then I fell to the ground on the far side, my shoes scattering dust and pebbles on landing. Hiking up the drive, I kept my eyes fixed on the front door. Behind the house the sun was setting and the sky was a radiant orange. I shielded my eyes from the light until I was in the broad shadow of the house. There were no cars parked before the many garages. No patio furniture remained in the courtyard. The fountain was silent and dry. Though it seemed apparent that no one was there, I couldn't shake the feeling that I was being watched from one of the screened windows. Maybe from the second floor patio and the glass French doors draped with long white curtains. I rang the bell. More a precaution than courtesy. There were stories now of squatters living in foreclosed homes. Crust punks and meth addicts and cartel chemists, any of them might want to hurt me to defend their ill-gotten turf. The stories were probably bullshit, but I rang a second time, bringing my ear close to the door to hear the chime. To search for movement.

Deftly navigating the lava rocks that formed an apron around the house, I moved like a burglar into the backyard, straightening myself only when I made it to the flagstone patio. The pool was empty save the moist layer of desert muck caking the floor in the deepest part of the basin. Here too, the furniture was gone. Leaning against the sliding door, I cupped my hands like I was holding binoculars to block the glare. The house was empty. Nothing moved. The sound of a car away on the road froze me in place, its motor coming high and leaving low. Though I couldn't be seen by anyone on the road, my heart still beat faster until the sound had faded completely. The wind blew. I zipped my hoodie. In the west the sun was halfway below the jagged rim of the Earth. In the door my reflection was nothing but shadow. A human shaped mass with only the world around it illuminated and alive with color. Gold and pink. Purple and blue. The oil painting of sky at day's end captured perfectly in the smooth glass. But me, I was a faceless void. An abyss where a man should have been. The wind blew again. I could hear a faint whistle. The door was open a crack.

Desperate for something, a relic, a sign, I reached for the wooden handle. My fingers on it, I lingered and breathed, building the courage needed to guide the door along on its track. Crossing into the house, I left the door open. The only light in the living room was what the polarized windows hadn't sheared from the falling sun, and that was only enough to see that the house had been stripped bare.

"Hello." I stood motionless, listening to my echo die. Waiting for a response. "Ashli? It's me. Riley." Still nothing but my own pulse beating in my ears.

I took light steps, but the vacancy of the house and my overcharged nerves magnified every footfall. I walked down the hall to the room where Ashli had lain next to me, telling me what I could have been. I climbed the stairs and went to the room where I had begged her to see me. Where she'd confirmed that I was nothing. Now there was nothing in any of the rooms. Only darkness and dust.

I left the way I had come in. No longer afraid of being caught, I lingered with my feet hanging over the edge of the pool. I smoked a cigarette and watched the great golden ball of the sun take its time in falling behind the serrated peaks those hundred miles away. Shadows on the near face of the Superstitions grew long and sharp, demon heads and snapping dogs, until the force of the sun gave out and the mountains were only mountains again. Exhaling smoke, I rested on my elbows and followed the lights of an airplane as it passed on course to touch down at Sky Harbor. The blinking red tail light shrank until it was made invisible by distance. My cigarette all but smoked, I flicked the cherry into the deep end of the pool and the glowing ember died with a hiss so small that I wouldn't have heard it had I not trained my ear to await its coming.

Waiting for the stars, I cried. Wept, really. Full on. Eyes hot and slick. Nose spilling a clear snot that fell between my shoes into the pool. I poured forth everything. Giving it to the night. Crying for Collin and Dom. For Michelle. For Cricket and the unnamed infant I would never know and the father I would never be. For the person I once had the potential to become. For my deep and unyielding love of the person that I was, despite my many resplendent failures. And for my unapologetic happiness defying the miseries that seemed intent to gather in my orbit like so many dark and unloved moons. I wept for the sand in the hourglass that falls into oblivion one priceless grain at a time and for that beautiful piece of infinity we had together unearthed so accidentally. So innocently. Like children in a future beyond counting who brush away dust from a long buried, long forgotten atomic bomb. Watching the night take hold, I pitied us because we thought what we had might be common. Like water or air. That it might be available to us again, and again, a million agains into the twilight of living, and this made me cry for the tragedy of being. For the mockery inherent in joy. The cruelty of the clock. For the devil who collects every time we utter the word "tomorrow." I cried for myself. I cried because I was in love with living and because I was afraid to die. I cried because it all happened so damn fast and it never once asked if I was ready.

"Hello?"

"Hey, ma."

"Riley?"

"Yeah."

"Oh."

We were both quiet for a time. Listening to the other breathe. She heard me sniffle.

"Are you OK?"

"I don't really know, to be honest. How about you?"

She took a moment to answer. "I don't really think I know either."

I slept in parking lots. Showered at gyms. Everything I owned was in my truck. Mattress and sleeping bag in the bed next to three stolen milk crates that held my clothes. At the old camera shop in Mesa, I'd bought a Canon. One that shot on film. I had nothing to do with my days so I took pictures. Mostly landscapes. Sometimes mundane things like a bit of graffiti or the texture of a wall. Sometimes only because I liked the feel of pulling the lever. The tension of the spring against my thumb and the clicking into place of the next frame when I would wind the roll. My camera bag was always at the ready in my passenger seat. My old skateboard on the floor in front of it. I'd never had the heart to get rid of it. Not before everything. Not after.

Caleb had moved to Los Angeles. He was riding as an amateur for Toy Machine and renting a house with three other guys. When I told him I was living in my truck, he offered me a couch to crash on. Said he could always use a good photog. Imagining myself in L.A, I knew better than to expect the glitz I had been sold by Hollywood. It would be a real place with cracked pavement and traffic and despairing people who drank and fought and fucked and let their sorrow steer their limbs, but it would also be a place where the winters were warm and my feet could touch the ocean, and palm trees set against the sky at day's end could calm my heart when questions about what exactly I was doing with my life began to claw at me, as I knew they would. It sounded great. If nothing else, it was clean. And it would have me. The decorations were up and I knew I couldn't do another Christmas in Phoenix. Ringing in another new year would kill me.

I typed out a message to Caleb telling him that I would take him up on his offer. I told him that I wasn't going to rush. That I wanted to take a meandering path to California. To avoid the interstate and see all there was to see between here and there. But he could expect me soon. I warned him that I wasn't taking skate photos anymore. Said I hoped that was OK.

The day I planned to leave I woke early and sipped coffee at a cafe in Tempe, watching employees unlock doors and sweep sidewalks. Cloistered in the short trees lining the street, thousands of grackles that had migrated to town chirped and squawked. Amidst their heckling chorus, I sat behind my laptop and looked at the profiles of everyone I knew. Hundreds of photos that I'd taken over the past two years were being ported over from Myspace to Facebook. The shrapnel of so many nights. All one could see was the glamor. The thrill. If I hadn't been the one behind the camera, I might have believed it. But having seen it with my living eyes, I couldn't help but focus on the negative space. The pain that lived between flashes. That void that didn't reflect light.

Thea had gotten married. A small ceremony. Reception at the Crowne Plaza in Chandler. Friends in dresses and suits touching cheeks over white tablecloths. Mingling on a plastic lawn that would never turn brown. Michelle would have worn a Versace dress. Instead she had a funeral I'd not been invited to attend. Back in Wisconsin. Somewhere cold. I clicked through her old photos. Smiled at her smile. There would be no new profile for her. Or Collin. Or Dom. No one was going to make sure they were carried along to the new digital hot spot. When Myspace was abandoned, its collapsing architecture useful only as a curiosity, a busted boomtown along the highway of progress, they would be left behind. Posed and beautiful and forgotten in a mausoleum of ones and zeros. I wrote a comment beneath the last picture she ever posted.

I'm sorry

When my page refreshed, I had a new message in my inbox. It

was from Ashli. She had left *XRXS* and gone to Las Vegas with Seth. He'd made her many promises. Then the crash came. It hit him hard. He'd become erratic and unpredictable. Borrowing and moving money. Drinking too much and flying into fits of rage. The last time she'd seen him, he'd terrified her. Now he was gone. She didn't know where. She was out of money. She had no way to get home. Nobody to turn to. I typed a response.

I'm coming

On a napkin I wrote the directions to Las Vegas. In my truck, I taped that napkin to the vinyl dash just above the stereo. It was a five hour drive. Leaving the valley on the 60 West toward Wickenburg, the city gave way to ranches and then the ranches gave way to open desert. In Kingman I stopped at a service station to use the bathroom and to refuel. As the dial on the antique pump rolled to count the gallons and the dollars, a flock of pigeons on a drooping line took to the air, flew in a wide circle and then back again, finding perch in that place where they'd started. Retaking my seat behind the wheel, I looked to my passenger seat and saw that I needed to make space for Ashli. Back on the highway and heading north, my camera bag was stowed away in the truck bed. My skateboard I'd left leaning against the gas pump. A gift to the first kid who wanted it. I hoped so, anyway.

Deep in the desert, the radio that didn't talk about Jesus was static, so I let the only CD I had, the new Kings of Leon, play through from start to finish and then over again. And then again after that. When I crossed the Hoover Dam I thought about stopping to take photographs, but I didn't want to keep Ashli waiting, so I made a promise to myself that I would stop on the way back. A promise that I broke. The sky was red when I took the exit onto Las Vegas Boulevard and passed the sign welcoming me to that fabulous city.

Immediately I was in traffic. Three times I passed the fake Arc de Triomphe and the fake Eiffel Tower before I found the road that led to the parking garage. I took a ticket at the gate, and wound my way up. After finding a spot, I sent a text to Ashli.

I'm here. What room?

Napoleon Suite.

Through the white walled lobby with its gold trim and heavy chandeliers, I followed signs to the guest services desk. A man in a black vest greeted me, and I explained that my friend, Ashli Rose, was staying in the Napoleon Suite. I asked if he would give me a key card for the elevator. He typed on his computer.

"I don't have an Ashli Rose registered in the Napoleon Suite. Are you sure she isn't in a different room?"

"She said Napoleon Suite." I checked what she had texted me and showed him the phone screen.

Looking at his monitor, he said, "That Suite is registered to an Ashley Kahn."

"What did I say?"

"You said Rose."

I smiled. "It's Kahn."

He held a phone receiver between his ear and shoulder and made a call. When he hung up, he said, "Just a moment." An older man with gray in his slick hair and wearing a suit complete with pocket square came from a doorway and took the place of the man in the vest. "You're friends with Ms. Kahn?" he asked.

"Yes."

He examined me like he was skeptical. Like he could smell wealth and could tell I had none, and so wondered by what circumstance I could be linked to the beautiful woman in that most expensive suite. "Unfortunately, I cannot give you access to the elevator."

"Why not?"

He cleared his throat. Spoke with the delicate precision of a politician. "We are currently in the process of removing Ms. Kahn from the hotel."

"For what?"

"For non-payment of her bill, unfortunately."

His face was grim. To him, being broke was no different than being dead. I mirrored his tone, and like I was asking for the particulars of her death, I whispered, "How much does she owe?"

He whispered back, "A substantial amount." The word substantial sent his chin down and his eyebrows up. At full volume he said, "Unfortunately sir, I am not permitted to divulge that information." He checked over his shoulders and mine. Whispered again. "But if I grant you access to her suite, would you be willing to impress upon her the urgency of contacting me? We really hate to have any unpleasantness with our VIP's."

I matched his volume. Spaced out my words. "How much, does, she owe?"

The man in the black vest led me to the polished brass elevators. I walked as if my flesh had been overtaken by a distant intelligence. I'd traveled these hundreds of miles on raw electric charge, never once thinking about why I was doing what I was doing because thought had no say in the matter. What falls and rolls down hill does so not by demand or intent, and people only pretend to be any different. Not me. Not anymore.

The golden doors parted and we stepped into the elevator car. The man in the black vest held a magnetic card to a black box and pressed one of the higher numbers on the panel. The button lit up. It sent my heart to drumming. I made eye contact with myself in the shine of the doors as the elevator began to lift, and the calculating part of my brain couldn't stand the cold discipline with which I was riding on the leading edge of the moment. It pleaded with me to prepare some simple motion, a few easy words. It was tortured by my refusal to predict the minutes that lay ahead, to prevision what she would be wearing. How she would greet me. How she would react to what I had to say.

The elevator seized as it came to a stop, and the doors opened, ripping my reflection in two. The man in the black vest made a sweeping gesture with his hand and I stepped out onto the dizzying carpet, all the while fighting my evolved self. Like a monk at meditation, I walked forward, and as my subconscious paraded images of Ashli before me - Ashli at the door, Ashli reaching for a hug, Ashli inviting me in - I destroyed them all. Celebrated destroying them. Laughed out loud and then laughed again because I had laughed out loud. Standing at her door, I was already brimming with the most delicious regret. I knocked, and as the stupidest version of myself stood waiting for her to answer, that cracked and broken boy, perpetual fool so addicted to the nostalgia he was always at the wheel in shaping, I looked back on him from a day some thirty years later and shook his hand, told him congratulations, gave him a teary thank you, elder self to youth, for having had such stolid disdain for anything like reason.

Footsteps approached on the other side. Soft, bare feet. "Riley?" she asked through the door.

"Yeah. It's me."

A series of locks turning and sliding. Then her.

"Am I glad to see you." She said it like I'd come riding in on a horse. She took my hand in hers and drew me into the room and shut the door behind us, fixing all the locks again, then turning on her toes, she gave me a hug. A real one. Or the closest thing to it. Her bright red hair recently washed. Curls pinned up. Pomegranate. Rain. "Come in," she said, leading me into the suite.

The room was a strict white with ornate moulding at the floor and crown. In the corner, a baby grand piano, white to match the walls and sofas. From the center of the recessed ceiling hung a crystal chandelier. Ashli took a seat on the couch and patted the cushion next to her. As soon as I was sitting, she sprang back up and said, "Drinks!" and on the balls of her feet, circled the furniture and moved toward one of the bedrooms and vanished through a doorway. Watery ice shifted in a bucket. She came back into the room with a dripping bottle in one hand and two glasses in the other. She set everything on the low mahogany table and replaced herself next to me. The bottle was half empty.

"Mescal?"

"I know. It's awful. Seth liked it, and now it's all that's left."

She pulled the cork from the bottle and poured the honey colored liquor into each of the two waiting glasses. She raised her drink and I raised mine to match and we touched rims and drank. I breathed away the heat. She drew up a leg so she could face me, and with her glass in both hands, she told me everything. When they'd arrived in town, Seth would leave her in the suite, his days spent dealing with the collapse of his real estate empire. He'd maxed out his cards to stem the outflow of money and he had Ashli put the room in her name. He was a millionaire several times over. He would move his money, liquidate assets, and everything would be fine. As time wore on, he became more unpredictable. Drinking and getting high. Coming and going at all hours. Bringing people into the suite who were clearly criminal. Furtive men. Armed. Loud when they should be quiet. Quiet when they should be loud. Once, Seth left for a couple of days, and when he returned, he carried a Crown Royal bag. While he'd showered, Ashli had felt inside that bag and found it was full of uncut gold. Shapeless and unpolished. He'd caught her examining one of the nuggets, and like that, he was an animal. Threatening to kill her. She had never been so scared. He left with the gold and now a week had passed. He'd changed his phone number. Kamran wouldn't take her calls. The hotel manager was losing his patience. She had tears in her eyes as she finished her tale. They may have even been real.

Glowing in the night sky out beyond the floor to ceiling windows, the names of casinos sparkled. Projected onto the side of a hotel, the bright face of a magician. She put her hand on my leg. "You might be the only friend I have left." Her eyes went to the top of my head. "You cut your hair." She ran her hand against the grain of the stubble.

"So what are you going to do?" I asked.

"I'm not sure," she said, sinking back into the cushion behind her. "Find a rich guy to pay it off." She laughed, and twisted her finger in a coil of hair. "Seriously though, I've been trying to land a modeling gig, but the economy is fucked and no one is buying anything." Out the window, the Magician was gone. A comedian had taken his place.

"What would you say if I told you that I took care of your bill?"

She straightened her back and looked at me sideways. "I'd say that I didn't believe you. I'd say that you were fucking with me."

I lifted my glass. "Merry Christmas."

She shifted her whole body so she could view me out the other side of her face, as though she needed to take me in from a different angle to examine me for the truth or lie of what I'd said. "You couldn't have."

"Why not?"

"It was too much."

"It wasn't. And I did. Just now, down at the front desk." I took another fiery sip.

Her whole body lit up. "Riley! How? Where would you even get that kind of money?"

"The accident."

She stared at me wide eyed, waiting for me to say more.

"The car accident I was in this summer. During the monsoon."

Still, she said nothing.

"The big accident, with Michelle. You didn't hear about any of this?"

"How would I have?"

Now I studied her, searching for a lie. "Why did you write to me?" I asked.

"Because I was afraid, and running out of options. I was trying to find anyone who might help me, and you posted those pictures of your truck and I thought you could at least get me out of here."

"You really don't know."

"Know what?"

"Michelle is dead."

"For real?"

"For really, real."

She was quiet.

"Didn't you notice my ear?" I set down my glass and twisted at the waist to show her.

"Oh, fuck!" She covered her mouth against a pop of laughter.

I unwound and took my drink again, sipping it as I settled back into the sofa. "Fuck, this stuff is awful."

She lifted her own glass and was about to sip from it. "Why did you do it? Why did you pay my bill?"

There were so many ways to answer her question. None of them adequate. My feelings shattered and dashed and no description of their pieces would have been capable of explaining my driving urge. I wished I could just show her. That I could turn a key and open my chest like a curio cabinet and expose the dense ball of glowing heat that was at the center of me. The animating fever that hated words and made such a terrible master if things like consequences mattered. It would be easier to show than to explain that when I shut my eyes to anything forward of impulse, that sacred heat moved through me. Set all of me to humming, vibrating in tune with the rumble and tick of the grand orrery of time. I paid her bill because it felt like falling. I paid her bill because recklessness was the only way I knew to see the shape of my soul.

She touched my leg. Called me back. I said to her, "Because I needed to know what it would feel like."

"What?"

"This."

We sat sharing a silence that wrenched the space between us, wringing the air until it risked breaking open, begging one of us to release it with a word. I let her face consume me. Buried myself in her eyes. Finally she drank and said something about the room, gesturing to the walls and fixtures. I swallowed the rest of my mescal and got up and walked to the center of the carpet. Beyond the window glass, the strip glittered. When I had taken one step too many, and the floor began to fall away beneath my feet, I stopped. Took one step back. Let the ground settle into place. "Dom is dead, too." I said.

Ashli's reflection found mine. We watched each other in the pane. "How?" she asked.

"She killed herself." I said it like I was only now accepting that it was true.

"Fuck."

"And she never had the abortion."

"I know. I told her not to."

I spun around to see the real Ashli. "Why would you do that?"

"Because she wanted the baby. She was crazy, and I told her so, but it's what she wanted. And you were saying all this stuff about leaving, about moving away, and I needed you."

"Until you didn't."

She wasn't offended. If anything, she was excited by my attempt to wound her. She perfected her posture, ready to parry. With a lift of her eyebrow, she tilted her glass in my direction, and asked, "Do you really think you have the right to judge me? To judge anyone?" She let her question land, but kept me from answering, pointing at me and saying, "You hurt her. Awfully. But you know that." She was enjoying dressing me down, pulling me into the swamp alongside her. "You used her. And you lied to her. And in that, you were like every other guy she'd ever been with, and when I spoke to her on your behalf, do you know what she said? She said she wanted something more. She wanted someone who might finally love her back. And she thought her baby was the answer. So in the end, I told her to do what felt right. How could I tell her anything else?"

I had no answer. Ashli held her gaze so my shame could be complete, and when she decided that it was, she sipped from her glass.

"What's your real name?" I asked her.

She was taken aback. "What?"

"Down at the desk, they said your name is Ashley Kahn."

"Rose is my middle name. Ashley Rose Kahn. Why does it matter?"

I consulted her reflection in the window, then locked eyes with her in the flesh. "It doesn't." She finished her drink with one large swallow. "So what does?" I asked her.

She stared at me like I'd caught her in a lie, or like maybe she'd caught me in one. She nodded small nods that reminded me of the detective. Grabbing the mescal bottle by its neck, she came to where I stood, and with a smile made of equal parts pity and contempt, she asked, "Why would there be anything?" She put the bottle to my chest. I didn't take it at first because taking it would mean bowing to her answer. But I could only resist for an insignificant second. What felt true might as well have been true. Was true. "How much did it cost you?" she asked, as I took the mescal from her hand.

"All of it," I said. I brought the bottle to my lips and took a swig, draining half of what remained. The fire ran my throat and stung my eyes.

She took the bottle back and finished the last of what it contained and dropped it to the floor. It hit the Persian rug with a thud. She gave me a look like we shared something hideous. Like we'd survived some unspeakable ordeal only by eating the bodies of our familial dead. She took both of my hands in hers. "Let's get out of here."

We walked the casino floor. A fake Paris with fake cafes under a fake blue sky that forced us around and through rows of gaming tables and slot machines before we could reach the exit. We took a cab ride downtown and slowly strolled the Fremont Street Promenade. Arm in arm. Stepping as one. I didn't know where the night would take us or how it would end. I didn't know that the next day when we loaded into my truck and left Las Vegas, that Ashli would be hungover, and that she would sleep most of the ride back to Phoenix. That we would hardly speak as we crossed the deadly expanse between those two cities of the plain. That I would roll us cigarettes and sneak glances at her as the sun danced in the black lenses covering her eyes. I didn't know that after checking into a Tempe motel where we'd agreed to spend a weekend figuring out what to do next, she would leave early the second morning, disappearing when I stepped out to buy us food, a nameless car having stolen her away.

Between the ceaseless *panging* of simulated coins in pans and the *tootling* of video poker machines, the *clack clack clack clack* of a little white ball caught up in the centrifugal force of a roulette wheel as it sought a place to be and the crowds laughing and shouting as they won and lost and won and lost,

I didn't know that the note she would leave for me would only say that she didn't know what to say, but that she was grateful, for whatever that might be worth, that I was really something, and that she loved me in a way, in a way, but there could never be an us, not one that would last, and that deep down I had to know that that was true, that she knew I knew, and that's what made her leaving OK. Good even. Better to get it over with. Better to not make a big fuss.

That brilliant night, her hand in mine under moon and planets, an illusion made possible by thousands of beads of colored light, heads turned to see her, to feel a bit of her glow, because she did glow, and those heads saw me there with her and in their minds they thought all manner of things about who I must be for her to cling to me so. For hours we made our way from one casino to the next, throwing dollars on tables and then walking away when the numbers weren't ours, pulling levers on machines and cheering when they returned small sums of money barely larger than what we'd wagered, holding our fingers high so cocktail waitresses who dressed like cigarette girls would have dressed in a time when there were such things would come our way. Take our order. Bring us more glasses to clink. And drinking them down, I didn't know that in three days I would never see Ashli Rose again. Not in person. On a billboard a year later when I lived in Los Angeles. Then in a perfume ad on the side of a bus in that same city. Much later, on the cover of a celebrity magazine, holding the hand of a gold toothed rapper.

I didn't know that I would see those images of her and that I would be sad when I saw them. That my ears would ring. That I'd itch with betrayal or loneliness or boredom or whatever it was. I didn't know that Caleb would never turn pro, or that Parson would open his own bar that would fail and leave him bankrupt. I didn't know that The Prospector would die when a pandemic swept the Earth, not from the disease itself, but from having been made to stay home, old and alone and despairing, or that hikers in the Superstition Mountains would discover Jesse's bones, meatless and bleached white, wedged in a crevasse where he'd died trapped, terrified, hating the last step he'd taken and the thousands before that, crying to a mother who couldn't hear his constrained sobbing, or that one day, I would marry a woman named Fallon, and that a number of autumns after vowing to always love me, she would tell me that she wanted a divorce, and that when I turned fifty I would long for home and make the slow drive back to Chicago, to the gray that had molded me, and there in the city of my birth, at fifty-six years old, the irregular rhythm of my heart, a symptom of traumatic brain injury, would at last claim my life. Sudden cardiac arrest as I descended my apartment steps, clinging to a handrail.

It's funny to me now because I didn't know anything that night on Fremont Street, and I couldn't have been happier about it. Knowing never did a damn thing for me. It only made everything twice as painful when it came. On the sidewalk outside a small wedding chapel, I said to Ashli that we should get married, and she looked at me like I had only two minutes to live. Like I was already dead in her arms. She kissed me on the cheek. "Don't say that," she said, then pulled me along, and hand in hand we steadied each other against the inebriated teetering of our collective gait. Eventually she asked that I carry her on my back, and so I did, tipping this way and that as she laughed, her cheek tight to mine. On a stage that blocked a cross street, a famous band played a famous song. Ashli banged on me with her open hand. "Stop!" she demanded, and so I did, lowering her to her feet. She took my arm and dragged me to the front of the crowd. "I love these guys," she said, and we sang along as the man at the microphone crooned that he was on his knees, begging for the answer. When the singer thanked the audience and declared that their next song would be the last, Ashli looked at me with glassy eyes and told me to dance with her. Her arms went up and fell in a loop around my neck. From the speakers, the singer's voice came slow. Penitent. His song a ballad of sorrow.

She rested her head on me.

I pulled her close.

At home among that wreckage of people drunk and raging against the dismal particulars of everything they'd become, I danced with Ashli Rose, and it made me so damn happy. The electric show hanging in place of the sky showed a rippling blue sea, a second firmament, manacled now, and begawked, the blue of it on us. Coloring our skin. Glimmering as though the water that we are was all there was of us. Oh, happy lie.

Ashli sang quietly, learning the chorus as I held her against my beating heart. "There's nothing I can say, there's nothing we can do now."

Moments come and destroy the moments that came before them and nothing at all can hold back this belligerent ruin. This perpetual treachery against loving. So we suffer it. And suffer it again. Her red hair beneath my nose, I breathed Ashli in, and like I was stripping the day's clothes, I stepped out of myself. Out of the part that has to go forward. The permanent hostage. The song was ending and everything that would come after would pale against the now and I couldn't bear it. I couldn't bear it at all. So I left myself there. I'm still there now. Dancing. Breathing the sweet air off her cruel neck. And I'll never leave. Why would I? The universe began and then it ended and somewhere in between there was a moment that meant more to me than any other ever could. See me there. Imagine me happy.

Acknowledgments

Thank you to Kira Rose and Benjamin Steinhorn for reading an early draft of this book and encouraging me to complete it. Thank you to my wonderful wife Dani for not only tolerating the madness that is living with a writer, but for supporting me and loving me as if it were an autonomic function. Thank you to my daughter Dahlia for giving my life dimension and color. Thank you to all the no longer young men who spent those days and nights with me, tearing skin, rolling ankles, and laughing away the pain eager to do it again, who loved nothing so much as the road west that secreted us away from winter, whose energy and elation certainly saved my life. And thank you to everyone who has ever reached out to say that something I have written has touched them. It keeps me going.

ALSO BY JOHN F. DUFFY

:

A Ballroom for Ghost Dancing

:

About the Author

John F Duffy was born in Palos Heights, Illinois, and lived as a child in the northwest suburbs of Chicago. A graduate of Columbia College Chicago, he is a Pushcart Nominee and his short fiction has been published in a variety of magazines and journals. His debut novel, *A Ballroom for Ghost Dancing*, was shortlisted for the Indiana Book Award and the National Indie Excellence Award and it won Best Midwest Fiction from the Independent Publishers Book Award. He currently lives in Bloomington, Indiana with his wife and daughter.